Follies Past

A Prequel to Pride & Prejudice

MELANIE KERR

Dedicated to Dr. Redwan Moqbel, the kindest and best of men, whom Jane Austen doubtless would have loved, if not for his rare sense then for his profound sensibilities.

ACKNOWLEDGMENTS

My heartfelt thanks go to Beatrice Nearey, for her generosity with her vast knowledge of all things Regency; to Nadia Rushdy, Martin Kerr, Roxanne Rout, and Cameron Rout, for their very helpful reviews and input; to Angela Rout for the exceptional original cover art; to Ania Telfer for taking such great photographs at such short notice; to Bryan Szabo for his prompt and painstaking edits; and to Raphael Marinho for all his kind assistance with the cover. I would be remiss if I did not also thank the Republic of Pemberley, Wikipedia and Etymonline, without which the research for this book would surely have taken decades.

The man whose virtues are more felt than seen,

Must drop, indeed, the hope of public praise;

But he may boast, what few that win it can,

That if his country stand not by his skill,

At least his follies have not wrought her fall.

- William Cowper

CHAPTER 1

Caroline Bingley had long known the name of Darcy, and she had always hoped to increase her family's intimacy with it. In fact, she was prepared, as soon as it could be arranged, to take it as her own. Mr. Fitzwilliam Darcy was the head of the very wealthy and well-connected family and was her brother's most esteemed friend. She thought, therefore, of the joy it would bring her brother if she could be the means of uniting the companions in brotherhood, of the many benefits such an exalted connection would bring for her own dear sister, of the future generations of her family and all that they would reap from their association with the prestigious house of Darcy. Of all these considerations, she took pride in none so much as she did in her own charity, for having considered everyone's interest but her own.

"I know not how I shall survive two fortnights without you, Louisa," she remarked to her sister as she packed her trunk.

"This may be the most important four weeks of my life."

Caroline had been introduced to Mr. Darcy by her brother at a ball earlier that year. He had not asked her to dance, but she had convinced him to sit down to a game of cards with her, and she felt she had outdone herself in conversation with him—particularly since he was somewhat taciturn with her at first. He had even gone so far as to express a hope of meeting again, which was more than she had heard him do for any other lady that evening. When she received from her brother the news that they were all invited to spend Christmas at

Pemberley, Mr. Darcy's Derbyshire estate, she attributed it to her personal charms and was very well pleased with her success.

Had Caroline known the true cause for the invitation, her pride and her hopes would have been quite dashed. The Bingleys had been invited with the pointed purpose of being introduced to Mr. Darcy's younger sister, Georgiana. Caroline always spent the London season at her brother's house in town and Mr. Darcy hoped that she might take an interest in Georgiana, that their acquaintance might ease his sister's transition to London and her coming out in society, both of which were to follow in the spring.

Caroline's sister, Louisa, was not able to accept Mr. Darcy's invitation as she was to spend the season with the family of Mr. Hurst, the man whom she had lately engaged herself to marry.

"If Mr. Darcy's affections were inspired on the strength of a single meeting," Louisa said, "then it would be best to imitate, as closely as possible, the conditions of that first encounter."

Caroline nodded her agreement with this wise counsel.

"To your first dinner at Pemberley," she continued, "you must wear the very gown you wore that night. This shall inspire in him a recollection of his obviously favourable first impression."

"But is not it a risk to wear the same gown twice in a row in the same company?" asked Caroline.

Her sister replied with confidence, "And so it must stand out in Mr. Darcy's mind for its anomaly and work to impress upon him even more deeply the significance of your first encounter. What is more, you must wear the same fragrance, as scent is known to act upon the mind and heart more potently than any other of the senses."

"An excellent point," remarked Caroline. She agreed to everything suggested by her sister, but most importantly, she determined to be everything charming and clever.

After several days and three nights of fair weather and tolerable inns, Caroline and her brother, Mr. Bingley, arrived at

Pemberley at dusk.

"We are dreadfully late in arriving, Caroline," said Mr. Bingley as the carriage entered the gate. "We ought to have left Allestree much earlier. It is, indeed, a duty to offer charity wherever possible, but I cannot understand why it was necessary to visit the alms houses in person. Surely a gift of some money would have sufficed. Christian duty or no, you risk inconveniencing our hosts."

"Oh Charles," Caroline sighed. "You are not accustomed to acts of charity as I am. It is the presence of the giver that is the true gift. The money is of assistance, certainly, but to receive it from the hands of the giver—to *see* the face of generosity—is a gift of hope and good will that far exceeds the value of the coins themselves. Surely you can see that this is worth delaying our arrival for."

In truth, it was the delay that had been Caroline's object. She always intended to arrive as the sun was setting, in order that her complexion might profit by the glow of evening light. She believed that there was never too much concern to be spent in making an impression. She wished her sister had been present to make a third as they alighted from the carriage, for a grouping of three is always more pleasing to the eye than two. She was cheered by the late but happy thought that the figure of the footman would suffice to complete the picture.

All her careful planning was thwarted, however, by the efficient courtesy of their host. Mr. Darcy was more eager to greet and welcome his friend than he was observant of the image so prettily constructed by Caroline.

Elegantly posed, profile turned to the setting sun, she watched him descend the stairs. From her brother, she had long known him to be clever, well-bred, and self-assured. When she was at long last introduced to him, she had been very pleased to discover how tall and how handsome he was. As he approached them at the threshold of his own home, she thought the grace and warmth of his demeanour added much to his already considerable assets.

Caroline held her pose as Mr. Darcy embraced her brother

with both hands.

"Welcome, welcome," said Mr. Darcy. "I am so glad you have finally arrived. I had looked for you some hours ago, but that is no matter."

Hardly looking at Caroline, he bowed and offered her his arm. "Miss Bingley, welcome. Please, come in. We are all assembled." She coyly accepted, and he led them both up the stairs into the house. Although it did not alter her intentions towards him, Caroline did think Mr. Darcy ought to have dwelt more on her person—or at least to have paid *some* attention to her appearance—and she wondered whether a want of appreciation for the virtues of others might not be one of his failings.

Mr. Darcy ushered his guests directly into the parlour, where the rest of the party was assembled in the large but cozy room. Immediately upon their entering, Mr. Darcy's formidable aunt, Lady Catherine de Bourgh, called out to them.

"Bring them here," she demanded. "I must have the honour of first introductions, followed by Anne, and then Georgiana, and then the Colonel. I do not approve of the relaxing of formal obligations, you know, and I see no reason to deviate from them in this case."

Lady Catherine was seated by the fire and showed no intention of rising to greet anyone, though she was not prevented by age or infirmity from doing so. Her figure was tall and straight, and though weathered by age and indignation, her features were still strong, and retained some of the beauty of her youth.

Mr. Darcy replied to her tersely. "There has never been any suggestion of doing otherwise, Aunt." He directed the new arrivals towards Lady Catherine.

Lady Catherine's imposing stare betrayed more consciousness of superior rank than any real superiority of mind, manners or taste. She found nothing in Caroline Bingley to inspire either alarm or praise. Her dress and her hair were suitable, but no more than suitable. She was nothing to her Ladyship's own daughter and Lady Catherine proceeded to disregard her for the remainder of her stay, excepting of course those moments when her Ladyship's conversation required either an audience or an object.

"Anne must be next," she instructed, gesturing towards her daughter, who was seated beside her. Mr. Darcy forced a smile and turned to a demonstrably unimposing creature, almost hidden behind Lady Catherine, whom he introduced as his cousin, Miss Anne De Bourgh.

Anne did not get up from her seat.

"And then Georgiana, and then the Colonel," Lady Catherine continued loudly to direct the proceedings to the obvious irritation of her host.

On the introduction of Georgiana, who was only fourteen and shy even for her age, Caroline was overjoyed. Although she had not initially factored the girl into her plans, she immediately saw the advantages of an intimate acquaintance with her. As Mr. Darcy's ward and beloved sister, here was just the vehicle Caroline wanted to contrive her way into his heart—if she were not already firmly established there. Georgiana did not seem a difficult conquest. The elder girl mistook the purity of the younger girl's heart for a ready and undiscerning affection, and the hesitancy in Georgiana's manner led Caroline to believe that her opinions could be easily dictated.

She did not account for the powers of perception and discernment which Georgiana possessed. When Caroline was presented to her, Georgiana did not instantly dislike her, but was quick to note the condescending nature and forced intimacy of their first conversation. When Colonel Fitzwilliam, Mr. Darcy's cousin, had been introduced, Caroline returned to Georgiana.

"I am so very pleased finally to make your acquaintance, Miss Darcy," Caroline began. "I have been longing for the pleasure of it more than you know. Ever since I heard that Mr. Darcy had a sister and that I should have the privilege of spending four weeks in her gracious company, I have been most anxious to make your acquaintance. As you may be aware, I have a sister from whom I am usually inseparable and she could not join us at this time. Therefore, I shall depend upon you for companionship these two fortnights, and I very much hope I shall not make too tedious a job of it."

Here Lady Catherine could not suppress a remark, as, in fact, she never could.

"If you had all come to Rosings for Christmas as I suggested," she chided, "there would be plenty of young ladies in the neighbourhood to keep any of you from loneliness. Here in the North, however, you do not have the benefit of society so much as we do in the South."

Caroline, agape at this insult against the hospitality of her host, looked about the room and noted the wide eyes and open mouths of several other guests. She turned to Mr. Darcy to see his reply, but none was forthcoming. It was long since he had heard anything his aunt said. Her conversation had something of diminishing returns. The more there was of it, the less value it had, and it was always in ample sufficiency, several times over.

Caroline, thinking to make herself agreeable with an obsequious reply, curtseyed in Lady Catherine's direction and was opening her mouth to speak when she was spared the task by the grace of her young new acquaintance.

Taking her brother's lead, as she did in all matters of propriety, Georgiana left her aunt to her own musings and responded instead to Caroline, with a humility that was lost on her guest.

"Miss Bingley, it is I who am grateful of your company," said Georgiana softly. "You know, my brother is always thinking of what most pleases me, and I have never known him to be wrong in anything. Therefore, I trust your presence here will bring me the greatest possible joy. I only hope I shall acquit myself tolerably of my duties as hostess. May I begin by showing you to your room? Your journey must have fatigued you, and I have taken the liberty of having some small refreshment laid out for you there."

Caroline tilted her head in acquiescence, and the two girls

disappeared together down the corridor. The three men retired to the library, and Miss de Bourgh and her mother continued their elevated silence beside the fire.

CHAPTER 2

So confident was Caroline of Mr. Darcy's affections that she felt it best to begin immediately the task of asserting her authority over the servants of Pemberley. If she were to become mistress of the house, it would be in everyone's interest that the staff respect her from the outset. Acting on this principle, she ordered that three maids come to her room to assist her in preparing for dinner. One was to assist her personal lady's maid, Jenny, with her hair and head dress, another was to put away her things, and the third was simply to attend in the event that Caroline should want anything and not be in a humour to wait for a servant to be called to fetch it.

The effect of her pains was indeed remarkable. Caroline did not want for fine features, and she was not negligent in making the most of them. She was tall, but light in her form, and she had always particularly prided herself on her excellent teeth and her very well-formed nose.

Dinner that evening began well enough. Georgiana complimented Caroline on her elaborate headdress. Caroline responded with feigned humility, glancing surreptitiously down the table towards Mr. Darcy, who was engaged in inspecting the wine.

Mr. Darcy had not failed to notice Caroline's garb upon her entrance, nor to recognize it from the evening of their first encounter, though it had not the effect she had hoped. Rather, it left him a little confused and led him to the conclusion either that she must have only one gown of that quality, or that she must not have very keen powers of recollection, for he knew young ladies never to wear the same dress in the same company twice in a row.

Lady Catherine, ever ready with a reproach, seized on the subject of Caroline's headdress.

"At Rosings Park, one need not be concerned, as it is such a very modern building and has very tall doorways throughout, but in such ancient halls as these, one must always take care of knocking such things off. In my day, we did not wear such things to dinner. It must be most inconvenient for eating soup."

Caroline was not usually contemptuous, if to be careless of the feelings of others is not contemptuous, but she was quick to take offense when her pride was wounded. On such occasions, her tongue could be every bit as sharp as Lady Catherine's.

"I should so much have enjoyed living at the time of your youth, Lady Catherine," she said sweetly. "I have read much about the last century, and I am convinced it must have been infinitely more pleasant than our modern times. Do not you agree, Charles?"

This response from Caroline drew the attention of Mr. Darcy, accompanied by a short cough. He could not approve such a speech, especially from one so freshly admitted to the house, but he was not sure he did not admire her for it. She was fearless, that much was plain, and, to be sure, his aunt was due a little of what she herself administered so freely.

Mr. Bingley attempted a reply to his sister. He got as far as saying, "well" several times before Georgiana saved Mr. Bingley from his predicament.

"Have you ever been to the seaside, Miss Bingley?" she asked.

Mr. Darcy was delighted to hear his usually reserved sister speak up in company.

"I am considering," he said, looking at Caroline, "whether I ought to send Georgiana to the seaside for the summer. Brighton is much too busy, but I thought Ramsgate might suit."

Caroline considered the broaching of this topic as an invitation to display her considerable expertise on the most fashionable destinations.

"Indeed, Brighton is frightfully crowded in the summertime, though I daresay it attracts the best society. I have been there on several occasions myself. My sister and I are very fond of it. But, of course, you do well to consider somewhere like Ramsgate for Georgiana. Brighton could well be overwhelming for one not accustomed to society."

"No, the seaside is out of the question," asserted Lady Catherine. "She had much better come to us, at Rosings Park. She shall have all the society she might wish for there, without any of the hazards. And she would have Anne as a constant companion. Yes, that is a much better plan. The seaside is far too perilous. There is no decorum in such a place, and people are permitted to mix wherever they please, with no regard for their place in society or anything."

Georgiana's heart began to sink. She feared lest her brother should heed her aunt's advice and she should be deprived of her holiday and forced instead to spend the summer with her insupportable relations. She did not understand how much secret pleasure it gave her brother to thwart the designs and ignore the counsel of Lady Catherine.

"Ramsgate is not quite the same as Brighton, though, is it Miss Bingley?" he asked, ignoring his aunt's suggestion.

Caroline took it as a profound compliment for her opinion to be asked twice on the same subject, and replied enthusiastically, "Oh, Ramsgate is charming, and yes, very different from Brighton in being quite a bit smaller. It is still very well regarded in highest circles, and I believe it would be very suitable—an excellent choice, Mr. Darcy." She simpered and returned to her meal.

"Well," said Lady Catherine, not content to let the matter be finally decided without any input from herself. "If she must go to the seaside, she must be properly attended. Who will travel with her? Who will accompany her, chaperone her while she is there?"

"We shall find someone," Mr. Darcy replied coolly. "I may even go myself."

Lady Catherine shot her horror and indignation across the table.

"You shall find someone?" she repeated. "Someone? You insist on sending her to such a treacherous place as a seaside resort and your great plan for her protection and companionship is that you shall find *someone*? That will never do, sir. You must send two manservants in the carriage. I insist. I shall furnish the servants myself if need be, but no less may be considered. And, as for a companion, you must leave that to me also. You know I am always happy to find ladies for such situations, and am constantly being applied to for my services in this regard. It would be the most convenient thing in the world, as well as the most suitable."

Mr. Darcy did not appear as though he intended to respond, and so the Colonel answered in his place.

"Thank you, Aunt. I am sure we will ask for your assistance if we have any difficulty in finding a suitable lady, and, as for the servants, there shall not be need for you to send any. Mr. Darcy will certainly provide everything in that way. You know he is always exceedingly attentive in all such matters."

"Very well," said Lady Catherine, composed but not entirely satisfied, "but I shall be most seriously displeased if I should learn that the strictest care has not been taken. Why has she been moved from school at all? I thought she had a very good place where she was."

A scourge of coughing sickness in several local seminaries that autumn had prompted Mr. Darcy to remove his sister from her West Midlands school, where young ladies of fortune were sent to procure all the knowledge, refinement and skills found in the highest circles of society. Though Georgiana could find no fault with the place beyond what is to be expected from a collection of privileged young ladies accustomed to having their own way, it could never rival Pemberley in her heart.

Caroline noticed that no one at the table was hazarding a reply to Lady Catherine, and began to make one herself.

"I believe Mr. Darcy was concerned—"

Lady Catherine spoke above her, answering her own question.

"I suppose the masters in London are the best, and a school can never offer the sort of individual attention that can be had from private lessons."

Mr. Bingley came to his sister's defense, saying, "Both my sisters were educated at a seminary, and I would say they are as accomplished as any in London."

"Yes Charles," Caroline agreed without apology. "But that really was one of the best schools in town, if not the country. They are not at all equal."

This led to a lengthy discussion on the relative merits of public and private institutions as well as education in general, during which Lady Catherine offended every member of the party in turns, Mr. Bingley never finished a sentence, and Caroline made several clever and well-phrased speeches of which she was very proud.

CHAPTER 3

The following day at breakfast, Georgiana received a letter in the morning post. From the tidy script she knew the author instantly as her schoolmate, Clare. With no surname of consequence and no fortune to speak of, Clare Langford of Maplethwaite was an unlikely pupil at the school Georgiana had attended, and at three years her senior, an even less likely choice friend of Georgiana, yet she was both.

Her attendance at the school had only been brought about by great sacrifice and economy on the part of her parents, who had spent the bulk of their capital and even borrowed against their income in order to furnish the fees. It was obvious that Clare would profit from an association with Georgiana, with all her wealth and connections to bestow. Less obvious was the service Georgiana received from Clare, who saw beneath the pretty gowns and skilled handwriting an orphaned and uncertain girl of fourteen, far from home and wary of the world. Clare gave to Georgiana some of the comfort and guidance which she wanted in her mother's absence. But the greatest gift that Georgiana gave Clare was not dependent on her position in life but lay in the sincerity of her friendship and the open and tender nature of her heart.

Georgiana received Clare's letter with a mock serenity that concealed her eagerness to read it. She laid the letter aside for the remainder of the meal, hoping to take it up to her room directly. As she excused herself from the table, however, Lady Catherine entered the room and addressed her abruptly.

"I intend to make my usual tour of the grounds this morning, Georgiana," she said, already tugging on her gloves. "It is some years since I have been to Pemberley, and I am keen to see how the improvements that I suggested on my last visit have come along. I must have some company, and I am afraid Anne is very dull this morning. She is still recovering from the journey." Anne was seated at the table, and, though it was clear she heard her mother, made no effort at a response. "Therefore," continued Lady Catherine, "it must fall to you to attend me. I have already sent for the carriage. We may leave straightaway."

"Of course, Aunt," Georgiana stifled a sigh. "I shall be honoured to show you what has been accomplished since you were last here."

As Georgiana anticipated, it was a long and tedious morning. Lady Catherine insisted on inspecting every corner of the property, including the orchards, the greenhouses and even the work sheds. As ever, she was liberal with her advice and so attentive that no detail was beneath her notice. Her condescension extended to every groundskeeper and under-gardener, each and every one of whom she instructed on every aspect of their duties, from where to plant which shrubberies, to how to construct a fence, to when to water the pineapples. In spite of feeling impatient, cold, weary, and more than a little embarrassed by her aunt's behaviour, Georgiana gracefully received all Lady Catherine's criticisms of her beloved home and dutifully facilitated her aunt's abuse of the staff with a promise in her heart to amend Lady Catherine's interference as soon as she was able.

Upon returning to the house, Lady Catherine retired to her chamber, where she ordered a fire be lit and some mulled wine be brought in to her. Georgiana sought the quiet of her own room for a few minutes' reprieve to read her letter. On her way through the house, however, she had the misfortune to pass by the drawing room in which her footsteps were heard and from which came the desperate voice of Caroline.

"Georgiana? Is that you returned? Do come and join us by

the fire. I am sure your feet and hands could use warming."

Caroline had been sitting with Miss de Bourgh and could simply find no topic on which to engage her in conversation. She must have started on a dozen different subjects, all of which solicited merely an "indeed" or a "perhaps" from her companion. Miss De Bourgh's constant companion, Mrs. Jenkinson, was also present, and might have offered some relief were it not for her unceasing attention to her charge; every time Mrs. Jenkinson was about to engage with Caroline, she would become distracted by her concern that Miss De Bourgh might be too far from the fire, or too close, that her tea had not enough sugar, or was too hot or too cold, or that the light of the window might be too bright for her eyes, or that there was not enough light from the window for her to see without straining her vision, or that her footstool was too low to be of any benefit without a cushion and then too high to be comfortable with one.

After nearly two hours of carrying on in this manner, even Caroline's usually inexhaustible supply of talk wore thin, and the women were in great danger of slipping into a dull and anxious silence.

Georgiana was therefore obliged to delay her own pleasure in order to redress her cousin's want of amiability.

"Do come in," Caroline said, rising from the sofa to meet Georgiana. She took her hand, and led her towards the fire, where Miss De Bourgh, occupying the only chair, showed no intention of giving up her place—indeed, Mrs. Jenkinson would not have allowed such an outrageous idea to be so much as proposed. Thus, still holding her hand, Caroline led Georgiana away from the fire and back to the sofa, where she sat her down and poured her some tea, clearly relieved to have something to do and someone to speak to.

"Do tell me about your tour of the grounds this morning. Are you undertaking many improvements?"

"Not so much improvements as maintenance, though I suppose the extension of some of the cottages must be considered improvements, and we are expanding the orchard."

"Of course, I am sure I should find Pemberley in no need of improvement." Caroline took in her surroundings, almost forgetting her companion in her deliberation over what alterations she should make on taking charge of the place. "But fruit trees are so charming" she continued, recollecting herself. "I simply adore blossoms in the spring. You know Charles is searching for a place to settle. I do hope he chooses a place for the grounds as much as for the house, for the landscape is as much part of an estate as the house, do not you think?"

"I do—very much so. In nature, one finds constant and evolving beauty which even the finest home cannot supply."

"Yes, I am absolutely devoted to the beauty of a garden, and there is so much one can do to enhance the natural setting, such as the addition of a hermitage, or a Grecian temple, which I believe all the finest homes are including now. When once Charles has found a place, you must come and offer me your thoughts on where he should place such things. I know you must have the most excellent taste in such matters."

Georgiana cheerfully agreed to such a scheme and left for another day the resolution of her dilemma that she considered the best place for Grecian temples to be Greece, and that hermits rarely—if ever—enhanced the value of an estate.

"This afternoon," Caroline insisted, "you must promise to show me the rest of the house and tell me all its history and secrets."

Caroline would not let Georgiana leave her side for the remainder of the day, so it was not until after dinner that she was able so much as to hope for a private moment in which she could read her letter from Clare. All had retired to the drawing room, and Caroline, Mr. Bingley and Colonel Fitzwilliam were sitting down to play cards. Lady Catherine, not being in a humour for cards, claimed Mr. Darcy for her conversation. As she had seemed to do for the entire day, Miss De Bourgh remained in the only chair at the fireside. Georgiana, seeing that everybody was thus occupied, rose and excused herself. Caroline called her back again.

"Dear Georgiana, you cannot be leaving. We need you to

make up our rubber." She then added, a little too sweetly, "You must think I have had enough of your company for one day, but I assure you, I could never have too much of it. Do say you will come and be my partner."

Georgiana looked to her brother with a pleading and helpless look which prompted him to interject, interrupting Lady Catherine in the middle of a long expostulation.

"I shall join you at cards, Miss Bingley, if it is all the same to you. Georgiana has had a long day and I believe the fresh air this morning has left her quite weary."

Had Caroline been in any doubt as to Mr. Darcy's regard, this would have been sufficient to dispel such uncertainty. He had disregarded his aunt and even ousted his sister in his eagerness to be near her. How could she be mistaken in her assumptions? What further proof of his affection could be looked for?

Georgiana silently thanked her brother and quickly excused herself before Lady Catherine could recover from the slight against her and claim Georgiana as Mr. Darcy's replacement.

Safely installed in her room, Georgiana sat down with her letter. Peeling it open, she began to read.

"DEAREST GEORGIANA,"

"It has only been three days since you quitted my company, but already I feel your absence. I hope your journey was not too tiring. I trust that you are well, and that you are enjoying the company your brother has assembled for you. I am certain that you can be brave enough to meet your aunt's gaze this year, and that you shall discover a true friend in your cousin Miss de Bourgh once you are able to find the subject of her hidden passions.

"My family are all well, including my mother. You will no doubt recall the fright my mother had in the autumn. She has not relapsed since and shows no sign of permitting it to disquiet her. I take her own fortitude as my guide. She writes to assure me that there is no cause for fear, that the Lord is kind and will keep us all whatever may come to pass. She has always been a woman of piety and charity, who has served her Lord by obeying her husband and caring for the poor. The knowledge of this is my solace and keeps me from the anxiety that might be mine had her character been less than unexceptionable.

"My mother has remained firm that my brother and I should not return home for the holidays, but the fees for staying on at school would be greater than the cost of traveling home. Therefore, my brother Crawley and I have been sent to stay with our Aunt and Uncle Watson, in Leamington Priors, as that is many dozen miles closer for both of us than Maplethwaite. Although I shall miss stirring the porridge with my own household, staying with my aunt and uncle gives me the opportunity to become better acquainted with them. Indeed, I have always wished for the chance to know them better. I believe it will be a charming holiday, and I hope will lead to my own improvement.

"Crawley does not seem at all inconvenienced by being kept away. There is much more society here than he is used to either at home or at school.

"I hope our presence is not too trying on my aunt and uncle who have four children of their own. The entire family has been very gracious in rearranging themselves to accommodate us. Their house is very comfortable, though not overly large, and though they insist that they are very glad of our company, I still do my utmost to ensure that my brother and I do not add overmuch to the burden of the household.

"I have even been teaching my brother some steps that he might attend a Christmas ball, which has had him practising with an application the likes of which neither his Latin nor his sacraments have ever seen. If one could dance a Catechism, he would be the most pious man in Christendom! I am told there are plans to construct a new Assembly Room here, and Crawley is forever expressing his wish to be a frequent guest at Leamington when the addition is complete. Everyone is very keen on these developments, but I do hope they do not turn this very pleasant town too much into the image of Bath, even if that is precisely what everyone is bent on. I suppose I must think of how it shall benefit my uncle and the other merchants in the town, for what we cannot alter we must learn to accept with gratitude.

"Do keep me and my dear family in your prayers, and do not be uneasy about your transfer to town. You shall shine as brightly in that place as you would in any other, and I cannot accept that you will feel my absence so much as you profess. Surely, London's many diversions cannot leave you wanting your old friend, but if they do, know that I shall always be with you in my heart and remain,

"Yours, sincerely,

"CLARE"

Georgiana's heart filled with pity for her friend. She felt the sadness in Clare's efforts to deny her loneliness and her longing for home; she felt Clare's resentment towards her parents for keeping her and her brother away; and she felt her want of a trusted friend. Such feelings, she sensed, threatened to overwhelm Clare were she to allow herself to feel their full force.

Georgiana had come to understand that Clare very often spoke more of what she believed it was right to feel than what she actually felt. Georgiana admired Clare's self-restraint and sense of right, and she always offered what solace she could to the wounded heart that Clare attempted to conceal from the world. It was this ability of Georgiana's—to understand Clare in ways that she herself could not—coupled with a reluctance to correct her friend that had endeared Georgiana to her.

The final lines of Clare's letter inspired Georgiana with an idea. She would speak to her brother about it in due course, though not immediately. She did not wish to distract him from the enjoyments of the season and she was willing to let the arrangements for London stretch out so that she might remain at home as long as possible.

In the autumn, she had been delighted to learn she was to return home that winter. When she learned what was to follow—her transfer to town and her coming out into society—she was filled with dread. She considered London, with its endless new acquaintances and unfamiliar dance partners, to be the very cauldron of all things terrifying.

And so she went to sleep, thinking what she might write in her reply and how she might contrive to find the time to compose it with all the demands of a houseful of guests. She also pondered over what hidden passions might be secreted away in the heart of her silent cousin Anne.

CHAPTER 4

The Friday following the arrival of the Pemberley party, Mr. Darcy and his guests were invited to attend a private ball. The ball was hosted by Lord and Lady Brackenhall, whose family had been settled in Derbyshire almost as long as the Darcys. Their children, Reginald Lord Branston and Lady Sofia, were home for the winter, and though this occurred every year, their parents still found it occasion enough to merit celebration.

The invitation was gladly received by nearly everyone.

"I say, it is very good of them to include us all," said Mr. Bingley cheerily. "I think they must be excellent people to extend such hospitality to the whole party."

"Indeed," replied Mr. Darcy. "They are old friends, and, as you say, excellent people."

Lady Catherine was of quite a different opinion and, turning to Mr. Darcy, declared,

"I daresay, it is very odd of them to invite all your guests to a private ball. It does not evidence any sort of discernment." Expecting some response and not receiving any, she felt obliged to continue. "It does not signify, however, for my dancing days are over I am afraid, and Anne's health shall prevent her from attending either." Miss de Bourgh made no objection to this pronouncement and Mrs. Jenkinson nodded her approbation.

"In that case, Aunt," began Mr. Darcy, "I shall be most happy to remain behind also, as your host. I cannot leave you here on your own, and I have never been overly fond of dancing myself."

"I should hope not, Mr. Darcy!" exclaimed Lady Catherine in dismay. "It is one thing to bring all your guests to a ball to which you are invited; it is quite another to send them along without *you* to justify their attendance. I have never heard of anything so shocking. Who should introduce them to their hosts? Surely you do not intend that Georgiana should go? She is but fourteen, and not yet out."

"Of course not, Aunt," Mr. Darcy answered, entirely unmoved by Lady Catherine's condemnation. "Colonel Fitzwilliam is well known to the family and very competent at introductions."

Caroline could not countenance the idea of giving up Mr. Darcy to his aunt for an entire evening and of relinquishing her opportunity to impress him with her skills in the arts of dancing and flirting with other men. However sure she was of his affections, she had always believed that a lady could never be too impressive in her accomplishments in the eyes of a worthy gentleman. She therefore began to say,

"If Georgiana is already to stay behind, then——" when she was interrupted by Lady Catherine.

"Georgiana is perfectly adequate company for myself and Anne. There is no cause for you to stay behind."

"Quite so, Darcy," added Mr. Bingley, grateful that Lady Catherine had saved him the task of contradicting his friend. "It would be unkind to the ladies to deny them another partner with so little cause. We shall have a very gay time, I am sure."

Mr. Darcy was not so sure as his friend on the last point, but could not argue with him in the main. Georgiana should keep her aunt and her cousin company, while Mr. Darcy should go to the ball.

When the anticipated evening arrived, Georgiana sat with Colonel Fitzwilliam in the drawing room while the others finished dressing.

"It seems a shame you cannot join us tonight," Colonel Fitzwilliam began. "I hope you shall not be too sorry to miss it. You shall be out soon enough."

"Do not trouble yourself on my account, cousin," Georgiana replied. "I should be very anxious at such a gathering, for I do not doubt it will be very crowded and I should be expected to dance with strangers, which I find a dreadful prospect. A dance may seem pleasant and be over quickly when one is easy with one's partner, but you know I should not be so with anyone I did not know very well."

"Well, there should be no cause for uneasiness on an evening such as this. Between myself and Mr. Bingley, there will always be someone to stand up with you, or, if you prefer, to sit down with you if you do not wish to dance."

"You must think me very silly, but even Mr. Bingley is too much a stranger to me as to make dancing with him enjoyable. He is a very pleasant gentleman in general, I grant, but I am so unaccustomed to making new acquaintances that it takes more than a week for me to be at ease with anyone, especially a gentleman—even my brother's most trusted friend."

"Well, if we should ever find ourselves together at a ball, I shall be delighted to sit with you for as long as you remain without a partner, and, if one cannot be found, to dance as many dances with you as you may wish. I am sure we shall always have much to say to each other."

"Truly, I am blessed," replied Georgiana with a sincere look of appreciation. "How many young ladies have even one guardian so kind and selfless as I have in either you or my brother? But to have two such, truly, I do not deserve it."

Colonel Fitzwilliam simply smiled and patted his cousin's hand. He did not lie when he said it would be a delight for him to spend a whole evening with her without once relinquishing her to any other gentleman.

When his Uncle Darcy died, Colonel Fitzwilliam—then merely Ens. Fitzwilliam—had been more than a little surprised to learn that he had been appointed joint guardian of his cousin. Surely, he thought, Mr. Darcy was sufficiently careful of his sister and nice in his judgments that a second guardian was not necessary. If the Colonel had been appointed alternate guardian, to take over should anything happen to Mr. Darcy, that would have been easier to understand, but the instructions in the will had been clear.

It was some time before he landed on an explanation that satisfied him. He concluded that his uncle had hoped that by throwing him and Georgiana together in this way, he would encourage the possibility of a marriage between them. This theory had not originally occurred to the Colonel as he did not think his uncle considered him worthy of his only daughter. Had he been heir to the earldom, it would have been obvious, so why was he made guardian and not his brother, who was indeed the heir? The answer eventually came to him that it was because of his brother's uncertain health, which had taken something of a downward turn not long before his uncle's death. Old Mr. Darcy must have planned a union between Georgiana and his younger nephew because he did not expect his older nephew to survive to Georgiana's maturity. The Colonel had felt troubled by this speculation and had determined not to take part in any arrangement that was so offensive to his sensibilities as a brother.

As of yet, this had not been a difficult promise to keep. Colonel Fitzwilliam had not had any inclination to think of his ward as anything but a child, but seeing her this Christmas had worked to alter that. A womanly grace had crept into her tall and once awkward frame; her naturally gentle air was utterly devoid of superficiality. Though her face was not particularly handsome, it was pleasing in its appearance of sense and good humour, especially when she smiled with shy affection, as she did now. Warmed by the softness of her voice, and the sincerity of her attention, the Colonel began to be tested in his resolve not to regard her as a prospective life partner. He felt that his connection to her was unique and precious, that the world did not see her as he did, and, indeed, could not perceive her true worth. He predicted that, when once she came out and began to be introduced to other gentlemen, they would see in her an enviable wife, for her fortune, her taste and her sweetness. But he saw her as more than these things. She offered disinterested affection and humble, intelligent conversation; she did not seek praise from others, which was more than could be said of many of the other rich, tasteful, and demure young ladies of society. These qualities drew him to her, as it would any creature of even moderate sensibility.

Mr. Darcy had quite a different plan for Georgiana's future. He intended to forward a match between Georgiana and Mr. Bingley. He had noted that this was not a plan to bear fruit in the very near future, as Georgiana was still altogether too young for such things, but this was not a reason to delay the introduction. He well knew that his sister was slow to develop intimacy with anyone, and so it would be better to begin right away, particularly with her going to London soon. In fact, though there were several motives for her removal to town, Mr. Darcy would not be honest if he denied that this matchmaking scheme were among them.

It would not be difficult to convince Mr. Bingley of the suitability of Georgiana as a partner. If her family and her fortune and indeed her own person were not sufficient to tempt him, there was no doubt that he would yield to the influence of his friend, whose judgment in all matters he trusted more than his own. And Georgiana was so timid that it would be unlikely for her to find a suitable match without some guidance. Better that her brother should provide someone so familiar and so trusted as his own preferred companion than that her choice be left to the world and all its devices. When Mr. Darcy had raised the matter with the Colonel, therefore, the latter had not seen any cause to object. But that was before Georgiana had arrived at Pemberley; that was when he had not seen her for almost a year, before she had ceased to be merely a child.

A rustling of taffeta was heard in the hallway and, as Georgiana and the Colonel looked up, Caroline Bingley passed by the open doorway.

"Shall you walk me to the door, and see the fruits of everyone's pains in dressing for the evening?" asked Georgiana. Colonel Fitzwilliam rose and offered her his arm, which was accepted.

"And when I return," he said, "I promise I shall recount to you all the finest and most ridiculous ornaments that I see while I am there."

"Indeed, you must," she made reply. "But the sport may be ruined for I doubt very much you shall see anything to rival Miss Bingley's turban."

The Colonel laughed at this unexpected joke, and off they went, all ease and merriment and pale yellow muslin.

CHAPTER 5

Mr. Darcy and his guests entered the ball to find rooms so crowded that it appeared as though the entire county were in attendance. Caroline was delighted with the event. Here were silk and lace and titles enough to please any young lady bent on climbing the rungs of society. Immediately upon entering, they found themselves pounced upon by the guest of honour, Lady Sofia, a sprightly and energetic creature close in age to Caroline, though infinitely less guarded. Displaying every appearance of amiable sympathy, Caroline succeeded in attaching herself to Lady Sofia almost instantly and set off with her to procure as many introductions as she could until the dances began. Although she spoke very highly of Georgiana to anyone she thought might think well of her for it, she at no time felt the absence of her dear new friend from whom she had grown so quickly inseparable.

As for Mr. Darcy, the thought of standing up with a total stranger for the duration of an entire dance filled him with nearly as paralyzing a dread as it did his sister. His shyness, which was widely misapprehended as hauteur, prevented his asking many ladies to dance. This might have invited some criticism from Mr. Bingley had the latter not been, as he was, so wholly occupied in dancing himself.

All was quiet at Pemberley when the party returned, and the silence continued well into the following morning as the guests recovered from the evening. Caroline was about a little earlier than some, keen as she was to meet with Mr. Darcy and recall to him all the gaiety of the previous night's outing. To this end, she sat down to breakfast with Georgiana, who, having retired well before the guests had returned, had risen earlier than the rest of the house. Colonel Fitzwilliam soon joined them, eager to keep his promise of recounting the evening's high points, and hoping to find Georgiana alone at table.

"Good morning, Cousin, Miss Bingley," he began. "You are both looking well for such an early hour. I trust you feel as well as you appear."

"I am very well rested, thank you," replied Georgiana. "I confess myself surprised to find you both up so early. I did not look to see you for a few hours yet."

Caroline broke a piece of her toast.

"Since we all left you alone so cruelly last night," she said with a look of condescension and concern, "I thought I should make up the deficit by coming early to see you. Though it was a charming evening, and I did manage to dance most dances, I confess I thought of little but your own poor self, not able to enjoy the amusements. I recall being quite wretched with jealousy and anticipation when my older sister was out and I was not. It pains me very much to think of another suffering as I did, especially one such as yourself, who are so sure to inspire praise and admiration at every ball, when once you do enter society."

Caroline smiled and tilted her head as she bit into her toast.

"You hid your pain remarkably well," Colonel Fitzwilliam responded. "I am sure nobody present suspected you of anything but unalloyed enjoyment. It is fortunate indeed that you were able to keep your true feelings concealed, lest our hosts should think your unhappiness reflected poorly on their hospitality."

Caroline was not immediately able to answer, and Georgiana considered whether this might be as good a time as any to raise with the Colonel the idea she had struck upon while reading Clare's letter.

"I hope your sympathies did not truly mar your evening," she said to Caroline, "for there was no cause for pity. I am quite ill at ease in a crowd, and was very happy here and not at all alone. I had my aunt and Anne for company, you know. I only wanted my dear Clare to make a perfect evening of it, for every fond memory I have of the last several months has her in it."

"Your dear Clare?" Colonel Fitzwilliam repeated. "Why, you are full of surprises cousin. Who is this Clare?"

"I must have spoken to you before of my closest friend, Miss Langford. She is the nearest to a sister I have ever had."

Caroline grew attentive at this. In her plan to endear herself completely to Georgiana, she had little counted on having to supplant a rival. She chewed her toast while looking across the table at Georgiana, thinking hard about what to say next.

"I cannot recall your ever having mentioned her in my presence. Then again, it has been a very busy week, and I may have been occupied or distracted when you mentioned her."

"I was ever so miserable at school, you know," Georgiana said, "that is, until this year when I made Clare's acquaintance. When I consider my spirits since, and compare them with what they were all the years prior, I wonder that I endured so long as I did with so little complaint; but then, I suppose I did not know what I missed, having never had such a friend before."

This introduction of the subject of Clare was part of Georgiana's plan to lead the Colonel to her idea in such a way that he would think it his own. She considered this preferable to approaching her brother with a direct request. To Georgiana, the idea of asking her brother for anything beyond the many thoughtful and generous things he already did for her reeked of that demanding and repugnant sort of privilege which she had encountered so often among the daughters of wealth that she had come to know at school.

"I am sorry to hear how little enjoyment you had for such a long time," said the Colonel, his eyes showing genuine concern. "I always imagined your time at school was pleasant, not to say delightful, amongst so many of your peers."

"Do not trouble yourself on that account, cousin; all is forgotten now, and I do not believe it is the place that can be blamed. It is my nature to be reserved and slow to develop friendships, and that is why I am so fortunate to have found such a friend as Clare, who I believe will be a friend for life, though I do not know when I shall see her again, now that I have left the school."

"Well, I am very glad to hear that you have made such a friend; I hope you shall make many more so when you go to London."

"I must not despair of making many new and agreeable friends in future, but none of them, I venture, shall replace Clare. She is so good, Cousin, and always so clear-minded. I rely so much on her judgment, and she has always shown herself very wise."

"Well, perhaps you should take Miss Langford on as a lady's companion when you go," interjected Caroline, intending a slight on Georgiana's friend.

Georgiana responded in earnest to Caroline's disingenuous suggestion, which was the very thing she had hoped for.

"Miss Bingley," she said, clapping her hands together, "you must be inspired! What a capital idea! Cousin, do you think it might be possible? That is to say, I do not think I should need a companion exactly, but if she could join me in London, I know her presence would be as much a relief and a comfort to me there as it was at school."

Caroline laughed inwardly at what she imagined was simplicity on Georgiana's part.

Colonel Fitzwilliam considered the advantages of inviting this friend of his cousin's to join her in London. He knew Mr. Darcy wished Caroline Bingley to befriend Georgiana, and if Miss Langford could depose her in this role, it would place a little more distance between the object of his affection and Mr. Bingley. What is more, after only a few days in her company, Colonel Fitzwilliam was already convinced that Caroline was not at all the sort of lady to guide his unspoilt and precious charge through the moral gauntlet that was London Society.

"Tell me more about this Miss Langford." Colonel Fitzwilliam inquired. Georgiana was only too happy to oblige.

"I must first tell you how we met," she began, "though I am

afraid it will not flatter me to do so." She cast a quick glance at Caroline, who, busy inspecting the milk before pouring it in her teacup, seemed little concerned with tales of Georgiana's school chums. Georgiana turned more towards the Colonel and continued in a more confidential tone,

"One evening in the first week of school, I was sitting in the dining room with a few other girls, and I noticed a new girl sitting quite alone. The girl was, of course, Clare. I was not really included in the conversation of the girls I was with, but I soon started to hear them speak of Clare, and imply that she would always be alone at that school, that she did not deserve to be there. Clare is not as wealthy as most of the girls at school, you see, but still you may imagine my embarrassment when some of the other girls began to voice their presumptions about Clare's parentage, her dowry and her marriage prospects. Clare must have been able to hear them, for she could not have been more than fifteen feet away, and the girls never made any attempt to lower their voices. If she did hear, though, she never showed it. My own face burned with shame. I longed to leave the table, to apologize to Clare for the behaviour of these girls."

Georgiana lowered her head as she admitted, "I am ashamed to say that I simply could not muster the courage to defend Clare to so many girls at once. It was only a minute or two before one of the staff approached our table and quieted their chat, but I regret having been complicit in their barbarism, even for those few moments."

Colonel Fitzwilliam smiled at her purity, to feel such deep remorse for a small sin of omission.

"Later that evening, as it had been rather a warm day, many of the girls were spending some time out of doors. Clare was seated on a bench beside the river, which flowed past the garden, and I begged a place beside her. I was shaking with anxiety, as I always do when speaking to a stranger, but I forced myself to speak to her, to say that I was very sorry for the things the girls had said over supper, and that I was even sorrier that I did nothing to stop it. I knew the girls to be better than they had shown themselves, and I asked that she accept my apology on their behalf. It was very difficult for me to say, however necessary, but Clare put me completely at ease. Truly, I think her so much above all the other girls at school, whatever their fortunes. Do you know how she replied?"

"Do tell me," said the Colonel.

"She said that it was nothing, that people so often speak without thought, and that we cannot allow these things to encroach on our own peace. If they pursue a path of ill-will and calumny, they shall only meet with their own misery and loneliness, for true friendship cannot survive such conditions and none can be truly happy without friendship. She also allowed that they would see their error now it was over, and shall not repeat such behaviour. Did you ever hear such magnanimity?"

"She spoke very wisely," observed the Colonel.

"And in earnest, I assure you," added Georgiana. "I have come to know her well enough since, and can confidently say that such Christian principles, without any trace of pride or vanity, govern all her thoughts and actions. Truly, she is no less deserving of a place at that school than any of the other girls. Her father may be of obscure birth, but he has been elevated to the rank of Admiral, which is not insignificant."

"Quite so," agreed Colonel Fitzwilliam.

"And her mother was the daughter of a baronet, which really is something, particularly since the fortunes of several of the girls who mocked her that night were made in trade," Georgiana remembered Caroline, whose family's fortune had also been made in trade, and quickly added, "which is respectable and I say nothing against it, but it does not elevate them to a station *above* hers. Would not you agree?"

"I would, yes," answered the Colonel. "She sounds a very deserving creature indeed, and would be an entirely suitable companion in London."

Clare was indeed an uncommonly virtuous and sensible girl—a secret weakness for horrid novels notwithstanding—but she was intolerant of her own faults and, in turns, valiantly battled, vehemently denied, and, to her own abhorrence, occasionally indulged them. By this is meant that, in rare, dark moments, she could be found eagerly enjoying a gruesome work of fiction, and loathing her own enjoyment of it.

Raising his voice a little so as to include Caroline, the Colonel added, "We must thank Miss Bingley for the idea of inviting her. I shall take the proposal to Mr. Darcy as early as possible."

Colonel Fitzwilliam followed through on his promise, presenting with all the enthusiasm and support that could be justified on the subject the idea of Clare's accompanying Georgiana in London. Mr. Darcy agreed to consider it.

This was joyful news to Georgiana, who then thought she had better ensure her friend would find the proposal equally agreeable before pursuing it further. She therefore spent much of that evening in writing to Clare on the subject.

CHAPTER 6

Georgiana had been correct in her assessment that Clare was not so far beneath the other girls. Clare's grandfather, Sir Geoffrey Crawley, had indeed been a baronet—and his seat, Farrow Hall, in Nottinghamshire, a very respectable one. Her father, however, was not of high birth. He had been merely a midshipman at the time of his marriage to Clare's mother, but with the help of the Crawleys—and of his own skill and bravery—he had worked his way through the ranks of the Navy to become Admiral Langford. Maplethwaite, the small property where they lived, had come into the Crawley family through a marriage a few generations prior and did not belong to the Langfords outright. It was Clare's mother's for life, having been set aside for her by a doting grandfather, but would pass to the Crawley heir upon her death.

Whatever status Clare had, her family estate and her limited import as granddaughter of a baronet, all depended upon her mother's continued survival. If anything were to take Mrs. Langford before she saw Clare well settled, there would be little chance of her ever being so.

With good regulation and restraint, the Langfords had expected that, in a few short years, they should be able to repay their debts and set aside enough money to provide an ample dowry for Clare and to purchase lands in freehold to pass on to their only son, Clare's younger brother, Crawley, but a sudden threat to Mrs. Langford's health that November had left them uncertain as to whether those years would be their own.

Neither of the children had been called home from school. To do so would both jeopardize their education and incur costs against their currently meagre inheritance.

When Mrs. Langford first proposed to her sister-in-law that Clare and Crawley might stay with them for the holiday, Mrs. Watson insisted that their home was not grand enough for the granddaughter of a baronet, that it would be impossible to house them in the luxury to which they must be accustomed, and that any attempt to do so would pain her as much with embarrassment as with expense. She bemoaned the fact throughout for she excessively wished to improve her acquaintance with her niece and nephew and to show them any kindness that it was in her power to bestow. Mrs. Langford replied with assurances that the Watsons' home was appointed more than well enough to satisfy Clare and Crawley, who had both been brought up to eschew ostentatious shows of wealth. What is more, she continued, both of the Langford children, having been at school for several months, would be delighted with the many charms of the Watson home and its inhabitants. The warmth and comfort of a family home would be everything Clare and Crawley could wish for. She assured Mrs. Watson that it could be very agreeable to have Clare and Crawley in the house for a few weeks, for their company and their assistance with the children. Mrs. Watson would not be required to wait upon her guests. Rather, her guests would dutifully wait upon her. All Mrs. Watson's fears that she could not meet every desire and wish of her relations were put to rest by such promises of their servitude to her.

Clare sat at the breakfast table with her aunt in a rare moment of tranquility when Georgiana's letter was delivered to her. Recognizing the post mark, she rejoiced.

"It is a letter from Miss Darcy! I have been so anxious to hear from her. May I be excused, Aunt, to read this?" Clare was, in fact, anxious to hear from Georgiana, and not a little because it might give her excuse to sit alone a while without disturbance.

"Of course you may read your letter. I should never forgive

myself if I should delay your pleasure for a moment. Only do make sure the breakfast things are tidied away first, and that the children are dressed and engaged in their studies. Miss Brown tells me she is feeling a little indisposed today. Truly, she would be indebted to you for your assistance with the children. And Molly already has so much to do. I do like to relieve her a little of her burdens when I can."

"Of course, Aunt. We must all offer what kindness is in our power."

Clare rose, and with admirable resignation set about realizing her aunt's benevolence towards the help, while their mistress remained at the table sipping her tea and reflecting with pleasure on her own magnanimity.

It was almost noon before Clare found peace and solitude enough to read Georgiana's letter.

"MY DEAREST CLARE,"

"I hope this letter finds you and your family in continuing good health and happiness. Do write and tell me how your brother's dancing has been coming along, and whether he has been to any balls and how he has liked them. I long to hear how you have been enjoying yourself this season.

"We have all been quite merry here. I believe I might even have seen Lady Catherine smile once, though Miss Bingley suggested it was merely indigestion. Sadly, the fullness of our days and the attention of our guests have meant that I have had little time to dedicate to writing to you, which I have been most anxious to do.

"I hope you will not be very angry with me for doing so without consulting you first, but I have asked my brother if you might accompany me in London when I transfer there, and he has agreed to consider it. He has not given his final approval, but I am confident he will find no fault with the idea, as he could not find any fault with you. I write to inquire whether this is agreeable to you or not. I know you will need your parents' consent, but I can see no cause for them to object; my brother shall provide all the best masters and he will arrange everything to meet the most exacting standards. I constantly tell myself of all the advantage it shall be to you if you accept, because I know it to be such a selfish request on my part. I shall not fear London half so much if you are with me. I shall restrain myself from making all the entreaties that my heart presses me to make, as I do not wish to burden you with my disappointment if you are not in a position to accept this proposal. I simply ask that you reply as soon as you are able with your own thoughts and feelings on the subject. If they be favourable, I shall advise you as soon as I hear whether my brother consents to my request. I pray that he does, for I can imagine nothing that should bring me more joy.

"And now I must tell you more on a subject that you raised in your last letter. You will be pleased to learn what an improving influence you have been on me regarding my cousin, Miss Anne de Bourgh. Your encouragement spurred me to seek out a greater intimacy with her. As you know, she is my elder and, as she has not attempted to further our friendship, I have assumed that she did not desire to do so and so I have not pursued a friendship with her. But lately I had begun to question whether I had judged aright. Timid as I am, I little suspected that I could intimidate anyone else, especially one of my elders. She is, though, very small and frail. I wondered if she might be like me: shy of others and uncertain how to enter upon a closer acquaintance, or even upon conversation in general. After all, with my aunt always present with her, Anne has had as little opportunity of practicing her conversation as she has had fair examples to follow.

"With this in mind, I sat up with Anne and my aunt on the night of one of the balls to which my brother and our guests had been invited. We sat in the drawing room by the fire—we being Lady Catherine, Miss de Bourgh, her companion Mrs. Jenkinson, and myself. As there was nothing much to be said—her Ladyship being the only one to say any of it—my aunt soon retired to bed, leaving strict instructions for Mrs. Jenkinson that my cousin do the same as soon as she had finished her tea. What I say next may shock you: I dismissed

Mrs. Jenkinson straight away, saying that I would answer to Lady Catherine for it if need should arise. I was determined to find a subject that would draw my cousin out, and I felt that, like me, she would be more likely to speak with fewer people to hear.

"Try as I might, I could not engage her. I entered on poetry, art, fashion, bonnets, architecture, landscape design, even carriages and horses, all without success. I began to wonder whether it would be necessary to resort to less polite topics, and was steeling myself to raise the war in France when I chanced a remark on a scar I have on my wrist from an insect bite that has refused to heal. My cousin asked me what sort of insect it was that had bitten me. When I said I was not sure, she asked me what it looked like. You must understand that two questions on the same subject is more than my cousin has ever asked me in the whole course of our lives, and so, though I could hardly remember the incident, I did my best to supply a description of the offending creature. I could never have predicted the onslaught of inquiry and information that followed. My cousin, dearest Clare, is a closet naturalist!

"Due to her delicate health, she spends most of her time indoors. It seems that my cousin has made a constant study of all of the books on natural science in the De Bourgh's extensive library.

"As such subjects do not often arise in the company of Lady Catherine, so my cousin is rarely induced to speak. Indeed, I cannot recall her saying more than three words together on any occasion, but ask her of beetles, spiders, or earthworms and she will hold forth every bit as copiously as a lady of fashion might speak of partners at a ball or gowns ordered from the Mantua maker.

"I was very eager to share this anecdote with you so you might see how fruitful your efforts with me have been, and how gratified I have been for my efforts with my cousin. Only imagine what you could achieve with me if I were under your constant guidance and example.

"Please let me know your first response to this proposal of

mine to join me in London. I shall await your reply in restless anticipation.

"Yours etc.

"GEORGIANA"

Clare set the letter down. She had been smiling for so long and with such enthusiasm that her cheeks were sore. She could not recall, since separating from Georgiana in November, feeling such happiness. In fact, she could not recall ever looking forward to a scheme with such felicity as she did to the prospect of spending the coming months in the society of her dearest friend. She would not have allowed that the idea of London and all its delights held any attraction for her, for she believed cities to be a hazard to the soul. She never questioned that she would have been equally overjoyed at the prospect of accompanying her friend to Sunderland. Fortunately, she never had occasion to test that belief.

As she folded the letter, Clare made several resolutions. She resolved to write to Georgiana that very day to express her unreserved acceptance of the proposal. She resolved to write to her parents and introduce to them the idea of her going to London, firmly believing their frugality would dispose them favourably to the savings it would afford them. And most importantly, as she was to be responsible for the development of the young Miss Darcy, she resolved to expunge all fault from her character. To that end, she took all her novels from their hiding places, wrapped them in a bundle and headed out to return them to the circulating library from which she had borrowed them under an assumed name.

CHAPTER 7

Four weeks after the arrival of his Christmas guests, Mr. Darcy found himself in the unhappy position of understanding less of the character of Miss Caroline Bingley than he had before ever she entered his house. He enjoyed her company despite the occasional impertinence of her remarks. He could not doubt that her wit and her spirit rather livened the household. He believed Georgiana might benefit from the influence of her self-assurance.

Yet still, he perceived in her character a disregard for the feelings of others, an exaggerated and misplaced self-importance, and a quickness of temper to which he did not wish to expose his sister. He was rather relieved at the introduction of the idea of Miss Langford, for she seemed, from Georgiana's account, to be more than suitable to accompany her in London. As the chosen friend of his sister, she would be the best person to make Georgiana easy in her new situation, and her presence would alleviate the immediate need to forge any new relationships for her.

Mr. Darcy had consulted the Colonel, whose opinion as co-guardian he valued highly. Interested in separating Georgiana as much as possible from the Bingleys, the Colonel concurred with Mr. Darcy on all the points in favour of inviting Miss Langford to join Georgiana in London. Among other things, he pointed out that in providing someone to be with her always, he would be relieving much of his sister's anxiety, which was considerable. Colonel Fitzwilliam could see that

Caroline was more than prepared to receive Mr. Darcy's attentions, and he did not wish to see his cousin grow too fond of that lady, for reasons which were beyond his own self-interest.

Had Mr. Darcy known the details of Caroline's behaviour while staying at Pemberley, it would have confirmed him to a highly unfavourable opinion of her. She had acted the tyrant with every maid in the house; she had called a servant to her chamber in the middle of the night nearly every night of her stay and always for the most trivial of reasons; she complained that the fire did not burn warm enough to keep her comfortable at night and when a larger blaze was prepared, complained that the closeness did not suit her constitution and that the windows must be opened to allow it to escape, which only redoubled her complaints about the cold. The staff grew to dread her call, but Caroline was little interested in the opinions of the servants.

The one whose opinion she *did* value was becoming every day more attached to her—of this she was certain. As the four weeks passed, she had grown ever more assured that her future at the estate was beyond doubt. She believed she detected, in Mr. Darcy's frequent and close attentions, a deep and irrepressible affection. It was clear that he wished her to befriend his sister, and what else could that signify but that he meant to prepare them both for mutual sisterhood? Her only point of vexation was that he had not attempted to speak to her alone at any time. She was certain that four weeks was sufficient to make him fall in love with her, for she never doubted her own charms. Her only explanation to herself was that Mr. Darcy was a man of consequence; he was not quick to make decisions of great importance. She consoled herself that a passion such as his could only be augmented by her absence and that she would not be long away from Pemberley.

A few days following the departure of the Bingleys and the De Bourghs, Georgiana's guardians broke the silence of the drawing room with long-awaited news.

"Georgiana," Mr. Darcy began, "I have something to tell

you—an answer for which I believe you have been most anxious, though you have borne your anxiety with admirable patience and control."

The young lady's eyes shot up from her cup. She spoke without releasing her breath.

"Please, do not keep me in suspense, Brother."

"Calm yourself, Cousin," interjected the Colonel. "It is good news." Mr. Darcy nodded for him to continue. "It has all been arranged; your friend Miss Langford shall join you in London."

Georgiana's teacup, which had hitherto been suspended before her open mouth, now sounded against her saucer, and her saucer against the table as she hastened to arise and embrace her brother. "Oh thank you, Brother, thank you" she said into Mr. Darcy's shoulder. "And you too, Cousin, thank you so very much." She took his hand and kissed his cheek with an uncharacteristic exuberance that caused him to blush, though the fact went happily unnoticed by either of his cousins.

That evening was spent going over plans—plans which were frequently interrupted by exclamations of rapture and gratitude from Pemberley's most joyful resident. Free to speak her feelings on the subject, since it could no longer be perceived as insistence on her own wishes, Georgiana shared with her brother what fears he had allayed and what a comfort and relief it brought her to know that she would have a true and trusted friend with her in a new and overwhelming place such as London. Indeed, Georgiana may have spoken more words— and these more quickly—that evening than she had done so far in all of the New Year.

The following day, the Colonel and Mr. Darcy were invited on a shooting expedition with Lord Brackenhall and his son, Lord Branston. Georgiana was to spend the day with Lady Brackenhall and her daughter, Lady Sofia, at Pemberley, and all were invited for supper following the hunt. Shortly after the meal, Lady Brackenhall enquired whether any progress had been made in setting Georgiana up in London.

"It will be charming for the girls," said Lady Brackenhall,

"both staying in Mayfair. I am sure it must be very pleasant to have a long-standing acquaintance near one, especially when one is moving to a new place, with so many new people."

"Indeed," replied Mr. Darcy. "I have begun making inquiries as to the best masters, and my cousin Ashwell wrote to me only just this morning to say that he is able to make some recommendations."

"Your cousin Ashwell?" Lady Brackenhall's expression was a mix of curiosity and surprise.

"You remember Lord Ashwell, Mama," Lady Sofia began, mistaking her mother's meaning. "He is the Colonel's brother who lives in Grosvenor Square. I invite him every year to at least one ball, though he rarely attends."

"Of course I remember him," Lady Brackenhall said impatiently. "Only I did not expect he would be much involved in Miss Darcy's education, not, that is to say, publicly, for his reputation, I would not have thought . . . I mean, do you expect she shall see much of Lord Ashwell while she is in town?" Lady Brackenhall attempted to recover from her stumble into an awkward subject. She did not like to gossip, but she was not able to restrain her interest, particularly where there was a history of scandal, however long ago. And a scandal there had been. She did not prevent her own daughter from extending invitations to him as he rarely accepted and she trusted to her daughter's very able and conscientious chaperone Mrs. Belfry to keep her from any danger.

"I believe I know to what your ladyship refers. All I am permitted to say on the subject is that it was a long time ago, that he is a faithful friend to my sister, and that what one hears and reads in the papers often leaves out the essential and exculpatory facts."

"Of course, Mr. Darcy. I did not mean to suggest . . . That is to say, it will no doubt benefit Miss Darcy to have such noble connections. And your house, it is in Berkeley Square if memory serves."

"Yes, it is," he answered.

"Very close to you then, Sofia dear," remarked Lady

Brackenhall. "You shall be able to visit as often as you choose."

"The roads in that neighbourhood are very serviceable," Lord Brackenhall noted with approval.

"They are, indeed, some of the best kept roads in London," Lord Branston agreed.

"Well then, on a fine day the young ladies might even venture to walk between the houses."

Lady Brackenhall could not restrain her horror.

"I should hope not, my dear," she huffed. "I do not think you should wish to see your daughter traipsing about the London pavement, wearing out her shoes and exposing herself to the multitudes. Please tell me you would not do such a thing, Sofia."

"I assure you, Mama, there are no multitudes in Mayfair. It would be a great deal more amusing if there were. And Mrs. Belfry always insists on the carriage no matter how short the journey, so your worries are without cause, though I would walk barefoot clear through Bow if a friend were in need of me."

"Well, let us be thankful that Mrs. Belfry takes such care of you as to have the carriage always ready should such an idea seize you."

Lord Branston was quick to join the conversation which touched on one of his favourite subjects.

"On a fine day, a phaeton is always preferable to traveling by foot," he said. "It allows one to see and be seen, and the pace is not to be rivaled. What sort of carriage will you keep in town, Miss Darcy?"

"You must excuse my brother," Lady Sofia joined in. "He thinks of nothing but horses and carriages. I, for one, see nothing fascinating in something that is merely a means of conveyance; it is the destination and the company that concern me. Pray, who will have charge of Miss Darcy when she is in Town?"

"I have a very dear friend from school who is to accompany me," answered Georgiana, "a Miss Langford of Maplethwaite, in Nottinghamshire."

"As for someone to preside over their education, we have not yet fixed on anyone," added Mr. Darcy.

Colonel Fitzwilliam continued, "It is a very exacting task to identify a lady with adequate credentials and a suitable character to run such a place. You can understand that filling this position is perhaps the most crucial step in the business."

"Oh Mama!" cried Lady Sofia, leaping from her seat and seizing her mother's hand. "You must allow me to recommend Mrs. Younge. It is too fortuitous." Turning to Mr. Darcy, eyes wide and gestures exaggerated, she continued before her mother could answer her. "Mr. Darcy, please excuse my impertinence, but I feel it is fate that this subject be raised before me at just this hour, for I am acquainted with a lady in London who has only just written to me this week to ask if I may recommend her to a position. She is an educated lady—a widow of a soldier who was fallen only last year, taken by fever while deployed on the continent. They had hoped he might make his fortune in the war, but he did not have the time to do so, God rest him. Her pension is barely enough to live on. Colonel Fitzwilliam, you must know the worth of your fellow soldiers. Is not it a duty to do a kindness to a late comrade's family when the opportunity arises? Please say you will consider it, please. It is such a tragic case, and I do so wish to bring the light of hope into this poor creature's dark and blighted life."

"That is enough, Sofia," interjected Lord Brackenhall. "I am sure the Colonel and Mr. Darcy are capable of choosing an appropriate person for the situation without any of your sentimentality."

"The name was Younge, you say?" asked the Colonel.

"Yes, Private Thomas Younge was her husband."

The Colonel turned to Mr. Darcy. "Well, it can do no harm to make inquiries, can it?"

In fact, Mr. Darcy was very grateful for the recommendation. As yet, a suitable candidate had not emerged, and he was beginning to think he may have to accept his aunt's offer to supply someone for the position. He would be very happy to give preference to any satisfactory alternative.

"No, indeed not, and if she can provide reliable references, we shall certainly not deny her application outright."

Lady Sofia gasped loudly and clasped her hand to her heart. "Oh, you must be the most saintly gentlemen I have ever known. You have my eternal admiration and gratitude. I know you will find no fault in her, for I never met with anyone of such true and worthy sentiments as hers." She tilted her head in acknowledgement and with a sigh returned to her seat and to her screen.

As the guests departed that night, Mr. Darcy knew his sister would wish to know the history of their cousin, James Lord Ashwell, but would not be so bold as to ask. He thought it would be unfair not to tell her something about it.

"I know you must wonder," he said, "what Lady Brackenhall and I meant about our cousin Ashwell. I know you are too good to inquire about old gossip, but, in case you find the hint of rumours troubling, allow me to set your mind at ease. You are too young to remember the story, and those old enough to remember it dismissed it long ago due to Lord Ashwell's longstanding reputation as a gentleman of worth and respectability. Old and idle gossip cannot alter the value of our connection with him. There is nothing you need fear on that account. And there is nothing more you need to know."

Mr. Darcy was sincere in his defense of his cousin. He did not merely wish him innocent out of family pride. If he had believed Ashwell capable of the kind of unscrupulous conduct of which he had been accused, he would not have risked exposing his impressionable sister to such a man. The allegations were of such a nature that Mr. Darcy could have no personal knowledge of their truth or falseness. Though he had never been given any entirely satisfactory explanation, he knew enough of his cousin's heart to be unconvinced by the appearance of the matter.

CHAPTER 8

It was a still, cold January morning when Clare departed Leamington to return to school, expressing a regret she did not feel at leaving her relations, and giving largely futile instructions to her young cousins to be good and to apply themselves to their studies. Had her stay been longer, her influence on the children might have been more enduring, but, with a mother and a governess such as they had, the chances her efforts would have lasting effects were negligible at best. Though she was little saddened by the thought of taking leave of the Watsons, parting company with her brother was quite a different matter.

"I hope you shall be happy to return to school, Crawley," Clare said as they awaited the carriages. "It shall not be too long until we next meet, and perhaps our aunt and uncle might invite you to come again, though I doubt I shall be able to accept any invitations for some time."

"Goodness, Clare," replied Crawley, "I shouldn't worry about me if I were you. School is very jolly. We have some sport or other nearly every day, though I should like it above all things to come back here when there is more dancing to be had, whether you are able or no. I am sure I can get a partner without a sister's aid."

"You shall never want for partners, Brother."

As she climbed into the carriage, Clare's heart was a mix of sadness, relief and anticipation, though her calm and practiced smile revealed none of this turmoil. The journey was like every other: long, uncomfortable, and short on diversion. She arrived at school just in time for supper, which she ate in silence, seated alone.

Upon returning at last to her room, she found two letters waiting for her, one from her mother, the other from Georgiana. In a moment of rare abandon, she left her mother's words to wait, unread, while she unsealed with alacrity the letter from her friend, eager for all the genuine and sisterly affection she knew it would contain, as well as anxious for news of her possible invitation to London.

"MY DEAREST CLARE,"

"I am sending this to the school, where I hope it will find you happy and well and safely arrived after a pleasant journey. I am sorry that you must now be apart from your dear brother. I know well the joy a loving brother can be to one who is separated from all other family. I trust you left him and your other relations well and in good spirits, and I cannot help saying that I hope your absence teaches them to love and appreciate you all the more.

"How I miss your company, dear Clare. I have missed you since the first moment we separated in the Autumn, but I feel it even more keenly now than I did then. We have lost the last of our company, and with it all our amusement. My cousin, Colonel Fitzwilliam, left this morning, and the house now feels so very large and empty. My thoughts cannot help but turn to those who once made it a home. But I shall not dwell on misery. This is to be a happy letter, full of good news.

"You must steel yourself for an arduous task, my sweet friend. Henceforth, most of your time will be spent in the company of a very troublesome creature. My guardians have advised me that they will grant my request for you to accompany me to London. The formal invitation is forthcoming, but how could I not tell you as soon as I was able?

"As you are far more disciplined than myself, I am sure you can bear the time between now and then without agitation, but

I am afraid I cannot. I am all nerves and apprehension and expect I will be thus until I am arrived and settled in town. How much comfort it will be to have such a friend as you with me at all times.

"And I shall have the pleasure of introducing to you all those of whom I have talked so much, for we shall live not far from several friends. I tell myself this when the thoughts of London overwhelm me. This may not be my first time in town, but it was quite different when I was younger. I never attended any public events then, and so, very little was expected of me. How I dread the idea of being out in society, though it should be such a pleasant prospect for young ladies of stronger constitution than myself. I know it cannot be put off forever, but I do not imagine it will take place before I am fully fifteen. I treasure the thought of evenings spent just the pair of us in our parlour, drinking cocoa and reading to each other, at least in the early weeks.

"You see how vexatious I can be? To bring you all the way to London, to the heart of all things diverting and pleasant, and then to keep you all to myself by the fire, as secluded as though we were a pair of Cornish spinsters, never seeing anyone or anything, our only distraction the possibility of a call from my cousin, Lord Ashwell. I do hope he shall visit us often, for his house in Grosvenor Square is so very close to ours in Berkeley Square. I do not think I have spoken much of him before, but it is not for want of love. I hope he shall not be too proud or too occupied to visit his little cousin. Though I have always known him to be congenial and never haughty, he is a viscount after all, and heir to my uncle's earldom, and I must not expect too much attention from him.

"It may be overly cautious, but still, I feel I should advise that if you should hear any untoward stories about Lord Ashwell, pay them no heed. My brother assures me that our cousin's friendship will only be to our benefit, and I have never known my brother to be wrong.

"My brother has also received a recommendation for a proprietor of our new institution, and as the referral came from such an old friend as it did, it shall likely be taken up. So matters are being settled quickly, and we may be in town as soon as Easter.

"And now, I shall leave you to settle back into your own life and lessons at school, all of which I am soon to disrupt again. As ever, I remain,

"Yours, etc.

"GEORGIANA"

Clare dwelt on Georgiana's words for some time before she was able to set down her friend's letter and turn her attention to her mother's.

"DEAR CLARE,"

"Your father and I received your recent letter with joy. We were pleased to read the news you sent of your aunt and uncle and were grateful to learn that they are in good health and free of worldly concerns. We are certain that your stay there was of benefit to yourself as well as to them and theirs, and we hope you did not miss any opportunity of being of use to your aunt, for acting in a spirit of selflessness and giving does as much good for the giver's character as it does for the life of the receiver. We trust that your stay afforded you an opportunity of mixing with an expanded circle of desirable society. We cannot stress enough how important it is that you maintain every suitable new acquaintance with a regular and frequent correspondence. You cannot rely solely on the connections you have formed at school to carry you through life when once you quit that place. The friendship of Miss Darcy is, of course, a great privilege, but you must not depend upon it exclusively.

"On the subject of Miss Darcy, your father and I have discussed the proposal which you conveyed of possibly joining her in London. We were both of us struck by a consideration. London will afford you the opportunity of mixing with very good society, the advantages of which cannot be overstressed. However, moving in such circles means that you are just as likely to encounter temptation and very poor society, which ever abound in London. We would be remiss were we not to warn you of the dangers thereof to a young lady such as yourself who has not lived in the world and who would not have her own protector. Your position will require you to be disciplined on behalf of Georgiana as well as yourself; you must take constant care that neither you nor Miss Darcy be exposed to anything untoward. What is more, you must take care to prevent any occurrence that might sour your relationship with Georgiana and cost you your intimacy with the Darcy family, which is an association of great value.

"After careful consideration, your father and I have concluded that the opportunity is one which cannot be passed by, and we believe that your own character is sure enough not to be overly susceptible to the ills of the city which might give us pause were you raised without such principles as you have been. Therefore, we can advise that if you are invited to join Miss Darcy in town, you must accept.

"If you require anything further, please do not scruple to ask. Though our means are not extensive, we shall not see our only daughter shamed by the unwarranted appearance of want.

Please be assured that your father and I are both well. My illness has not caused me to slow in my charity work, praise be to God, and your father urges me to include his affectionate regard. I do so and remain,

"Yours, etc."

Clare set down her letters and considered the responsibility that should in a short time be hers, and the weight of her parents' expectations, and all the work she had to do before her lessons began again on Monday. Anxious from all these considerations, she reached beneath her mattress and retrieved a copy of Vathek, which she took to reading with equal parts repressed delight and wretched self-contempt.

CHAPTER 9

Caroline Bingley entered her London house, removed her bonnet, and looked about herself. She saw the fashionable residence which had long been a source of pride and satisfaction, and she saw all the improvements it wanted— improvements which the Darcy fortune could bring about. She took the stairs to her room, calling the housekeeper after her.

"Mrs. Cooper, please accompany me. I have some instructions for you."

Mrs. Cooper followed with as much haste as her stout and aging frame would allow.

"Please have Thomas look into the cost of having the plasterwork in the entrance replaced. It is in a shocking state, and really ought to have been seen to while we were away. I should also like to know whether it is possible to replace the mullioned windows on the upper floors with sash. It should have been done years ago. Finally, I should like to have the candles refreshed every evening that I am at home."

"Yes, madam."

"Oh, and tell Pimm to prepare only a light meal this evening. Traveling always wreaks havoc on my appetite. And remember that Louisa arrives tomorrow, so her room will need to be prepared. I imagine Mr. Hurst will also be joining us for supper.

"I have several calls to make tomorrow morning, so I will need the carriages ready. And my gowns will likely need pressing after being packed. Louisa and I shall be out much these coming weeks, preparing for the wedding, and she will likely have many callers, so I shall need all my best gowns at my disposal."

"Yes, Madam. Will that be all?"

Caroline waved the housekeeper away. She had just crossed the threshold when Caroline called her back.

"Oh, and Mrs. Cooper? I should like a bath this evening."

Mrs. Cooper muttered to herself as she passed Mr. Bingley on the stairs. He was coming from speaking with the butler, whom he had asked to tell Pimm to prepare a hearty supper as long journeys never failed of increasing his appetite.

Caroline sat at her dressing table as the servants brought in her trunks and Jenny unpacked them. Caroline, watching them go about their work, reflected on the servants—something she almost never did. Mrs. Cooper was a dependable housekeeper, but was not so refined as might become the future Mrs. Darcy. Caroline and Mr. Bingley had brought her down from the North when they had relocated; she had been with the Bingleys since the early days of their wealth. She had kept many of her northern mannerisms and idioms, and Caroline now questioned whether this would really do. Furthermore, Caroline was always having to instruct Mrs. Cooper on how things were to be done. Perhaps a southern housekeeper would take the lead in improving the household. After all, was not it the role of the servants to keep abreast of how things are done in the best houses and to direct themselves accordingly?

As for Jenny, she was well-mannered and competent enough, but she knew little of fashion. It may be preferable to engage a French ladies maid, who would know all the best ways to arrange hair and other accessories in accordance with the latest styles. Caroline was certain that the most fashionable ladies all had French maids.

She knew she would face opposition from her brother on these improvements, especially as regarded Mrs. Cooper, to whom he was excessively attached. Caroline thought such fondness for the staff to be undignified and sentimental. Surely, her own feelings and wishes were of greater import than those of the help.

Nevertheless, to avoid confrontation, she decided it was best to wait until the engagement was formal before she embarked on any alterations to either the house or its staff. Once her future as Mrs. Darcy was sure, she would discuss these matters with her future husband, who would persuade her brother of her opinions in an instant, for Charles never questioned the judgment of his friend. And Caroline never questioned that Mr. Darcy would be entirely of her mind in everything.

In fact, Caroline spent almost no time thinking of Mr. Darcy at all. It might have entered her head, had she let it, that it was odd for a woman set on marrying a man never to think of him, but being made almost entirely of mercenary ambition, Caroline believed Mr. Darcy to be constantly on her mind because his income constantly was.

The following day Louisa arrived. The two sisters had much to discuss and the house exploded with chatter and laughter on Louisa's entrance.

The Bingley sisters spent the hours until supper sharing their respective visions of their soon to be married lives, describing the fashions and the houses observed in their respective sojourns, and intermittently giving long lists of tasks to their respective maids, most of which was to be repeated over supper for the benefit of their brother, which repetition had allowed the ladies to perfect their news with embellishment and wit thought of only after the first telling.

CHAPTER 10

The following week, an invitation arrived from Lady Sofia and Lord Branston to attend an evening party at their London house. To everyone's gratitude, the invitation was not limited to Caroline and Mr. Bingley; it extended to Louisa, who had returned from her holidays, and to Mr. Hurst as well. The heart of Lady Sofia was always most generously inclined towards strangers. She always gave the most to those she knew the least.

The Bingley sisters brimmed with anticipation as they entered the ball. They were not disappointed. Upon spying them, Lady Sofia rushed forward to greet their party with all the passion of a long-separated lover.

"Dearest Caroline! Mr. Bingley! How pleased I am that you could join us. It is almost a month since we last met in Derbyshire, and I have every hour longed to see you again. Now," she continued, "this must be the sister of whom you spoke. I should know her for your sister anywhere. You share the same interesting sensibility in your manner."

"Indeed, Lady Sofia, allow me to present my sister, Miss Bingley."

Louisa curtseyed.

"I am delighted to make your acquaintance, Miss Bingley," said Lady Sofia, "but I insist that you call me Sofia. Only the servants ever call me Lady, and I feel a kinship with you already."

She turned her head to examine Louisa's companion.

"And this," she said, "must be the worthy gentleman who has been so fortunate as to secure your hand."

"Yes," answered Louisa. "May I introduce Mr. Hurst."

"You are most welcome, Mr. Hurst. I so hope you will enjoy the entertainments this evening. We are simple people, and enjoy the simplicity of company and conversation, but I do not doubt there shall be some sport before the evening is through. Do you play cards, Mr. Hurst?"

"A little, madam."

"I never knew anyone so fond of cards as Mr. Hurst," interjected Mr. Bingley.

"Well, we must introduce him to my brother then. Reginald has been keen to make Mr. Hurst's acquaintance since he first learned from Caroline that he drives a Curricle. This, plus their common interest in cards, must secure their eternal friendship."

Lady Sofia looked around the room in search of her brother.

"Come, Mr. Hurst," said Mr. Bingley, "let us go and find Branston. I am sure the ladies can occupy themselves." And with that, the two men departed, leaving the ladies with Sofia, who immediately began to inquire all about Miss Bingley's wedding clothes and honeymoon plans.

Just as Louisa was opening her mouth to make answer, a party made their entrance to the drawing room. Lady Sofia, recognising the new arrivals, let out a short, sharp cry of surprised delight, causing Louisa to catch her breath.

"Oh, I do apologise, Miss Bingley," said Lady Sofia, hurriedly, waving over the newly arrived guests. "Only I am so thrilled that dear Mrs. Younge has been able to join us. I have been most anxious to introduce her to all my acquaintance. And she brings with her a friend of her late husband's. I suppose we ought to have met him in Derbyshire as he is a very old friend of the Darcys. If I am not mistaken, he is to return there shortly—and to a very excellent living. I am sure others may find it improper for a lady to be out alone with a gentleman, but I do not think such a rule applies to widows, do you? And besides, I believe those in grief should be afforded every flexibility in rules of decorum. Society is cruel to judge those who have suffered as deeply as Mrs. Younge. Shall I introduce them?"

Caroline and Louisa were always keen to expand their acquaintance, especially amongst the circle surrounding the children of nobility, and thus they readily assented to the introduction.

Lady Sofia practically dragged Caroline by the arm towards them. Mrs. Younge moved cautiously forward to greet Lady Sofia, clearly unaccustomed to such large gatherings of genteel society. She was small and dark, no more than five and twenty, with a downcast look that seemed to justify Lady Sofia's fascination with her as a tragic heroine.

The truth was that she was not quite so tragic a figure as Lady Sofia had made her out to be, or, if she were, it was her husband's life rather than the loss of it that had made her so. He drank what little they had, and gambled what they did not, and to all who knew the unhappy wife of the deceased, it was plain that she was glad to have seen the last of him. Unfortunately, although he left her a pension, his substantial debts wiped it out entirely, leaving her less than nothing with which to make her way in the world. Her companion at the ball, a former gambling mate of the late Private Younge, had made, if not a wager, then an arrangement with the widow. The gentleman had a little money—just enough to assist her with her debts. He was handsome, and able to make himself agreeable to ladies in particular; he thought he could make a very good match for himself if he could get the right introduction. Mrs. Younge could be equal parts pitiable and charming, and, as a lady, she was better able to procure the kinds of introductions that he desired. He had therefore agreed to lend Mrs. Younge the money she needed to pay off her debts; and, if she were able to assist him to a fortuitous marriage, he would forgive the loan. And so the pair entered the ball with all the appearance of goodness that avarice could inspire.

"Mrs. Younge, do please come in. I have just been speaking

with two of London's most engaging ladies to whom I must introduce you." Mrs. Younge was not given time to respond.

"Miss Bingley, Miss Caroline, allow me to present my dear friend, Mrs. Younge." The ladies all curtseyed at one another.

"And you must introduce your friend," insisted Lady Sofia, "though I am certain we must have met if he is from the neighbourhood of Lampton, as you have told me. I believe I know everyone in that region."

Mrs. Younge's tall and uncommonly handsome companion stepped forward.

"Of course, madam," said Mrs. Younge. "Allow me to present Mr. Wickham."

The gentleman bowed, but not before his eyes met those of Caroline in a moment which demanded all of the latter's powers of composure, for she was unprepared for the sudden and arresting engagement of her heart occasioned by this single look from a perfect stranger.

"How do you do?" he said.

Caroline was glad of the opportunity to curtsey and bow her head, for she was not certain of her knees just at that instant.

"May I leave Mr. Wickham to your care for the present?" Lady Sofia asked, taking Mrs. Younge by the arm. "There are so many people here to whom I should so like to introduce you. Mr. Wickham, these ladies were recently in your home county, so I am sure you shall have much to discuss."

"Of course, Sofia," answered Caroline, surprised at the steadiness in her voice. "We should not wish to keep you from your purpose."

Caroline was more than content to have a greater share of the attention of this Mr. Wickham. For the first time she could recall, she was aware of a desire for the absence of her sister. If it had not seemed remarkably out of character, she would have urged Louisa to leave her with this stranger and instead to take an interest in her future husband, which Caroline had certainly never previously encouraged her to do.

"Lady Sofia seems a very devoted friend," began Mr. Wickham. "Have you been long acquainted?"

"My sister had only made her acquaintance a quarter of an hour before you arrived," answered Caroline. "I have known her a little longer, however. We were introduced this Christmas at a ball in Derbyshire. It may be called a short acquaintance, but there are those whom one can know only a short time and yet feel such a bond as years of acquaintance often cannot accomplish."

Mr. Wickham tilted his head in agreement, holding Caroline's gaze, which was returned in a way that told him much more than her words had expressed.

"I believe I know precisely what you mean," he said. "It is a rare treasure to find such a friend. Introductions are, in a way, so much out of our control that when they lead to an instant closeness, it is providential indeed. I do not often speak metaphysically, but I feel it must be fate which is at play in such cases."

Louisa had never heard her sister speak of Lady Sofia with any sort of affection. Indeed had never known Caroline to form a bond with anyone but herself, and that could not be called an immediate bond formed upon a short acquaintance.

"What brought you to Derbyshire at Christmas?" Mr. Wickham tore his gaze from Caroline's and addressed himself to Louisa. "Do you have family in that county?"

"Our brother Charles is very steady friends with Mr. Darcy of Pemberley," she replied.

"My belief in fate is strengthened!" Mr. Wickham laughed. "Mr. Darcy is very well known to me; he and I were like brothers. We have known each other since childhood. His father, God rest his soul, was my godfather. Tell me, how are they all? Is Mrs. Reynolds still running the house as a bastion of order and efficiency?"

Louisa thought it odd that he should ask after the housekeeper before the principal members of the family; Caroline took it as a mark of his thoughtfulness that he remembered those whom others would quickly forget.

"We were very well looked after," replied Caroline. "And everyone was in excellent health. I wonder that we never heard your name while we were there, your being so close to the family."

"Well, it is some time since I was there. We were very close as children, Mr. Darcy and I, but over time he developed interests quite different from my own, and, as the years passed, we somehow grew apart. My godfather and I were very close, however, and remained so all his life. His death was nearly as crushing to me as that of my own father; and when Mr. Darcy's life ended, so did my association with Pemberley—though I do hope it will be revived when I return to Derbyshire in the spring. It has been too long that I have been away from what is truly my home."

"After so long an absence, what takes you back to Derbyshire now?" asked Louisa, who was not content to sit out the conversation.

"The position old Mr. Darcy left to me has become vacant. I shall occupy it as soon as I settle my affairs here in town."

Caroline wondered what sort of position he meant. Could it be a mayoralty? Surely that would go to Mr. Darcy. But then, perhaps Mr. Darcy did not like to go into politics. He was not a great speaker, and she could not recall him ever talking of local affairs or expressing opinions regarding the many issues facing the country. Instead of raising this, she directed him towards a subject she hoped would be dear to him.

"Were you at all acquainted with Miss Darcy while you were in Derbyshire? I ask because she and I have become very fast friends since my visit there. I do not know that I have ever met such a sweet girl, so wise and accomplished for her age."

Louisa was certain Caroline had never used such language in reference to Miss Darcy before. Could she mean to impress this Mr. Wickham with this praise?

"The last time I saw her, Miss Darcy was still a child," replied Mr. Wickham, "but a delightful creature. I was very fond of her, and she, I believe, was equally fond of me. I recall she always called me *Dawdy* for she could not pronounce my Christian name, George. I am glad to hear she has turned out so well."

"And what brings you to London?" asked Louisa.

"The same things that bring anyone to London: society, and everything that goes with it."

"And shall you not miss those things when you are in Derbyshire?" asked Caroline, restraining the entreaty in her voice.

"I certainly shall, though I am not without hope that I may draw some of them there." Mr. Wickham looked at Caroline as he said this. She hardly knew whether or how to respond. It was only an instant before he explained his meaning, saying to Louisa—

"I hope to have many visitors, and, if I am fortunate, to encourage some local entertainments." But it was too late; the moment could not be reversed, and it was evident to both sisters that he was as transfixed by Caroline as she was by him.

"I do not doubt your powers of persuasion," Caroline made bold to respond.

The first dance of the evening was announced, and Mr. Wickham offered Caroline his arm saying—

"Well then, may I persuade you to join me in the Minuet?"

"With pleasure," she replied. She took his arm, leaving her sister quite alone and more than a little vexed.

CHAPTER 11

When the Bingley sisters returned home, Louisa could not help but remark upon her sister's behaviour at the ball. She had never seen Caroline so discomposed by anyone as she seemed to be by this Mr. Wickham, and she feared lest he might supplant Mr. Darcy and his great estate in Caroline's heart.

"I hope you do not intend to throw over Mr. Darcy in favour of this obscure friend of Sofia's widow protégé," she said as she removed her cloak.

"Do not speak nonsense, Louisa," Caroline laughed. "I should not think it worth overturning Mr. Darcy for anyone short of a Lord. Besides, I have not been acquainted with Mr. Wickham more than a few hours. I should not make a decision about anyone on such brief acquaintance. Still, I do not see why I must rebuff a gentleman who has not proved himself to be unworthy. Mr. Darcy has not proposed, and I am by no means certain of him. He has not so much as included a note to me in his letters to Charles, nor in the letter I received from Georgiana. I must not forestall alternatives lest I be proven mistaken in Mr. Darcy."

The pair ascended the stairs.

"Well, Caroline. I doubt very much that your motives are as benign as you say, and I also doubt that you have done everything in your power to secure Mr. Darcy. You say he has not included any message to you, but you are equally guilty of indifference, for you have not included any message to him in any of Charles' letters, nor have you yet replied to Miss Darcy, though it has been almost a week since her letter arrived. A gentleman takes all the risk in revealing his affections in a proposal. How can he see fit to act unless he is absolutely certain of the lady's regard? You must assure him by every means propriety affords that you are disposed to accept him. Only if he is then indifferent shall I allow you to entertain doubts as to his intentions."

"Of course you are right, Louisa," Caroline yawned and nodded her head as they reached the top step. "You always see so clearly in these matters. I shall write to Georgiana tomorrow, first thing. I would do it now, only I am so sleepy. I doubt I could hold a quill."

"I shall say goodnight then." Louisa left her sister at her chamber door, then stopped and turned back. "Promise me you will not dream of handsome strangers," she said in playful admonishment.

"Goodnight, Louisa." Caroline made no such promise and would not have kept it if she did. She had never dreamt of strangers before, only handsome properties and handsome incomes. But this evening was as unlike others as Mr. Wickham was unlike other gentlemen. She could not criticise Mr. Darcy, but as she readied herself for bed, reflecting on her past conversations with him, she realised he had failed to leave any lasting or remarkable impression on her mind. She could not recall any details of anything they had said to each other, or at least that he had said to her. They had spent weeks together, but she had not noticed any alteration in her person; whereas, upon only being introduced to Mr. Wickham, she felt so transformed that she believed she never previously knew herself. Even Charles, the very picture of affability, had not Mr. Wickham's power of engagement. She could not think of a single gentleman who could match Mr. Wickham in conversation, in gentility of manner, in wit, or in taste, and he displayed all of this so effortlessly in but a single evening, indeed, in but the first hour of their acquaintance. If given the opportunity, what further qualities might he reveal?

Although she told herself repeatedly that she would never give up Pemberley for a novel infatuation, as she searched the secret, unfamiliar corners of her heart, she discovered a wish that Mr. Darcy might give her up first and spare her the decision.

With no small effort, she diverted her thoughts back to Mr. Darcy and Pemberley. Lying in bed, she considered what she might write to Georgiana, and what message she might ask her to relay to her brother. Even in the midst of these thoughts, Mr. Wickham's image again rose to the surface. She realized that she could ask Georgiana for information about Mr. Wickham. It would be entirely proper and could be naturally raised, as Mr. Wickham had spoken of Georgiana. Surely, his intimacy with the Darcy family would mean that she would have some information to share, even if she had not seen him since childhood.

Caroline roused herself from her bed, crossed the room, and sat herself at her writing table. She made a decent start of the business, but found that the combination of the candle's dim light and the fatigue from the evening's exhilarations was more than she could withstand. She retired to her bed once more, determined to finish her letter by morning's light.

As it happened, morning was not sufficient for her to complete her letter. She slept too late to take it up before breakfast, and shortly after breakfast a visitor was announced.

"Begging your pardon, Miss Bingley," the butler said, entering the breakfast room, "Mr. Wickham to see you." Caroline had only a moment to compose herself before the previous night's dream came striding into the breakfast room in the flesh.

"Mr. Wickham, what a surprise!" Louisa addressed their guest but looked towards her sister.

"Please, come in," Caroline's welcome was markedly more inviting.

"I am sorry; I seem to have caught you at your breakfast. I did not realize it was so early."

"Not at all, we were just lingering here while we planned our day," Caroline answered before her sister could. "I am sorry; you have just missed my brother. I should have liked to introduce you, as I did not have the opportunity last night. Mrs. Cooper, bring Mr. Wickham some tea."

"Yes, Miss Caroline."

"Thank-you Miss Caroline," he said, "but I am not sure I shall have time to drink it. I am on my way to see Mr. Hurst. Last night, he expressed an interest in one of the horses I was driving, and I offered to let him inspect her this morning. Unfortunately, I have mislaid the address; I was nearby and thought I might stop here to inquire whether you might give me the direction."

"In that case, there is no cause for haste. You shall not find Mr. Hurst in a state to receive visitors for at least another hour. Is not that correct, Louisa?" asked Caroline. "Please sit and have some tea."

"Well, in that case, I would be delighted to. And to fill the remainder of the hour, perhaps you ladies would like to join me for a turn about the park—that is, if you are at liberty."

Louisa responded first. "I find myself engaged with wedding preparations this morning, so I am afraid I cannot join you." She was, in fact, not half so occupied as she claimed to be, but she did not wish to spend any more time on the fringe of Caroline's flirtation with Mr. Wickham. If Caroline intended to throw herself at this relative nobody, Louisa was not going to be party to it. With a stern look at her sister, she excused herself from the table and from the room.

"Well, I have no wedding to plan for at present," stated Caroline, "and I am sure I could profit by a little air."

"Excellent," said Mr. Wickham, donning his hat. "That settles it."

Rising from the table, Caroline ordered her bonnet and coat be brought to the door. Accompanying Mr. Wickham out of the room, Caroline said—

"I hope, Mr. Wickham, that you will not find my company the most tedious way to pass an hour or so."

"Quite the opposite, I assure you, Miss Bingley," he said, taking the spencer from the servant and helping her into it. "I am convinced I could never find your company the least bit tedious."

Caroline was not the only one to have begun inquiries following their first encounter and Mr. Wickham had been more than satisfied with the results of his. He learned from Lady Sofia that Caroline was quite unattached and had a substantial dowry. With these virtues added to her beauty and personal charms, Mr. Wickham was determined to have her.

"I am not afraid to say, Miss Bingley, that I had hoped I might find you at home and at liberty when I called this morning," Mr. Wickham began as he helped Caroline into the carriage. "It is true that Mr. Hurst inquired after my horse, and I do intend to stop there when we return, but I would have set out a fair bit later if I had not thought to steal a little more of your company by passing by here first."

"You are bold, sir!" replied Caroline, feigning shock when really she was elated. "To invent such a pretence is one thing, but to admit to it so openly is hardly proper."

Mr. Wickham, smiling and taking up the reins, replied, "You are entirely correct, of course. I should behave more like a gentleman and pretend I care only for riding horses and shooting birds, but I never could tell a lie." He snapped the reins and the horses pulled them out onto the road. "In fact," he added, "that is not entirely true. When decorum demands it, I am very skilled at telling a lie. Just the other day, I told a young lady that I admired the fruit in her bonnet, and I daresay she never suspected me."

Caroline laughed. "I do not call such flatteries lies, for, if I did, I must condemn all society as liars of the most accomplished sort."

"And do you think otherwise?" he asked. "If society tells young ladies that gentlemen prefer women who pile fruit atop their heads to those who adorn themselves more modestly, that society must be guilty either of deceit or, at best, of very grave delusion."

Caroline thought of the many extravagant bonnets she had purchased that year and wondered whether any of them might garner Mr. Wickham's condemnation.

"Fashions are all in how they are worn," she said in light-hearted antagonism. "They must always be tempered with taste and some can only been worn to advantage by those who possess a certain superior air, a graceful carriage."

"That may be so," he concurred, "but then I have always observed that those ladies who have sufficient beauty and poise to appear elegant in the most ridiculous fashions have no need of such embellishment and would be far better served by simplicity. I cannot be the only gentleman to find natural, unenhanced beauty preferable to ostentatious fashion."

"It is you who are deceived then," returned Caroline, "as are all gentlemen who believe they have ever seen a natural, unenhanced beauty out in London society. Those ladies you have thought to be so have merely succeeded where those who appear ostentatious have not, but all have as their object the appearance of effortless perfection. I should say, all truly elegant ladies do."

"In that case, Miss Bingley," he said, careful to keep his gaze on the road, "*you* have far outdone *me* in the art of deception."

Caroline slid herself along the seat towards Mr. Wickham. "Begging your pardon not to return the flattery," she said, reaching out her hands and taking the reins from his grasp. "But, if your driving were any more ladylike, I might dress *your* head in cherries and call you a very ugly wench."

She cracked the reins and the horses leapt into a gallop, causing Mr. Wickham to fall back into his seat, laughing and holding onto his hat.

The pair spent over an hour traversing every park in the neighbourhood, following which, Mr. Wickham returned Caroline to the house.

"I am afraid I have kept you much longer than the hour you intended to stay," she said, as he helped her down from the carriage. "I hope you shall have adequate time to show Mr. Hurst your horse. I daresay the morning will be quite gone by the time you are done there. I apologize if I have delayed you from any pressing engagements thereafter."

"Not at all. I am at leisure today."

"Make sure you do not keep Mr. Hurst as long as you have kept me," she said. "Louisa expects him here this evening to discuss their wedding plans."

She leaned closer to him and lowered her voice: "I should say, to be *told* the wedding plans, for 'twould be more accurate." She lingered for a moment before she returned to a more moderate distance and a less confidential volume. "Tell me, does Mrs. Younge often call upon Lady Sofia in Park Lane?"

Mr. Wickham looked a little confused. "I do not know. I believe so. In fact, now that I think of it, yes. Last night I heard her repeat an invitation to Mrs. Younge to call on her at any time."

"And was she so magnanimous as to extend the invitation to you?"

"I believe such an invitation was implied, yes."

"Lady Sofia is always so cordial. I have been terribly remiss in not calling upon her since I returned to town. Preparations for the wedding have been excessively consuming. I do hope to visit with her tomorrow morning, at about eleven o'clock. In fact, I am considering making a habit of calling on her at around that time. Do you think that a good idea?"

"Eleven o'clock is a very convenient time for a visit," he said with a knowing smile.

"Very good then," Caroline offered her hand. "Thank you for a very diverting outing, sir. I hope our paths may soon cross again."

CHAPTER 12

The following weeks witnessed a marked alteration in Caroline's manner. It did not escape the notice of her family, and what pleased the brother worried the sister. Caroline had softened somewhat. She was not so abrupt with Jenny as she had previously been, and she had even been heard openly inquiring after Mrs. Cooper's family. Louisa was not even aware Mrs. Cooper had a family, and neither of them suspected Caroline of any such knowledge either. Caroline seemed to smile more readily and did not always insist on displaying her talents at every opportunity. She was more attentive to guests at home and was easier with others in general.

Mr. Bingley, although he was pleased with Caroline's recent behaviour, could not identify the cause of the transformation and so could do nothing to encourage it. He little suspected that a man was at the centre of it—indeed, he did not even know Wickham existed, and so could do nothing to promote or prevent the growing intimacy between him and Caroline.

Louisa was not as satisfied as her brother. It seemed to her that Caroline was growing unscrupulous, and she feared for her sister's reputation as well as that of the family. Even more disturbing to Louisa was her suspicion as to what, or rather who, was responsible for this decline.

Caroline did not speak of Mr. Darcy so often as she did when first they returned home after Christmas. Louisa could not be certain she had even responded to Georgiana's letter. She attempted to raise the matter with Caroline, but was dismissed with assurances from Caroline that she was only more at ease

69

now that she considered herself future mistress of Pemberley. Not liking to quarrel with her sister, Louisa did not press the matter further, hoping Mr. Darcy would bring the affair to a swift conclusion with a forthcoming proposal. Her hopes were to be given some fuel shortly thereafter by an announcement from her brother.

"I have heard from Mr. Darcy this morning," began Mr. Bingley over supper one evening. "I have a few pieces of news to share that, I hope, will be pleasing to you both."

Louisa and Caroline raised their eyebrows in simultaneous anticipation.

"He is coming to town in a few weeks and hopes to visit us all while he is here."

The sisters caught each other's gaze.

"What business could bring him here while his sister is still at home?" asked Louisa.

"It is his sister who causes him to come," he answered, watching Caroline, who had taken a pressing interest in her napkin. "He is coming to ensure that all is settled for her transfer here. If all is satisfactory, he shall send for Miss Darcy to join him. He wishes first to meet the woman who is to run the institution. She is someone of your acquaintance, I believe, Mrs. Younge, a widow and a friend of Lady Sofia's."

Louisa's eyes widened. Caroline shifted her gaze from her napkin to her plate and began adjusting the silverware.

"When can we expect him?" asked Louisa.

"He is to arrive two days after your wedding, I am afraid, and so you shall miss seeing him."

"Well, that is no matter," replied Louisa with a shrug. "I am glad he shall not be in town at the time. I should not have known whether to invite him. He may be your closest friend, but we have never been introduced. It might have been awkward. But it is unfortunate that I shall be gone to Brighton by then. Caroline shall have the whole task of making him feel welcome, though I am sure she shall not mind."

"I shall be delighted," responded Caroline brightly; "even more so when his sister joins him. It shall be such a joy to welcome her here, and I shall look forward to introducing her when you return, Louisa. If I am to lose you to Mr. Hurst, Georgiana shall be a comfort to me. I hope she and I can be as close as sisters in time."

"Perhaps you should write her and tell her so," was Louisa's curt reply.

"Where is Mr. Darcy to stay?" Caroline asked, ignoring her sister's implication. "Does he have a house in town?"

"Yes, in Berkeley Square. But that is not the end of it. His cousin, Lord Ashwell, lives in Grosvenor Square, and we are all invited for an evening *there* as soon as Georgiana arrives."

"How delightful!" replied Caroline. "I only wish Louisa could be there. I am sure she is very anxious to make the acquaintance of your closest friend, Charles. I fear you shall never have the chance to introduce him to her, for he will no doubt have concluded his business and be off again before she should return from her honeymoon."

"Well, then let me put your fears to rest," said Mr. Bingley, eager to share one last piece of news. "After Mr. Darcy has settled his sister in her new surroundings, he has proposed that we all travel to Hertfordshire for an extended stay. I find myself increasingly drawn to that part of the country, and I should like to spend a little time there before I settle. I should take up residence without a second thought, but Mr. Darcy thinks it prudent to proceed with caution, and all of us, I think, will profit by a holiday in the country together. Is not that a capital idea?" Mr. Bingley beamed.

"I believe it is," Caroline concurred. "And a very charming time we shall have too, I am sure. I only regret that Miss Darcy will not be among us." Turning to her sister, she continued, "She plays and sings so beautifully, Louisa. I cannot think your taste would be anything but gratified by it." Looking down at her plate, in a confessional tone she added, "I am afraid I did not pay her so much attention as I ought when we were in the North. I should be grateful for the opportunity to redress that deficit. She is such a sweet creature." Caroline continued quietly with her supper.

Louisa and Mr. Bingley were both taken aback. Neither had ever heard such a speech from their sister; the latter, at least, very much enjoyed hearing his sister speak with kindness and humility, without any evident prospect of gain from it.

Whatever their differences that evening, neither Caroline nor Louisa could help but speculate on the significance of Mr. Darcy's invitations. There was no cause for Mr. Darcy to have extended his invitations to Mr. Bingley's sisters. In years of very devoted friendship, he had never shown any interest in including them in his engagements with their brother. Both were certain that this development was due to Caroline's success in winning the heart of Mr. Darcy, but while this soothed the anxieties of the elder sister, it only served to augment those of the younger, whose mind was more occupied than she would admit with an approaching public ball, at which she expected to see a certain gentleman whose name she would not speak.

CHAPTER 13

Darcy and Georgiana sat opposite each other at the breakfast table, each with a newly arrived but unopened letter before them. Brother and sister eyed each other's correspondence with curiosity, but neither would open their letters in the presence of the other. Each tucked their own away for future reading.

Georgiana thought she glimpsed the name of George Wickham beside the postmark on the letter to her Brother, but could not think why a letter from such an old friend—a friend long absent from the Darcy home—would not be readily shared. She hoped that if she revealed the nature of her letter, her brother would be forthcoming about his own.

"It is from Caroline Bingley," she said. "I shall read it over this morning, and if any of it merits sharing, I shall read those parts to you after supper if you should wish it."

"I look forward to it. Of course I would not pry into any private communication between ladies, but I should enjoy very much Miss Bingley's reports of the goings on in London."

Mr. Darcy offered nothing of explanation regarding his own letter, and Georgiana did not dare ask. Her brother did not share information with her unless it directly concerned her, and she had long since learned that he did not like her to inquire. He never spoke harshly to her, but the cold denial of a response had, on previous occasions, taught her to suffer her questions in silence.

Still, if the letter were from Wickham, it gladdened Georgiana to think that the two men were in communication again. It had been years since she last saw Wickham, and she regretted that he and her brother had drifted apart so, given how much a part of their family he had once been. She had only fond memories of Wickham from her childhood. She was not aware of any cause for distance between him and her brother. Perhaps he only stayed away because of the recollection of fond memories grown painful which Pemberley would excite for him, now that both his father and godfather were gone from the place and from the world. She could certainly understand that. There were times, even now, when certain scenes, smells and sounds about the house and grounds would call her mother to mind so keenly that she was overcome with feeling.

The sender of Darcy's letter was, in part, the subject of Georgiana's. Caroline remembered Mr. Wickham to her, stating that he had been introduced to her by Lady Sofia, and that Pemberley and the name of Darcy were mentioned at the time. Georgiana weighed whether to share this with her brother, and decided it might not be fitting, if, indeed, there was some unpleasantness between the two men. She would not risk raising a subject which may cause her brother any awkwardness. She could not tolerate the idea of offending her brother in any way, not because she feared his response so much as because she cared so deeply for him. She, more than anyone, knew the weight of the responsibilities he carried. He had been quite a young man when he became master of Pemberley and guardian of his sister. He had many tenants and a large staff as well as business interests that kept him steadily occupied. He was privileged, to be sure, to have come so young into his inheritance, but the burden of it did weigh on him. Though he was never demonstrative in his affection and sometimes severe in his manner, Georgiana could not fault him for it. He was always gentle and encouraging towards her, and what is more, he always acted with much fore-thought and the highest moral consideration.

Georgiana answered Caroline's inquiries on the subject of Mr. Wickham with sincere praise of the man as an affectionate and well-loved friend. She told Caroline that she had not seen him in the years since the passing of her father, who had been his godfather, and knew nothing of his current situation.

Mr. Darcy's response to the correspondence he received that morning was significantly more heated. Mr. Darcy rarely, if ever, lost his temper, but the letter from Mr. Wickham was of such an insolent nature as inflamed his indignation. Mr. Wickham referred to the recent vacancy of the living at Kympton as if it were quite his own, and inquired merely as to the arrangements which had to be made for his taking it. He proposed dates of arrival, expressed preferences as to the household, and gave instructions as to payment of his remuneration, all as though he had never renounced the living and the entire notion of ever taking orders; as if he had never been compensated more than adequately for his resignation of it; and as if it were his by right and not on condition, as it was, of the previous holder's preference, which was never settled on Mr. Wickham.

After the reading of his father's will, Mr. Darcy had received from Mr. Wickham a declaration that he did not intend ever to occupy the living that was left to him, and Mr. Darcy had paid him the significant sum of £3,000 as consideration for giving up any claim to it. When the living did fall vacant, it never entered Mr. Darcy's mind that Mr. Wickham would try for it, so vehement had been his rejection of it and so ill-suited was he to any clerical position.

Mr. Darcy was swift in issuing a reply, which he posted the same day, though the expense of the express was not considered necessary. Let him wait on his disappointment, he thought. Mr. Darcy was not a spiteful man, but he felt that Wickham's presumption in the face of the many generosities shown him by the Darcy family was offensive to the memory of his father.

He remained in an ill humour the whole of the day, that is, until evening, when he and his sister sat by the fire, where she regaled him, in her ever-pleasing tones, with the wit and good humour of Miss Caroline Bingley.

Mr. Darcy expected her letter to contain many oblique attempts at communication with himself, for he did not doubt she was resourceful and very clever. He found himself disappointed when none was forthcoming, for the contents of her letter were not designed to inspire anything but genuine friendship between author and recipient and, though well-penned and engaging, were clearly not intended to catch the heart of a gentleman. During the Bingleys' stay at Pemberley, Caroline had exhibited that odd sort of behaviour typical of young ladies who sought to attract a mate. Mr. Darcy had flattered himself that this was for his sake, though he could see nothing in his own actions that might have inspired any hope in her.

Mr. Darcy anticipated that he should think no more of Caroline after she had gone, and yet even now, some weeks later, he found himself recalling her presence there. He attributed this to the feelings of deprivation which are to be expected when one loses one's company.

If he had grown fond of Caroline, his fondness might have increased with her absence, but he was not fond of her at all. He thought her self-absorbed and often irritating. Her presence had, however, put him in mind that Pemberley would, in time, require a lady to preside over it. In addition to his own wishes, he considered that a wife to him would be a sister to Georgiana, and that this must be a desirable notion to the latter. If he were married, Georgiana could return home indefinitely, and both brother and sister would be gratified by such a happy occasion.

He did not fail to consider also that it must be pleasant to have a wife, and by it an excuse not to be required to attend balls and other engagements which necessitated mixing with strangers. A wife would bring select society to their home, would ensure Georgiana was exposed to other people, but always the right sort of people, and would save him the trouble of making friends himself.

In such wise would Caroline be eminently suitable for the post. She was the kind of active, unreserved sort of person who would always be meeting new people, but she was self-important enough not to allow less desirable people into her circle. Furthermore, she was clearly willing to accept the role.

As he was not in the habit of receiving young ladies to Pemberley, Caroline was the only eligible person that he had lately witnessed about the place. Therefore, when he imagined a lady of the house, he imagined her as Caroline.

He only wished that she were not so objectionable. Mr. Darcy dreaded making new acquaintances and dreaded even more the uncertainty which might attend a proposal to any lady of whom he was less sure than he was of Caroline. Had her heart been more tender and her manner less affected, her virtue of being familiar to him alone might have sufficed for him to make her an offer. Unfortunately for the lady and her hopes, he was too fastidious to give himself up for a mere wish of avoiding introductions.

Therefore, he had no thought in his mind of Caroline when, a few weeks later, he set off for London to make arrangements for his sister's education.

CHAPTER 14

Amidst the joyful tumult of Louisa's wedding preparations, the day came for the public ball to which both Caroline and Louisa had been looking forward with great anticipation, though not for entirely the same reasons. The wedding itself was only days away, but the Bingley sisters did not intend to miss the opportunity of mixing with the best of London society. Mr. Bingley, obliged to ride out to the country to see a solicitor about a property, could not attend, so the two ladies went with only Mr. Hurst for company.

The Assembly Rooms were bursting with starch and elegance. Caroline and Louisa saw Mr. Hurst to the card table and made their rounds. They charmed where they could, rejoiced as their dance cards began to fill, and kept their countenance when the figure of Mr. Wickham came into view. Caroline was especially impressed that she remained ostensibly unperturbed even as Mr. Wickham, seeming not to notice her presence, was immersed in conversation with another young lady.

She accepted the offer of a dance from a short man in a handsome uniform with an array of medals displayed on his chest. They took their place, she taking care to position herself in Mr. Wickham's line of sight. The effect was as desired; Caroline was a graceful and accomplished dancer, and, being taller than most of the ladies present, demanded, almost as if by will, the attention of many young men, including that of the only young man whose attention she cared for at that moment. Seeing Caroline in animated and amused conversation with her partner, he forgot to finish his sentence and had to be called to rather shortly by the young lady who had been giving him her very rapt attention. He did not finish his thought, and without looking away from Caroline said only—

"I am sorry, I just remembered something." He quit the company of the shocked and dismayed young lady and crossed the room to where he could intercept Caroline when the dance concluded and her partner escorted her off the floor. Caroline, seeing Wickham thus positioned, broke into a smile as her partner took her arm to lead her towards the very spot where he stood. The uniformed man, seeing Caroline's face light up, felt very pleased, believing himself to have been the cause of his partner's merriment. Her smile might have made him so bold as to request a second dance had Mr. Wickham not stepped between them to take Caroline's arm the instant they had made their bows.

"Miss Caroline," he began, offering her his arm, which she accepted, leaving the uniformed man disappointed and a little embarrassed. "May I prevail on you to allow me a space on your card, and a few minutes of your conversation?"

"Certainly, Mr. Wickham," she replied as they made their way to the edge of the room. "I believe I have yet a space on my card, and I should be only too pleased for you to have it."

"How long has it been since we last danced together?" began Mr. Wickham.

"I believe it has been five weeks."

"Can it be so short a time? I suppose it must. I have never known five weeks to be so long." Although they now stood still, Caroline did not remove her arm from his.

"Time is a strangely relative thing, is not it? Anticipation can transform five days, or even five hours into an eternity."

"Quite so," Wickham concurred, also refusing to drop his arm. "This ball shall last several hours, and yet I expect to find it over long before I wish it to be."

"Then you must live from ball to ball, Mr. Wickham. And when I am able to attend, I shall promise to be very plain and dull that I might always be free to dance, if you should not be afraid to stand up with such a lady."

"I defy you ever to be plain or dull, Miss Bingley." Mr. Wickham's voice was low and betrayed an earnestness which had never previously been his wont. Suddenly aware of the picture they were making, Caroline broke their stare, retracting her hand from his in order to gesture towards Louisa on the other side of the room.

"Indeed, I do wonder how my sister regards time just at the moment. Her marriage is a very happy occasion to anticipate, and yet she is so occupied with preparations that her time must not seem sufficient."

"I see also that she may not be entirely impatient to change freedom for matrimony" added Mr. Wickham, noting that Louisa was surrounded by a circle of young men, all of whom she seemed to have engaged in animated conversation.

"Everything gains in value just as we lose it. I can assure you, my sister little esteems spinsterhood."

Mr. Wickham laughed. "Will you be attending the ball for Branston and Sofia, to send them off to Brighton? I already know you are invited."

"I am, yes, and I should like nothing better than to attend; however, I do not know how I shall be able to, for my sister and Mr. Hurst shall be gone on their honeymoon and my brother will, in all likelihood, be engaged with Mr. Darcy, who is not fond of dancing. And so I shall have no chaperone. There are several young ladies whom I could ask, but none of them have been invited. So you see, circumstances beyond my control may prevent me from attending."

"I am afraid I cannot accept that anything should be beyond your control. If you should will it, it shall be. I look forward to our meeting there, and, though it may be presumptuous, I insist on my claim to the first two dances. If you do not appear, I shall be left wanting a partner, and very lonely for it."

"Then I suppose I am bound to engage all my resources and will my way there, for I should be loath to bring loneliness of all things upon any of my friends."

"Well, let us not lose this opportunity." Mr. Wickham offered his arm again. "The dance is about to begin again." Caroline accepted, and the couple joined in the set.

Had Louisa not been so wholly immersed in enjoying her last outing as a single lady, she might have been shocked by her sister's behaviour, and may have brought the latter's enjoyment to a swift end, for Caroline danced twice with Mr. Wickham and spent most of her time between dances conversing with him as well.

As the ball drew nigh its end, Caroline and Mr. Wickham stood near the edge of the room, talking and laughing with ease. Caroline remarked that they should be departing soon, and Mr. Wickham grew quiet, his expression solemn as he turned his whole person to her and said, "Miss Bingley, I would pray one further favour from you."

"Anything you wish," Caroline freely replied, her spirits high from an evening of unmitigated enjoyment.

"I should like to ask, if I might beg a few minutes of your private audience."

Caroline sobered very suddenly at these words, taking in his earnest look and apprehending the gravity of the moment. After a brief stupidity, she was able to reply.

"What, presently?"

"Yes," he plainly answered. "There is something I should wish to say to you which I should not wish to say before the eyes and ears of a crowd."

Anxiety seized Caroline's heart and she could barely form a polite reply.

"Certainly, sir."

Mr. Wickham reached for her hand, placed it on his arm and led her out of the ball room. When they were quite alone, he took her hands in his and, keeping his eyes on them, began his address.

"Miss Bingley, I have no right to speak to you in this way, but you have been so good as to permit me, and so I am encouraged to say what has been resounding in my heart since the night we first met. It has been such a short time that I have known you, and yet I feel it has been my whole life, so much has your friendship eclipsed everything that came before and so little else have I dwelt on since. Truly, I have never felt for anyone what I now feel for you."

He had not looked up from their joined hands since he began, but he did so now, albeit only for an instant. He read panic in her expression. She, too, kept her gaze on their hands, though she felt his stare. He continued with more gentleness and restraint.

"I think I may have alarmed you, madam. You must forgive me for speaking so abruptly. My feelings have overpowered me, and I am afraid I have not the discipline to restrain them in the face of their object. You need not make any answer now, but I could no longer be silent. If you would only bend your mind to the question of whether you will have me, and know that, you have but to will it and I am yours."

After a very brief pause, which felt to both parties like an eternity of silence, Caroline, though still unequal to raising her eyes to Mr. Wickham's, was able haltingly to reply, "I do not know what to say, sir."

Mr. Wickham, easy now that the worst of his ordeal was behind him, was bolstered by the thrill of having unburdened himself. He smiled and bent down to meet Caroline's gaze.

"Come," he said with a reassuring smile, "you need not say anything. Let us return to the ball. Your sister shall be wondering what has become of you."

Caroline nodded in relief, for she was utterly unprepared to give any answer. Were her feelings her only consideration, she would have yielded instantly, but there were so many questions yet unanswered.

As they walked back to the ball room, Mr. Wickham said, "If you are able to attend the ball we spoke of earlier, will you give me your answer then? It need not be a final one, only an indication whether I have cause to hope. Ten days shall feel very long indeed, but I should be obliged if you might give me a date to which I may look forward as an end to my suspense."

By this time, Caroline had regained some degree of her wonted self-possession and was able to promise with a modicum of composure that she would answer him in ten days' time.

Mr. Wickham returned Caroline to Louisa, and he and the Bingley sisters bid each other good night, he with a flourish, Caroline with a curtsey, and Louisa with a look of suspicion and silent discontent.

Louisa did not like seeing her sister with Mr. Wickham, as she had done that evening, but she told herself that what she witnessed was a relatively harmless flirtation and nothing more. As far as she knew, the two had only seen each other only three times: the ball at which they had met, the carriage ride the following day, and the ball which they had just left. Louisa well knew—and remembered fondly—the vain pleasure of dance, banter, and flirtation in the company of a handsome stranger, but she had always understood the importance of keeping such flirtations at a distance from oneself. Had she been aware that Caroline and Wickham had been meeting each other almost daily in Park Lane, she would have been grievously concerned; but she little suspected her sister could be so foolish as to behave thus when her future with Mr. Darcy was in the balance.

The disapproval of Louisa Bingley did not affect Mr. Wickham's buoyant mood as he floated out the door and into the carriage. He had been sure of his own intentions towards Caroline from the start, set as he was on winning any tolerable lady of fortune who would have him. He had not expected to meet with such cause for real affection as he had found in her. To his surprise and delight, he not only discovered a lady he could truly love, but, from all he had observed, the lady seemed to return his affection. He had come to the ball that night in order to observe her behaviour towards him and determine whether she might consider his hand; and she had given him the utmost encouragement. His proposal might have been hasty, but he felt that delay could only weaken his chances, that she might discover the nature of his circumstances and throw him over. The sooner he could secure her, the better.

In the carriage home, Louisa seemed to forget all about Mr. Wickham as she recounted the evening's raptures. She talked for some minutes about the ball's many diversions—the partners, the conversations, and the gossip—before Caroline was able to hear a word of it.

When she was asked about her own evening, Caroline shared every detail that did not involve Mr. Wickham. Had Louisa not been so distracted with her own recollections, she might have wondered how Caroline, usually so active and unreserved, could have had so few partners and so little conversation, so much of her evening did she fail to recount.

Though Caroline spoke of everything save Mr. Wickham, her mind was full of nothing else. All that night, Caroline turned over and over again in her mind the conversation between herself and Mr. Wickham. How could she reply to him? She could not accept him. That was clear. She wished to continue indefinitely their encounters exactly as they had been. Concluding the matter with a definite engagement so soon would exclude the possibility of providing for herself a more prosperous future with Mr. Darcy, whom she still believed she might win. Comparing the two men in her mind, she found it difficult to summon any affection for the latter that did not stem from a longing for the prosperity and privilege that a marriage with the Darcy house would afford. When, however, she dwelt on the thought of Wickham, she imagined many different causes of happiness, all unconnected with the comforts of wealth.

She repeated to herself again and again all the advantages that a life as Mrs. Darcy would hold—advantages not only to herself, but to her family as well; and yet she could not deny her feelings of joy at the prospect of a lifetime in the company of Mr. Wickham, feelings that threatened to dash all her lifelong concerns for her own advancement.

Seeking to excuse the consideration she was giving to Wickham's proposal, Caroline turned her thoughts to her sister's engagement. Louisa, so opposed to Caroline's flirtation with Mr. Wickham, had settled for a match far below that which she insisted on for Caroline. Mr. Hurst was fashionable enough, but he was certainly not a man of any substantial fortune. Mr. Wickham was at least connected with the Darcy family, which in itself was a mark in his favour, and he was to receive a very good living in the North very shortly. The match could not rival a marriage into Pemberley, but Mr. Darcy's proposal was, as yet, uncertain. Now that Caroline had experienced the reality of genuine mutual affection, she understood how contrived her imagined romance with Mr. Darcy really was. Her perception no longer coloured by a blinding desire to be admired by Mr. Darcy, she could see that she had never actually been so. He had never behaved with any partiality towards her that could not be explained by other motives. Her confidence in his regard, she thought, must have been misplaced; all the subtle signs of affection she had previously regarded as irrefutable proof of his intentions, all of these were illusions and nothing more.

Louisa's wedding would only serve to further the cause of Mr. Wickham in Caroline's heart. To see her sister marry a man whose conversation she did not seek, whose company she did not enjoy, and whose interests she did not share, would only convince Caroline that Louisa was not the authority on matrimony that she had always purported to be. Therefore, Caroline would make up her own mind on the subject of her future happiness. If she perceived no encouragement from Mr. Darcy when he arrived, she would accept Mr. Wickham's offer.

CHAPTER 15

Grosvenor Square was one of the only quarters of London that appeared to advantage in the rain. Hooded ladies glided into sparkling houses; horses, their manes and forelocks dripping, shimmered in the torchlight; and through the windows shone dazzling jewels and gaiety. Near a dozen guests had already gathered at the house of Lord Ashwell as Caroline and Mr. Bingley were announced to the drawing room. Their only acquaintance among the company, Mr. Darcy, stepped forward to greet them.

"Welcome, welcome," He said. "I am so pleased you took the trouble to come out on such a wet night."

"Not at all, Mr. Darcy," answered Caroline cheerfully. "Good company is the only way to bear such a night as this. I am sure Charles would agree, it is we who are grateful for the invitation."

"Quite so," said Mr. Bingley with a smile, "quite so."

"Well then, allow me to introduce you to our host, Lord Ashwell." Mr. Darcy ushered his friends across the room to a high dais in a corner opposite the fire and away from the window. On it sat a tall, fine-looking gentleman, dressed in garb simply cut—but from the richest cloth. He was near in age to Mr. Darcy and bore a slight resemblance to that gentleman, though his features were finer and his complexion more pale. His eyes were large and dark and he wore his hair longer than was the fashion.

He may have been the heir to the earldom, but Lord Ashwell had never taken that prospect to heart due to his health, which was threatened by a long-standing weakness in his lungs brought on by a childhood illness. He had long anticipated an early demise and so had very little regard for his expectations. As his father was in excellent health, with every anticipation of living many more years, the eldest son did not think he would live to take his place. His brother, Colonel Fitzwilliam, had always shown himself to be quite worthy of the title, and Lord Ashwell believed it would be the Colonel who would both receive and do justice to it. This resignation lent him an air of conviviality and light-heartedness, which some mistook for triviality.

"Cousin, may I introduce my friends Mr. Bingley and his sister Miss Bingley. Their sister you also invited, but she is lately married and gone from town on her honeymoon, I believe."

"Yes," said Caroline, "my sister is very sorry not to be here. Louisa is very fond of an evening party and of meeting new and charming people. It was so kind of you to invite us."

"It is delightful to make your acquaintance, Miss Bingley," said Lord Ashwell without rising, acknowledging Mr. Bingley with a bow of his head. "I understand from my cousin here that you are acquainted with my brother John, Colonel Fitzwilliam. Unfortunately, he could not join us either. His is posted too far to travel for an evening's enjoyment, I am afraid."

"One can never seem to gather all one's loved ones in one place at the same time, can one?" remarked Mr. Bingley. "Such a time we live in. It is a wonder that we should be all over the country all the time."

"You speak my very thoughts, Mr. Bingley," replied Lord Ashwell with enthusiasm. "*Such* an age we live in. Not only are we all about the country, but we are all about the world! Never have we lived with so few boundaries. It seems that anything is possible . . ." Lord Ashwell stopped suddenly as if remembering himself mid-thought and then continued, "I am sorry. I forget myself. Please, be seated." He indicated a few chairs placed near him. "Now, where is a servant to bring us some refreshment? I have not offered you anything. You shall think me a shocking host. I am far too easy on my servants, and now when I need them, they are nowhere to be found. They shall all end in idleness and ill-repute I do not wonder."

Here, Mr. Bingley took his chance to be useful. "Do not trouble yourself, sir. I shall fetch us all some punch. I shan't be a moment." And off he went to be active and amiable.

Mr. Darcy resumed the conversation, speaking to Caroline.

"Have you seen much of Branston and Lady Sofia since you returned to town? I thought I understood from your brother that you had."

"Indeed, they have been very active friends, very generous in their invitations. I believe Sofia is the most unspoilt creature ever to be out in London society."

"I have no doubt of it," said Mr. Darcy. "Her life is a bounded indulgence. I do not believe she has ever been given an opportunity of being spoilt by the world, for she is forever being rescued from it, and from herself, by the very diligent attentions of Mrs. Belfry. I have often wondered what she might be like if she were ever to feel the consequences of any of her follies."

"Mr. Darcy, you challenge me with the impossible," said Caroline playfully, "to hold my tongue in the face of temptation to mockery. But I feel it would not be right for me to disparage someone who has shown me nothing but kindness—not when I have so many faults of my own that I should hate to be made the subject of idle chat."

Caroline found it impossible not to be perfect that evening. She was flawless in her manners and her conversation, and this without so much as a trace of effort at being so. Her attachment to Mr. Wickham had, for the first time, shown her what it was to love and to be loved, and she did not rely on the approbation of others to buoy her. She wished her own happiness for the world and was generous and unassuming with everyone.

Mr. Darcy wondered how he had ever thought this lady impertinent or self-important, for here was no false virtue, no forced humility. As the conversation continued, he found her uniformly delightful. Her humour was evident more in heartfelt laughter than in stinging criticism, and her talent for conversation was displayed with more thought of listening than of being listened to. Mr. Darcy was incredulous.

Had his own vanity and prejudice shaped an image of Caroline more affected and vain than the true one that stood before him now? He began to doubt the judgments he had formed of her while she was at Pemberley. Here was no simpering, preening, ill-mannered creature; this was a true lady, the sister of his dearest friend, who was himself the embodiment of humility and good breeding. Surely Mr. Bingley's sister, raised in the same family, by the same parents, must have been taught the same principles and share the same qualities to some degree at least. It was true that her wit was sharper and her disposition more decisive than her brother's, but to be self-assured and clever was hardly something to which Darcy could object. Was this not, indeed, the very ideal of womanhood?

Caroline believed she caught in the gaze of Mr. Darcy more than a passing or indifferent regard, and she laid aside for the present all thoughts of her reply to Mr. Wickham. She was not yet sure of Mr. Darcy, but she enjoyed the way he was looking at her and it caused her to believe she may yet hope for him. There was no need to make any decision about her future just at that moment. She had until Thursday evening to consider her alternatives.

"Do you plan to attend the ball on Thursday?" Lord Ashwell asked Caroline, interrupting her reverie.

"Oh," she started a little, "I should very much like to, only I know not how I can achieve it. You see, my sister is gone on her honeymoon, and my brother will soon be engaged in the country with Mr. Darcy. I have no companion, Lord Ashwell. If my new sister in law, Mrs. Purser, had been invited, I might easily have convinced her to join me. Her husband is away on the Continent at present, and I am certain she would have accepted. Though Lady Sofia's hospitality is vast, I should not wish to trespass upon it by bringing a guest who has not been invited."

"Miss Bingley, I am in the happy position of being able to offer you the means you have been wanting," interjected Lord Ashwell. "Mrs. Purser must come as my guest and you shall both attend with me. Lady Sofia is so admirable in her tenacity for she always invites me, though I am rarely able to accept more than once in a season. I must make this the one occasion this year, for they leave for Brighton for the remainder of the season, and there shall end my opportunity. What is more, I should hate for you to miss it merely for want of a companion, particularly when I am in a position to render it possible at no inconvenience whatever to myself."

"Sir, you are too kind," Caroline replied. "If I were less desirous of going I should object for politeness sake, but I should not like to miss attending out of ceremony alone. Therefore, I thank you for your offer, and I accept it wholeheartedly. Mrs. Purser is a very obliging and unobtrusive lady. I could not impose her company on you if I thought for even a moment that she would in any way detract from your enjoyment of the evening."

"It is quite settled then. I shall see you on Thursday."

Mr. Darcy wondered at this offer of his cousin's. He was certain Lady Sofia and Lord Branston would not be offended at his not accepting any invitation that season, given they were to be absent for half of it and his cousin was not in such health as to enjoy the activities of a ball. He did not dance, and evening outings often aggravated his condition. Mr. Darcy, therefore, attributed the offer to the personal charms of Miss Bingley and a wish on the part of his cousin to become better acquainted with her.

This caused in Mr. Darcy a marked feeling of jealousy which he did not enjoy, and which reinforced the idea that he had been too quick to dismiss the lady. If she were able to engage the attentions of such a one as Lord Ashwell, perhaps he had been wrong about her and ought to reconsider his opinion.

A few of the guests had got up a dance, and Mr. Darcy thought it prudent to take advantage of the present opportunity.

"Miss Bingley," he began, rising stiffly from his seat. "Would you care to join me in the set? It seems they are short a pair for the quadrille."

"Of course, Mr. Darcy," she replied, taking the hand he offered. "I should be delighted." With a light step and a smiling countenance, she followed him into the dance.

This invitation by Mr. Darcy confirmed Lord Ashwell in his suspicion that this young lady was of peculiar interest to his cousin, for he had never known Mr. Darcy to do anything so spontaneous and so demonstrative as to ask a lady to dance without being firmly and repeatedly pressed to do so.

As the music began, Caroline was the first to speak.

"Your cousin is very kind to have invited us this evening, and to such a small party. Charles and I are very sensible of the honour of it."

"Ashwell is a very quiet sort of person. He does not enjoy elaborate affairs, and I think I must have spoken to him so often of your brother that he thought it time he made his acquaintance himself."

"Well, I hope we shall not embarrass you. Charles at least is liked wherever he goes."

"It seems that it is you that has made the strongest impression on him this evening. My cousin has agreed to attend Branston's ball, which, I assure you, is a compliment to yourself. Congenial as he is, he is not a great one for going about in the evening."

"I see. I shall be sure to see him home early then."

Mr. Darcy laughed.

"As you know," he said, "I am engaged to accompany your brother to the country tomorrow to view a piece of property. I imagine it is of some importance to you where he settles."

"You imagine correctly sir. It shall be as much my home as his during the winter months."

"And you trust his taste to choose the place?"

"I do indeed," she said, "all the more so for his having your opinion on the matter. He should make a very hasty decision on his own, I expect, but with you there, I am quite sure any decision will be a sensible one. It is always advisable to consult a trusted friend such as yourself on so significant a matter as the purchase of a piece of property."

"Well, since it is so important to you, I could, perhaps, stop by when we are returned and give you my opinion on the place—that is, if you should wish it."

"That would be very kind, Mr. Darcy, and most welcome, thank-you."

"It would be my pleasure."

Caroline was amazed at the suddenness of these attentions. She had done nothing to encourage him. She had not taken any of her sister's advice regarding winning his affection. In fact, she had been shamed by her negligence in that respect. And yet his interest in her was unmistakeable. What was she to do now about Mr. Wickham? She wished to accept him, wished for no cause to waver in her decision to do so. But how could she justify so rash a decision when she might yet have Mr. Darcy, who had so long been the object of all her ambitions?

As the dance continued Caroline also began to realize that this might be her last opportunity for obtaining information on Mr. Wickham from so reliable a source, and so, though prudence might have held her tongue, she was compelled to inquire after him, in as unremarkable a way as she could contrive. In the midst of an allemande, she remarked—

"Recently we made the acquaintance of a gentleman, who I believe is known to you. I am not certain whether I ought to remember him to you. By the way he spoke, it seemed he was quite familiar with Pemberley. His name, if I recall correctly, was Wickman, or Wickham, or something like. Did I understand correctly that he is a friend of yours?"

Mr. Darcy nearly lost his step, so unexpected was this reference.

"Indeed, Miss Bingley, he is very well known to my family, and he would be familiar with the estate of Pemberley, particularly its grounds, for his father was my father's steward."

"I see." Here, it was Caroline's turn to recover her steps. Mr. Wickham the son of a steward? To such a man she had almost surrendered her life and her heart? This was a shock, though she was careful to conceal her surprise from Mr. Darcy.

"That is very odd," said Caroline, forcing a light and indifferent tone. "One does not expect to meet with such a person at a private ball in Park Lane. And he seemed such a gentleman."

"Yes, he was always very graceful in his manners, and my father provided him a gentleman's education, so the mistake would be easily made." Mr. Darcy was not as practiced as Caroline at concealing his emotions, and he could not resist adding, hotly, "I expect he would not correct any such misapprehension, but probably try to profit by it. I would not be surprised if he had imposed himself on Branston by artifice in the first place. I assure you, he is not a gentleman—not of leisure, nor of any profession."

"I must not have paid very close attention. I thought I understood he was to accept a position in the North very soon. Then again, it was such a brief conversation."

"Mr. Wickham is not to take any position that I am aware of. He did inquire of one living which recently fell vacant, but he was not qualified for the post, not having taken orders, nor having studied to do so, and the recent proprietor was not of a mind to leave it to him. And so, all connection between us was truly in the past. But I thank you for your thoughtfulness in remembering him to me."

Mr. Darcy did not wish to spend any more time talking about Mr. Wickham. It was an unpleasant topic.

"Well, as I say, it was a very brief encounter. It is most likely I misunderstood him." Caroline also did not wish to linger on the subject of Mr. Wickham, and turned the conversation.

"You know, I cannot even recall what connection he had to Branston. A shared interest in horses is all his Lordship might require, I should not doubt."

Mr. Darcy laughed. "Quite."

Caroline's thoughts spun in her head. Fortunate it was that the dance concluded quickly, for she felt she could not support herself. She claimed fatigue from the dance and the heat of the room in seeking some outside air to refresh herself. As she stood on the balcony, tasting the damp night air, a host of emotions overwhelmed her. She burned with shame that she had been so duped by Mr. Wickham, but, more than this, she was relieved; she was sensible of having narrowly escaped a dreadful fate. To have married the son of a steward, whose claim to prestige was the living of a clergyman! And to all this she must add the fact that he could not even make that claim, for the living was not his for the taking. How fortunate she was to have inquired after Mr. Wickham, for what if she had accepted him? How could she have been so foolish to consider it when she was so uncertain of his circumstances? How could she be so fortunate as to receive the attentions of Mr. Darcy this evening, thereby giving her cause to hesitate in accepting Mr. Wickham? She had come too close to danger, and saw now with stark clarity how blinded she had been by her feelings. She was happy at least that nobody had been witness to her folly.

CHAPTER 16

Just as Caroline was renouncing him in her heart and in her mind, Mr. Wickham sat at his writing desk executing a plan to secure her hand.

He had received a reply from Mr. Darcy rejecting his application for the living at Kympton, and he had been attempting to draft a response ever since. He knew Mr. Darcy was not a sentimental man, so he dared not appeal to his pity, but he did know him to be a rational man and not unfeeling, and so he sought to set forth arguments in his response that might induce Mr. Darcy to reconsider his position.

Mr. Wickham was willing to admit that it had been impudent and rash to renounce the living once set aside for him. These were, however, the actions of impetuous and hot-blooded youth. He felt he had matured a great deal since then. He should very much like to settle, and the living would give him the opportunity to do so. It had been weeks since he had been to the races—even longer since he had indulged any of his other vices. He was impatient to explain to Mr. Darcy that this alteration in his character was an enduring one, and that his resolution was strengthened by a powerful agent.

An engagement to Caroline would give force to his claim that he desired no more to be the man he had been. He had mended his ways, and a wife would give him lasting motive to keep them thus mended. Furthermore, with her dowry and the income from the living he sought, he would eventually be in a position to repay the amount given to him in compensation, for he did not believe Mr. Darcy would allow him both the living and the funds paid in consideration for renouncing it.

Therefore, he could not deliver his letter until he had confirmed that Caroline would consider his proposal. He only hoped that he could continue to delay the revelation of his circumstances, at least until he was able to assure her of their being in every way favourably settled, for, though she had never given him cause to doubt her affection, he knew she would not accept him with such tenuous expectations as he could presently claim. And so, with an unsteady hand, he raised his quill to begin again his attempt to secure his lady, his fortune and his happiness in one evening's work.

The night of the ball, Lord Ashwell arrived in his carriage to collect the ladies who were to accompany him on his annual visit to Lady Sofia and Lord Branston. Caroline had thought it to best advantage to show herself to Lord Ashwell as a lady worthy of his cousin in every respect, as well as far above the legitimate hopes of Mr. Wickham. She therefore wore her highest head dress, her fullest silks, and her heaviest jewels. There could be no doubt of her appearing regal, her frame being tall and elegant enough to support such decoration, but Lord Ashwell could not help finding it a little much for an intimate evening with friends. It was, after all, a private ball they were attending, not a royal one.

Mrs. Purser, no less presentable for being more simply dressed than her companion, was precisely as Caroline had described her: timid and obliging to the point of near invisibility. Caroline had quite understated the case when she had said that Mrs. Purser would not be a burden to the gentleman. She danced only one dance, during which she spoke hardly a word to her partner, and she seemed relieved to be returned to Lord Ashwell, by whose side she spent the remainder of the evening in almost complete silence. Caroline, keen to demonstrate her skill to Lord Ashwell, had danced the first two dances. She hoped he might convey his admiration to his cousin and further her cause. So concerned was she with putting on a display for Lord Ashwell that Caroline did not notice Mr. Wickham arrive. At the same moment as he made his entrance, Lady Sofia entered from the other side of the room, sallying over to speak to Caroline and Lord Ashwell.

Breathless and emphatic as always, she began, "Dear sir, I am so pleased you were able to join us. You do us such an honour. I daresay, I did not trust to see you at all this season, so early do we leave for Brighton. Lord knows I should not wish to quit all my friends so soon. It is all Branston's doing, though I wager I shall make my way back here before too long. I always get my way in the end, you see. And who is this charming creature you have brought with you this evening, sir?"

"Lady Sofia, allow me to present Mrs. Purser. She is Miss Bingley's new sister-in-law, and we are delighted with her, are not we Miss Bingley?"

Mrs. Purser curtseyed in silence.

"Indeed we are, sir," Caroline replied.

"Miss Bingley, how majestic you are this evening!" remarked Lady Sofia, turning to Caroline. "And how do you like our arrangements here tonight?" she asked, indicating the curtains and fabrics which had been hung about the room to create tent-like areas around the corners and walls. "As you see, we have done it up in an Eastern style. It is in honour of our visit to Brighton, for I am given to understand His Majesty intends to expand and embellish his residence there in an Eastern style also. I am so pleased, for I adore all things Eastern. Do not you think them magical, Miss Bingley?" She did not wait for Caroline to respond. "I should not say so in public, but I confess that I have been reading the Arabian Nights, and I can scarcely sleep a wink so swept away am I by it. I am certain I shall be able to recount every story in detail by the time we are returned from Brighton, so devoted am I to reading it. Though I suppose Mrs. Belfry shall prevent me from saying anything about it in public. She worries so about my reputation."

"Well, in sympathy with your banishment from town, we shall all wear turbans in your absence," interjected Lord Ashwell, barely suppressing his amusement. "Will not you join me in this mark of solidarity, Miss Bingley? For I am sure it is preferable to arm bands."

"As you see, I am devoted to exotic headdress," replied Caroline, gesturing towards her crown. "I should be happy to oblige."

Lord Ashwell, noticing that the ladies were without refreshment, and looking for an excuse to step outside a few minutes, excused himself on the pretext of seeking out something for them all to drink. He could never stay in crowded, close places for very long before needing to take some air. Moments later, the others turned to acknowledge a new arrival to their party.

"I hope I do not interrupt," began Mr. Wickham.

"No indeed, sir. It is very good of you to come and send us off," replied Lady Sofia. "Shall I find Branston for you? I am sure he should wish to tell you all about the equipage we are to take to Brighton."

"That would be delightful, when he is free from the card table where I passed him just now. In the meantime, I should like to claim the dance which I believe has been promised me by Miss Bingley." He offered his arm with a look that spoke assurance as well as intimacy. Neither his arm nor his look was well received by the lady.

"I am sorry sir, if I misled you," she said coldly, "but I do not recall promising any particular dance to anyone. I am engaged here just at present and I should not wish to abandon my friends when there is a whole evening of dances to be had. I shall find you when I have quite finished here." She turned away from him, and addressed Mrs. Purser in the least condescending tone she could muster.

"Are you quite comfortable, my dear? Lord Ashwell will be back with some refreshment presently."

Mr. Wickham, visibly embarrassed, dropped his arm, and stood wondering how he ought to proceed. Lady Sofia, who did not like to see any soul injured, looked anxiously at Mr. Wickham, then at Caroline.

"Oh, Miss Bingley," she entreated, "you need not refuse Mr. Wickham on our account. Mrs. Purser and I may keep each other company, and I should never delay a friend's enjoyment for my own sake. Please, dance. It shall gratify me above all things to see you enjoy yourself."

Mr. Wickham stood awaiting Caroline's reaction. After a moment of hesitation, she forced a smile and said, "Come, Mr. Wickham, let us dance."

She stepped towards him. He offered his arm. She strode past him without accepting it, taking her place among the dancers before she finally turned to face him, her face sterner and prouder than he had ever seen it. If she sought to deter him with her contempt, she was not successful. He loved her for her strength and her wit; the fire that burned in her eyes as she glared at him worked only to further enchant him. She had never appeared to him more beautiful than she did now.

She refused to engage with him in the conversation on which he did not tire of entering. When he said, "I have missed you," she returned, "Oh." When he remarked on the overwhelming beauty of her person that evening, on the superior grace of her dancing, on the selfish delight he felt at the privilege of being her partner, her reply was a curt, "thank you," and nothing more.

Mr. Wickham could in no way account for the humour in which he found Caroline that evening, but he so trusted in her attachment to him that he was convinced her affection could overpower whatever might have altered her behaviour towards him. She did seem very cold and very angry, but perhaps there was some misunderstanding that he could explain, some misdeed that he could remediate in an instant. He had come too far to be turned aside now; he would have her answer.

As he bowed to her at the conclusion of the dance, he said, almost in a whisper to her lowered head, "Please, Miss Bingley, I must pray that audience of you which you did not refuse when last we spoke."

"And if it does not please me to hear you now?" she asked.

"I shall not leave your side until it does," he countered.

Caroline wished above all things to avoid any public unpleasantness, and so she led him from the house to the garden where they could speak without fear of being overheard.

They stood beneath a window, their faces barely illuminated by the light that shone through it. Caroline did not invite him to speak.

"Miss Bingley, you know what I have come here to ask you."

"Indeed, sir, though I do not know by what right you do so," she said archly.

"I do not understand, Madam. You assured me that you would give me some answer. Please remember that it is all my happiness you trample with your contempt, and that I have no hint as to its cause. I beg you would consider what you say and what you have said to lead me to offer you my unending love and devotion. I assure you, Miss Bingley, I am in earnest."

"In *earnest*, sir?" Caroline's voice dripped with indignation. "You have deceived me. You have been false, and you have imposed on me by artifice. How can you *think* that I would accept you?"

"My affection has been constant and unwavering," he pleaded. "Truly, I love you. I am undone by you. There is no falsehood in my declaration."

"You have told me nothing but lies! You are not who you presented yourself to me to be, and I can trust nothing that you say."

A cold pulse ran through his heart. She knew everything. He could see his hopes wilt in the heat of her scorn. He could only plead the truth in his defence.

"Please, Miss Bingley, my cause is not so hopeless as may have been conveyed to you. If you will only agree to consider my suit—only consider it—I am certain I may secure my future on the strength of that consideration alone."

"Consider you, sir? Consider *you*? You insult me with your request. Should I consider a man with no prospects, no connections, nothing to recommend himself, who requires my condescension merely to aspire to any expectations? And to what expectations? To the living of a *clergyman*! It is not to be borne. I am not so desperate as to accept the proposal of any man who will have me. Do you think me devoid of any other prospects? I assure you, sir, it is not so. I expect an offer from a gentleman of wealth and consequence—neither of which you possess—and I intend to accept it."

"What gentleman?" Mr. Wickham straightened.

"Do you not recall where I was at Christmas, for four whole weeks? Does that give you no hint? Well, I shall leave you the joy of reading about it in next week's papers."

Mr. Wickham froze. When they had first been introduced, Caroline had just come from spending Christmas at Pemberley. She could only mean Mr. Darcy, yet he was certain she did not love him, could not love him. She had never spoken of him with any sort of affection or regard. Could Mr. Darcy really be intending to propose? Could Caroline actually accept him? His heart pounded with panic and futility.

"You would throw yourself away on one you do not love?"

"You speak of throwing myself away—you, who would see me in rags? It is you who ask me to throw myself away—on poverty and obscurity—when I may have everything good in the world from another."

"I do call it throwing yourself away, when you give up on happiness, on love."

"You offer nothing that can make me happy, and it is no concern of yours whether I be so. I shall accept riches and honour—with or without the love to which you pretend. Good night, Mr. Wickham."

As Caroline turned to go, Mr. Wickham caught her hand. She stopped, allowing her hand to rest in his, but not turning back. He saw his only chance and took a step closer, pressing her hand to his lips. Still, she would not look at him, but she would not pull away either. "I pretend to nothing," he whispered. "Caroline, please." At the sound of her name, she turned to him, her jaw fixed and her breath rapid. His voice was low and soft. "You have forever robbed me of any pretense. I can only stand before you, in the confession of my love and beg you to do the same, for I would swear that you loved me last week. And I do swear that we can be happy, as happy as the greatest property in the world could allow. And together we can be great. We shall mock their false happiness with the truth of our love. You must believe me."

For a moment, Caroline's resolve wavered, but the moment quickly passed. She pulled her hand back as though from a flame, recoiling from him and from the temptation to mediocrity. She looked up at him, her eyes narrowed.

"I must do nothing. You are nothing," she said. Her cheeks burned with spite, with stifled regret and with a longing to surrender that she would never acknowledge. "I would strongly advise you," she said, "not to raise this subject again for I shall not demean myself to any alteration in my position."

With a set expression but trembling hands, Caroline turned from him and marched, flushed and breathless, back into the house. Her anger was as complete as her affection had been strong, for she could not hate him so much if she had not loved him so well. Her eyes burned, but she would shed no tears for Mr. Wickham or for the life of happiness with him which she forfeited that night. She would not permit herself to mourn the loss of the content but humble wife she might have been. She had made her choice and she abandoned any remorse, any second thoughts, when she walked away from him.

Mr. Wickham remained beneath the window a few moments longer, kicking the earth beneath him and cursing to himself, the name of Darcy spitting hot beneath his breath. He knew his chance had passed, that Caroline was gone from him forever, and he was convinced that Mr. Darcy must be to blame. He was as certain that Mr. Darcy had been the cause of his loss as he was that he would have succeeded with Caroline in the absence of that gentleman's interference. He turned his back to the house and walked towards the drive, unaware of the figure, unseen in the darkness, and only steps away—a silent witness to all his misery.

Lord Ashwell had returned to Mrs. Purser's tedious company while Mr. Wickham and Caroline had been dancing. By the time the pair had left the ball room, the warm and scent-laden air had again become oppressive. He excused himself and stepped outside to clear his lungs in the garden. Caroline and Wickham had just begun to speak, and they had not heard his approach. He grew still, half out of politeness, half out of curiosity, for he had come out that night with a secret purpose: Ashwell had observed a marked partiality for Caroline in Mr. Darcy, and he wished to observe the young lady's behaviour and character, especially outside of his cousin's company.

He never expected to be thus rewarded for his efforts. This episode between Caroline and the unidentified gentleman beneath the window showed a very different side of her character from what he had seen of her in his drawing room. The gentleman's protestations were clearly those of a man who had been encouraged. It was unmistakable to Lord Ashwell that Caroline's true affection was for this gentleman; and the lady herself had admitted that pecuniary considerations led her to throw him over for Mr. Darcy. Lord Ashwell would not see his cousin blindly led into matrimony to a fortune-hunter—especially when her heart clearly belonged to another. He could not stand idly by and watch it happen, not when he alone had the opportunity and the knowledge to prevent it.

CHAPTER 17

Morning found Caroline at her writing desk, sharing with her sister reflections on the events of the previous evening. Following her confrontation with Mr. Wickham, she had returned to the ball, full of animation and looking to throw off the nervous strain and ill-feeling which flowed from that encounter. All evening, she spoke louder than was required and danced with exuberance and spirit. She fancied herself the object of envy of every lady present, and the object of desire of every gentleman. Her wit flowed freely and more than one innocent guest felt the sting of her haughty spirits and severe tongue. She thought herself merely gay and energetic as well as masterfully clever in her repartee. Men and women alike found Caroline's boisterous shows distasteful. Lord Ashwell, whose favourable impressions from a week previous had already been thoroughly undone, saw in all of her actions an indelicacy and pettiness entirely consistent with her behaviour in the garden. Convinced as she was that each and every guest either envied or admired her, Caroline neither saw nor felt any of the disgust with her behaviour that rippled through the rooms.

Taking up her pen the next day, she wrote—

"DEAREST LOUISA,"

"I hope your honeymoon is exceeding all your expectations and that you are taking every opportunity of enjoying yourself. Charles is off in the country again, and I am exceedingly anxious for his return, for I hope very soon thereafter to have the most excellent news to send you. I am frightfully ashamed of my behaviour of late. I humbly acknowledge your superior judgment in all matters connected to my matrimonial prospects, and I beg your forgiveness for my imprudence. You must rejoice to hear that I have severed all connection with Mr. Wickham, whom I now regard as the most black-hearted and cunning creature ever to presume to call himself a gentleman. He is not at all who he represented himself to be. I find I am too deeply ashamed of my credulity to relate either the truth of his condition or the circumstances surrounding my discovery of it—or at least to commit any of the details to paper. Perhaps when I see you again, I may find myself equal to relating it all in person. Let it be sufficient for the present that I no longer consider him an acquaintance of mine, and as your only sister, I know I may trust in your discretion. I would be very happy indeed if I could erase forever the fact of my brief association with him; I must content myself with the erasure of any public knowledge of it.

"I have at last come to my senses, dear Louisa, for I believe that I have been living in a daze these past few weeks, and that my recent dalliance influenced me in my perception of the facts, falsely leading me to believe that I had no cause to hope for an offer from Mr. Darcy. But that nonsense is over now; the fog has lifted, and I am able to see with joyful clarity that I have been, all along, the only object of Mr. Darcy's affections. Although I did not see it for all its significance at the time, I am now convinced that he meant, by some recent remarks, to prepare me for a proposal. And when I review all his behaviour towards me when we were in Derbyshire, I find that I was a fool not to have expected it.

"You will recall that we were all invited to dine with Mr. Darcy's cousin, Lord Ashwell, in Grosvenor Square last week. Mr. Darcy maintains that it was his cousin's idea, but I cannot accept this explanation. I am certain that he pressed his cousin to invite us so that I might be introduced to more of his family, and so that he might have the opportunity of dancing with me and speaking to me in a semi-private manner. It is well known how little Mr. Darcy cares for dancing, so you can imagine all our surprise when he, quite unbidden, asked me to join him in a quadrille. Then, during the dance, he spoke to me of Charles' choice of residence in the country and its import to myself, which was clearly intended to show his interest in where I might be required to settle, as if to suggest I must prefer to reside at Pemberley. And if that were not sufficient to demonstrate his intentions, he actually requested an audience with me, which I will happily grant when he is returned from Hertfordshire. How else can I interpret this but as a gentlemanly forewarning of his plan to propose, so that I might prepare my reply? It is a very courteous gesture, but I require no time to deliberate. I have never been more certain of anything than I am that Pemberley suits me perfectly as a home and Mr. Darcy perfectly as a husband.

"And there is more. While we were dining at Grosvenor Square, I was treated with such cordiality that can only signal that Mr. Darcy's family already consider me as all but one of their own. I had been conversing with Lord Ashwell for not more than five minutes when he raised the subject of the ball at Sofia and Branston's. When I happened to mention that I was in want of a chaperone, he offered to take me himself! I could only attribute this to a wish by him to extend every kindness to his future kin. I did not detect from him any peculiar interest at the ball, and it would have been extraordinary if I could have inspired any in so brief a time.

"The fete itself was splendid, and I do not mind saying to you that I felt I was in rare form. I wore my gold silk and my blue sapphires, and I do not believe I saw my equal for coiffure all evening. I was singled out for honour when Sofia herself invited me to join her in Brighton. You will recall that Sofia's family is very close with the Darcys and, therefore, I do wonder whether she, too, was influenced by a suspicion, if not a knowledge, of Mr. Darcy's intentions towards myself. Whether that is so or not, it is a mark of undeniable distinction to be favoured with such an invitation. I would have been exceedingly happy to have accepted, and was indeed vexed to be required to refuse. It would have allowed me to visit with you in Brighton, and could have done nothing but good for my reputation to be seen as Lady Sofia's particular friend. But how could I consent to leave town just when I am expecting Mr. Darcy's proposal any day? It would be foolishness of inconceivable magnitude. I could not risk it.

"Please write soon and do tell me what a charming time you are having as Mrs. Hurst. Charles sends his love and best wishes, or rather I am sure he would if he were here. I look forward to seeing you soon in Hertfordshire.

"Your loving and faithful sister,

"CAROLINE"

Caroline posted her letter early in the day and spent until early evening seated near the window watching for her brother, hoping that Mr. Darcy would be with him when he arrived. He was not. Mr. Bingley entered the parlour, cheerfully announced that he was utterly fagged, and retired to his chamber.

The following morning, Caroline was at her toilette very early. She prepared herself to receive Mr. Darcy with every expectation of sealing a lifetime of ease and privilege. Mr. Darcy had not set a date to call, but, given his haste to return to town, Caroline expected he would not tarry long. At breakfast, Caroline ventured to inquire of her brother as to the success of the previous days' expedition.

"I am afraid the house we went to see was not suitable," Mr. Bingley told her. "It was a charming old place, but in need of a great many repairs. I would gladly have taken on the challenge, but Darcy forbade it. He thought it was a swindle, that the owners ought to invest their own money in their own property, and he said that once the place was fixed up, they might be of a mind to cancel the lease and get themselves a higher price from another party, or even from myself. I told him I did not think they could do such a thing; their solicitor represented them as being such good people. But you know I cannot defy Darcy, and so, our search continues."

"Have you any other leads then?" Caroline asked.

"Indeed, there are several. Some of them sounded very promising. I shall go to see them next month when we are in Hertfordshire. We might have seen a few on this trip, but Darcy seemed keen to get back to town."

Mr. Bingley had caught Caroline's attention with this comment, but he carried on without remarking it.

"He never seems able to enjoy himself in the country. I thought we could at least have stayed another night, as there were dances at the local assembly rooms, but you can imagine how that was received by Darcy. He is an impeccably good fellow, and the best friend I could wish for, but I do sometimes think he could stand to be a bit more jolly. He is good enough company when he is with friends, but why he cannot enjoy the company of new friends is beyond me. For myself, I always find the most recent acquaintances to be the most interesting."

"You must be careful not to speak too ill of Mr. Darcy, Charles. He is, after all, your most faithful friend, and you may come to regret any slight you make against his character, particularly to me."

Mr. Bingley did not at all understand what his sister meant, and was not accustomed to hear her defend anyone's character. He did recall, however, that she had been rather altered of late. This last remark, therefore, he took as further proof that she had, in recent weeks, grown kinder than he had ever before known her to be.

"Of course not, Caroline," he said. "I never meant to speak ill of my friend. He has been so very kind to us, so steady, and so faithful in every matter. I never knew anyone as careful of others as Darcy."

"I am very glad to hear it," said Caroline, pleased to hear such words of praise spoken about the man she regarded as her own. She looked forward with the greatest anticipation to the moment when she could announce to her brother that his most respected friend would soon become his brother.

After breakfast, she sat in the drawing room, a book open before her, though she was not enough mistress of her attention to absorb its contents. When she found herself reading the same line several times, she removed her hands from the page, allowing the book to close on itself. Rising from her seat by the window, she walked to the door, then back to the window, then back again. Her brother, who sat reading his paper, was distracted by her agitation.

"Are you quite all right?" he asked. "What is the cause of all this fidgeting? If you are so restless, why not take a walk?"

Before Caroline could answer, a carriage was heard outside. Caroline returned hastily to her seat and again took up her book, awaiting the announcement of Mr. Darcy.

"Are you expecting someone?" asked Mr. Bingley.

Caroline ignored her brother's question, feigning interest in her book. After a few moments, it was clear that nobody was calling, and she answered her brother.

"What? No, I do not expect anyone."

She could not resist walking out of the room and calling out to the housekeeper, "Who was at the door just now, Mrs. Cooper?"

"Nobody, ma'am," Mrs. Cooper replied with a curtsey.

"But I heard a carriage outside just now," Caroline insisted. "Who was it?"

"It was only the wine seller, ma'am, making a delivery." Mrs. Cooper curtseyed apologetically, confused at Caroline's interest in the goings on below stairs. Caroline dismissed her with a wave and returned to the drawing room, where she sank into her chair, ignoring her book.

"Truly, Caroline, you are very odd this morning," Mr. Bingley persisted. "Can I be of any assistance?"

Caroline stared blankly at her brother, considering whether, in fact, he could be of any assistance, and considering what, if anything, she should tell him. She sighed heavily.

"It is nothing, Charles," she finally replied, once more picking up her book and flipping through the pages. "It is only that I am so bored. With Louisa gone, I have no company. I have had no amusement since she went away."

"That is not true, Caroline. Only two nights ago you were at a ball, and the night before I left we were dining at Grosvenor Square. Do you feel the loss of Louisa so keenly that you forget these things?"

Caroline sat up in her chair and said, "Since you raise the subject, I do recall that Mr. Darcy said something to me that evening, in Grosvenor Square, before you went out of town. He said he would come by, after you were returned, and tell me about the place you had seen, since it would be of such particular interest to me. Did he happen to mention anything about this to you?"

Mr. Bingley folded his paper. "Is that what all this agitation is about, a call from Mr. Darcy?"

"Not at all." Caroline's tone was calm as she sank back in her chair, bringing her book up in front of her eyes. "I had quite forgotten about it until you mentioned it just now."

Mr. Bingley gasped in sudden remembrance.

"Do forgive me, Caroline," he began. "I am quite remiss. I entirely forgot about this note I received at breakfast from Mr. Darcy himself on that very subject. It arrived before you came down, and then when you did come down, I was in the midst of giving instructions to Mrs. Cooper about my trunks, and it quite slipped my mind."

Caroline's eyes darted from her book to her brother. She dropped her arm. "Well?" she urged.

Mr. Bingley reached into his pocket, pulled out a note, and began, "He says:

"Please let your sister know that, as the property in question is no longer under consideration, there can be no purpose in my giving her any description of it. Therefore, she need not wait for me to call as previously suggested. I shall contact you shortly regarding next month's plans for Hertfordshire. In the meantime, I expect to be very busy preparing for my sister's arrival, so do not be offended if I am not a frequent visitor, and know that I remain,

"Yours, etc."

Caroline felt winded at this cursory dismissal of all her hopes. "How insupportably fickle Mr. Darcy is!" she exclaimed, tossing her book onto the table. "I never heard of such poor manners, to send a note when a visit was promised. Truly, it is shocking."

Mr. Bingley was the one shocked by Caroline's abuse of Mr. Darcy, particularly in light of her comments to him that very morning. He only managed to say, "I say, Caroline—"

"I hope Mr. Darcy is ever grateful for your friendship," she interrupted, rising from her chair and crossing the room. "I know of no-one else who could tolerate him, for you never take offence and he gives it wherever he goes."

"I am not sure that is entirely true, Caroline," Mr. Bingley attempted to defend his friend. "I mean, I know he is not easy with strangers, but with his friends, he—" Caroline cut him off again.

"I believe I shall accept Sofia's invitation to go to Brighton. If we have not even the pleasure of Mr. Darcy's company, I do not believe I have any reason to remain in town another day. I may call upon Louisa there, to wish her joy and benefit from her chaperonage. I am sure I am quite lost without her."

With that, Caroline quitted the room and left her brother in dismay. She went upstairs and sent word of her intention to Lady Sofia, to Louisa and to Mrs. Purser, who had promised to chaperone her for the remainder of the season.

Caroline packed her things with fierce impatience, nearly tearing one of her best gowns. She barked at the servants and paced the room in a fury, huffing loudly and frequently as she did so. She was utterly wretched, and she could not see how she was to blame for her own misfortune. She had been certain that Mr. Darcy had intended to propose to her when he called, and she would not admit the possibility she had been mistaken. Something had altered his intentions, but, search as she might, she could find no reason to be thus abandoned. Since their last meeting, Darcy had been in the country with her brother, and, though he so rarely said the right thing, Charles could have said nothing to so affect Darcy's sure intention to propose. The Bingleys had no other common London acquaintances than Lord Branston and Lady Sofia, and Mr. Darcy would not have seen them since his arrival in London. He had only returned the previous evening, and besides, she could imagine no motive for their slandering her. Lord Ashwell knew nothing that would prejudice Mr. Darcy against her. Indeed, she knew of no honest criticism that could even be made of her conduct. She had done nothing that could soil her reputation.

There was only the business with Wickham in which *she* had been the victim, and which she had escaped without blemish. She could not imagine what Mr. Wickham might have told Mr. Darcy, let alone what Mr. Darcy might credit, given his frankly expressed opinions concerning that gentleman. Yet there was no other explanation. Mr. Wickham must be to blame. He was, indeed, cunning enough—and had cause enough—to lead the former to some damaging misinformation.

She left for Brighton with hopes that Mr. Darcy might feel her absence, that Mr. Wickham might have no more opportunity of wronging her, and, finally, that her sister might supply some plan for regaining the affections of Mr. Darcy.

Mr. Darcy had returned to London with every intention of fulfilling his promise to convey to Caroline his opinion of the house. It was of no moment that it was no longer under consideration; the subject had been a mere pretext for a call, though not for anything so serious as Miss Bingley had imagined. He had hardly begun to think her amiable, much less as his fixed choice of a wife. In calling on her, he hoped to resolve the discrepancy he had found between his very differing observations of her at Pemberley and at Grosvenor Square. He was not accustomed to making incorrect assessments of others and was perturbed to have an unsettled opinion on the subject. Furthermore, if he had been wrong, if her character were not so disagreeable as he had observed it to be, perhaps he might consider her after all.

He was at his breakfast when he received a most unexpected visitor. Lord Ashwell presented himself at the door, anxious to convey to Mr. Darcy his observations from the ball he had attended with Miss Bingley. The effect of the information on the recipient was immediate and exactly as Lord Ashwell had predicted.

He could not tell Darcy the name of the gentleman involved—Caroline had never called the man by name, and, from where he had been standing Lord Ashwell could not see his face—but, from all that Ashwell said, Mr. Darcy knew it could be none other than Mr. Wickham. He found the news shocking indeed. Not only did it unnerve him to learn that Caroline was in love with another man, but with Mr. Wickham of all people—the idea was insupportable. It cast his own conversation with her in quite a different light. No doubt she had been seeking information about Mr. Wickham in order to decide whether to accept him, and this while he was inviting himself over to call. The idea made him shudder, but it was not the worst of it. She had boasted of expecting a proposal from himself when he had only just begun to think of her. Moreover, she had boasted not of his love, but of his wealth, showing herself to be the fortune-hunter he had at first suspected her to be. He despised every form of deception, and any possibility of regard for her was now extinguished by his discovery of her insincerity.

He ought to have known that a lady who is too sparkling and clever is also cunning and insolent and not to be trusted. He had always believed strongly in first impressions, and here was evidence that he had been right to do so. He felt foolish for having doubted himself. He had wished Caroline to be suitable. It would have been very convenient if she were, being Mr. Bingley's sister and being already known to him. He concluded that his perceptions of her at Grosvenor Square had been influenced by this wish—perhaps helped along a little by Lord Ashwell's rather excellent wine—and that the opinion he had first formed of her at Pemberley was the correct one. Caroline was amusing enough to be tolerated as the sister of his friend, but no more than tolerated.

He therefore composed the note which Mr. Bingley read to his sister that same morning. In sending it, he resolved to think no more on the subject. It was not a difficult task, and he found that Caroline ceased from that moment to enter his mind.

CHAPTER 18

Though it was easy for Mr. Darcy to do so, Mr. Wickham was less able than he to dismiss Caroline from his thoughts in the days that followed her rejection of him. In a cloud of vicious misery, he had left the ball without taking leave of his hosts, returning to his room, where he snatched from his desk the letter he had so carefully composed the night before, crushing it in his hand and thrusting it into the fire. He cast about for a drink but, finding his only bottle empty, he became suddenly aware of his solitude and his utterly hopeless circumstances. He had no income, no property, and now no prospect of obtaining any. What is more, for the first time in his life, Wickham felt the sting of a broken heart. He let himself drop into a chair and began to weep.

He did not remain more than a few minutes in this state, however, as he was not prone to melancholy and preferred to dissipate his sorrows as he dissipated his life—in amusements he could not afford. He rose from his seat, and with a glance in the mirror, set out to find some solace in his old habits. He spent several days in pursuit of such diversions and had only just gone to bed on Tuesday morning when Mrs. Younge sought him out.

A bashful-looking servant girl answered the front door.

"Good morning, Mrs. Younge," the girl said with a smile. "I am sorry, but Mr. Wickham is not about yet."

Mrs. Younge had already begun to remove her bonnet, coat, and gloves. She handed them to the girl and brushed by her, ascending the stairs towards Wickham's room.

"That is alright, Polly," she said. "I shall rouse him."

Polly, with her arms full of Mrs. Younge's things, followed that lady up the stairs, protesting as she went: "He was ever so specific that he should not be disturbed," but there was nothing she could do to turn back the older woman from her purpose.

Mrs. Younge stopped at Wickham's door and turned back to the girl.

"He has not been abusing you, has he?" she asked sharply.

Polly lowered her head: "No ma'am." Mrs. Younge took a step back towards her, trying to see her face.

"He has not been making you any promises, or telling you stories?"

"No ma'am, nothing like that." Polly's eyes were fixed on the floor.

"Good." Mrs. Younge caught the girl's gaze and raised it to her own, reassuring her with a smile. "Mind you don't believe him if he does," she said. "There's a good girl."

"Yes ma'am."

Polly curtseyed to Mrs. Younge, who waved her away, and she descended, reluctantly back down the stairs.

Mrs. Younge rapped hard on Mr. Wickham's door.

"Mr. Wickham!" she called out. "Mr. Wickham! Arise and let me in, sir. We have work to do." When there was no reply, she beat upon the door again, harder, calling out, "You are not still pining for that Bingley wench, are you?"

After a moment, she heard a muffled "go away" from the other side of the door.

"I shall not go away, sir, and if you do not let me in, I shall shout your business to you through this door, and the whole building shall hear it." When the door still did not open, she continued. "Miss Bingley is not worth breaking your heart over, Mr. Wickham. She is a fortune-hunter like yourself, and she would never have had you anyway. Her rejection has only spared you the humiliation of being rejected later, after a public engagement, which would have been—"

The door opened.

"Very good of you to let me in, sir," she said to a bleary-eyed and very dishevelled Mr. Wickham. "Make yourself presentable sir," she chided, striding past him through the door. "You are a frightful disgrace."

Mr. Wickham closed the door and stood leaning against it for support. "I told Polly," he said, "I did not wish to see anyone."

"She did try to stop me, if that is of any consolation. Now, I shall sit behind there," said Mrs. Younge indicating a standing screen across the room. "You shave and dress. I may not be the highest lady in London, but I shall not sit with you in your shirtsleeves. I may tell you what news I bring from behind here." Mrs. Younge pulled a chair behind the screen and took a seat.

"If you have quite finished playing the Werther, there is still the matter of seeing you settled with a woman of some property, and I may be your angel of good fortune, for I bring you glad tidings on this front. I have received a communication of the most enticing nature, and it is all due to that flibbertigibbet, Lady Sofia. She may be a silly girl, but she has exactly the sort of connections we have been seeking. Had you not been so abominably pre-occupied with that jezebel Miss Bingley, you might even have got Her Ladyship for yourself, and she must be worth ten times as much. What's more, *she* might have had *you*—she seems just silly and romantic enough to fall for a man like you. She lauds suffering every distress that poverty can inflict with the object of one's most tender affection. In truth, I would like to see her survive on anything short of five thousand a year. I doubt very much her ideals would last her beyond Park Lane. But that is no odds. Lady Sofia is not the subject of my visit today, though I shall say that romantic ideals like hers can be very useful to one seeking a fortune from an unsuspecting young lady. Now," Mrs. Younge continued, "who do you think the lady might be? Have I piqued your interest?"

There was no answer. Mrs. Younge continued her prodding.

"She is known to Lady Sofia, and also to yourself, and I am to have charge of her education while she is in London. Do you have any idea whom I might mean? Come on, Mr. Wickham, have a guess."

Mrs. Younge, still receiving no measure of response from beyond the screen, peered into the room and let out an angry cry when she saw Mr. Wickham lying prostrate on the bed— neither dressed nor shaven, showing no sign of having comprehended anything she had said.

She rose furiously from her chair and marched over to the bed, picking up a cushion and beating him about the head with it.

"If you think I do not know how to rouse a drunkard and force him to his duty, you are mistaken. Mr. Younge was ever as insensible of a morning as you are today, and I never failed to move him to his task. I beat you with a pillow now, but there is a poker within my reach, and I shall wield it if you will not shake off this stupor."

Mr. Wickham, attempting to ward off Mrs. Younge's onslaught, shielded himself with his arms and cried, "What do you do? Take pity, please, I am in such a dreadful state!"

Mrs. Younge threw the cushion back onto the bed. "Sit up," she said.

He hesitated.

"Fine, I'll get the poker," she said, moving towards the fireplace.

Mr. Wickham knew her too well to believe her to be in jest. He reluctantly drew himself up and sat on the edge of the bed, hanging his head between his shoulders.

"There are your shaving things," she said, pointing stiffly across the room. When he did not look up to see where she was pointing, she struck him hard across the back of the head with her open palm.

"I say!" he exclaimed, rubbing his head and moving from the bed to the basin.

Mrs. Younge softened and continued.

"Now, shall I tell you who is to be your conquest after all?" she said sweetly.

"Have you no heart, Mrs. Younge?" Mr. Wickham stood, leaning on the wash stand, staring at his razor. "Cannot you see that I am wretched and that I have no heart to consider any other lady? I wished to marry Caroline. Cannot you see that it is too early for me to think of marrying anyone else?"

"Forget about Miss Bingley. She will not have you, so it is best for you to put her out of your mind immediately. You must have something to live on, and Miss Bingley's fortune is no longer within your grasp. The creditors will not be bought off by your tales of woe."

"You are very cruel, Madam, to force reality upon me at such a time as this." Mr. Wickham picked up his brush absent-mindedly and began to lather it.

"It is life that is cruel, sir," she said, returning to her seat behind the screen. "If I could have got Miss Bingley to marry you, with no fortune and no expectations, I would have. My seeming tyranny is only kindness in disguise, you know. A gentleman must be active to be happy. You must have some purpose, and you must find something to sustain you or you shall end up in the Marshalsea. You think yourself depressed now, but matters will only worsen if you do not take action."

Mr. Wickham, never one to consider with any gravity the consequences of his actions, focussed his attention on the sight of his excellent jaw, which began to make an appearance in the glass as he scraped it clean.

"Yes, yes," he muttered. "I shall think of something, no doubt. I always do."

"I have already done much more than think of something!" exclaimed Mrs. Younge with impatience. "If you would only listen to me, you would learn that I have discovered the key to all your future happiness, and that it is entirely at my command."

Mr. Wickham always enjoyed dressing, and, as he set about refining his appearance, his mood improved apace.

"Go on," he said.

Now she had his attention, Mrs. Younge measured her response, reveling in the suspense. "The young lady I am

119

thinking of stands to inherit a very pretty sum. She is very fond of you already, and young enough to be persuaded into anything. Lady Sofia tells me she is a sweet, unassuming creature with a tender heart and a passive nature. She shall give you no trouble, shall never impose on you, and shall never embarrass you. She shall be the perfect wife, and there is no obstacle to your having her. It is as good as done. You need only play your part, and in a few months it shall all be settled. You shall be rich, happy, and almost as unfettered as you are now."

"She is a friend of Lady Sofia's?" Mr. Wickham asked.

"Yes, I said that already!" Mrs. Younge huffed. "Without knowing what she was doing, Lady Sofia has arranged the whole thing so that it could not be more perfect for our designs. This is an excellent spot of luck for us."

"You say she is already fond of me?"

"Well, I confess that is an assumption, but not an ungrounded one. She was very young when she knew you, and we all know childhood memories cast everyone in the best possible light. She cannot but be predisposed to love you—if she does not do so already. After all, who is not fond of you?" Mrs. Younge knew this sort of flattery would interest Mr. Wickham. His vanity was the bridle by which she led him.

"All right, Mrs. Younge," he said, stepping away from the sink, "you have my attention. Who is she?"

Mrs. Younge paused, gleefully increasing his eagerness, before she slowly and quietly pronounced the name, "Miss Darcy."

"Georgiana?" Mr. Wickham's face appeared suddenly around the screen, giving Mrs. Younge a start.

"Yes, Georgiana Darcy," she replied, catching her breath. She looked up at him and grinned. "The house of Darcy is an unexpected quarter for such good fortune to come from, but rather poetic in a way. The son has been such a source of grief and disappointment to you. Now, the daughter shall be your recompense. What the brother denied, the sister shall supply."

"Georgiana," he repeated, staring above Mrs. Younge's head. He reflected silently for a moment, considering the implications of all Mrs. Younge had said. "But she is just a child," he objected.

"She is nearly fifteen," countered Mrs. Younge, "and likely to be out by the spring. Mr. Darcy is sending her to town for her education, and Lady Sofia has convinced him to allow me the honour of presiding over it. What is more, there has been some talk of my accompanying her to Ramsgate for the summer. Any obstacles that might have prevented your association with her in town will have no power to keep you apart at a seaside resort."

"She must be worth at least thirty-thousand pounds," he mused aloud. "And you are right; she was always very fond of me."

"How could her childhood affection not be renewed when she sees you now, as a young lady embarking upon the world? How could she possibly be insensible to your charms?" Mrs. Younge smiled.

Mr. Wickham needed little convincing to consider Georgiana as his destiny and his prize. Mrs. Younge left him much more cheerful—and much less full of Miss Bingley—than she had found him. As she closed the door behind her, Mrs. Younge rolled her eyes and sighed to think of his purported state of melancholy when she arrived only minutes ago and of the capricious nature of an ambitious man's heart.

CHAPTER 19

Northampton's midnight rain continued unrestrained as Georgiana finally surrendered to her fatigue and carried herself to bed. Clare was to have met her at that inn several hours prior, and Georgiana had waited for her in an anxious state of anticipation that had superseded her sleepiness, until that late hour. Some hours after retiring, she thought she heard the hushed commotion of an arrival, but she was not able to rouse herself, and only in the morning did she rise with the hope that the late arrival had been her friend.

She was not disappointed, for she received a knock on her door before breakfast and hastened to receive Clare to her room.

"How relieved I am to see you," said Georgiana, embracing her friend. "You must have arrived very late, for I did not retire until hours after I expected you. I hope you were not disappointed that I was not there to greet you when you arrived."

"Heavens no!" answered Clare. "We were unfortunately delayed, and I am the one who should apologize for causing you to lose so much sleep."

"What happened?" asked Georgiana, leading her friend to a seat.

"Some trouble with a horse," Clare explained. "We all got quite wet and had to warm ourselves and change our clothes at an inn, which took some time, in addition to the time spent on the horse. But I may tell you more on that later. I am so pleased to have arrived, and to see you again. Are you well? Have you had a pleasant journey so far?"

"As much as can be expected," Georgiana replied. "We have had nothing but rain, but I am very well, and very pleased with this place, particularly as it has brought me you. How have you been these past months? And how is your family, your mother especially? Have you really not seen her since the autumn?"

Georgiana knew Clare had not been allowed to return home since learning of her mother's illness, but she could not help expressing her disbelief at the fact.

"The doctors cannot say what kind of danger she is in," said Clare, shrugging in resignation. "Since I can be of no material use at home, my mother wished me to continue my schooling. It would give her the most peace to know that my education was not sacrificed on her account."

"Did she not consult your feelings, your wishes on this point?" Georgiana could read in Clare's brave and smiling face, the hurt and anxiety that necessitated the effort of cheerfulness.

"She does not act out of selfishness," Clare said plainly. "She thinks only of my welfare. And is not she correct? The journey home would be long and costly. And when I arrived, what then? She does not need nursing. I should simply sit wondering when the worst should occur. Instead, I have had the double benefit that my schooling was not interrupted and that I was kept busy, which is the best safeguard against constant worry."

"But if she should go soon, and you had not seen her, would not you regret . . . ?" Georgiana trailed off.

"Pessimism cannot be allowed to dictate the course of our lives. I must act on the hope that she may live many more years. If the worst comes, I would not have it that my last act towards her be a betrayal of her express wishes. I could never forgive myself if we were forever parted on bad terms."

Georgiana was struck by the nature of her friend's response, so different was it from her own reaction to the news of her own mother's illness some years ago.

Although they loved their children with devotion and sacrifice, the Langfords were so unskilled at intimacy as to fail to attribute to it any genuine value. They often lavished more affection on the furniture than they did on the children, for furniture cannot be spoiled by excessive demonstrations of emotion. They saw the advancement of their children's station as the chief means of promoting their happiness and did not indulge anything which might diminish their prospects.

"But tell me about your time at home," Clare inquired. "Was it as remarkably pleasant as I imagine it?"

"Oh yes, more so, I would guess." Georgiana could never refuse the opportunity to speak of Pemberley and Mr. Darcy. "And my brother has convinced me that London will not be so terrifying as I imagine. At the very least, it will be easier for him to visit me there, as he is often in town on business. He is so thoughtful of me. He says it is for his pleasure that he should see me more often, but I am sure he thinks of my pleasure in seeing him, which I do not doubt is many times his own."

"You were at school for so many years. Shall not you miss it?" asked Clare.

"I do not like to say that I doubt I shall think much on it. Everyone there was kind to me, but I was always sick for home. As I have brought you with me, I cannot say that I shall regret leaving anything behind. You shall be such a comfort to me in town—I do not think you shall ever know how much. I do not know how I should have fared without you, with all the bustle of the city, the calls, the balls, and all the people to whom one is obliged to speak. I shall only survive it because I shall have you to consult on every question of proper conduct, and to keep me company when there are no familiar faces in the crowd."

Clare assured Georgiana that her brother would never have allowed her to be lonely, that her conduct needed far less correction than she believed, and that she would never want for friends. In sum, Clare felt that some time spent in the world might add to Georgiana's self-assurance, which was all she wanted, if she wanted anything, to be the embodiment of every perfection.

Uncertain how to respond to such praise, Georgiana suggested that they visit the chapel next door to light a candle for Mrs. Langford. And so they went, not to eat their breakfast until their hearts were emptied and their knees were very sore.

CHAPTER 20

As they pulled into the house at Berkeley Square, Clare and Georgiana both expressed relief on having finally reached the terminus of their journey. Mr. Darcy welcomed them and the greeting between brother and sister was warm and affectionate, and might have gone on a deal longer were not the sister eager to introduce him to her friend.

"Clare, allow me to present to you my brother, Mr. Darcy," she said, looking at her brother as if for approval, which he gave by way of a warm smile.

"Miss Langford, it is a pleasure finally to make your acquaintance. I hope your journey was uneventful. I dare not hope such a lengthy one could be pleasant."

"We only had a small upset near Daventry, but after joining your sister, all went as smoothly as could be hoped. I am refreshed by the mere act of exiting the carriage, though I suspect that shall soon wear off and we shall both be quite ready for our beds when the time comes."

"Clare is such a stoic traveler, brother," added Georgiana. "It is true, the last leg of our journey was without incident, but she speaks of only a small upset when indeed it was a lame horse which caused the carriage to overturn into a slough leaving its passengers to wait nearly three hours in very cold rain with very wet feet. If such a thing had happened to me, I would have spoken much more plaintively of it after the fact and have behaved far more desperately at the time of it."

"As much as you say otherwise, I am convinced you would have behaved no differently in the circumstances," Clare protested. "There was nothing to be done but wait, which is in itself no meritorious feat. I am certain the incident could not have been prevented, and besides, nothing could be accomplished by complaint."

Mr. Darcy was very pleased with this evidence of Clare's sense and resignation. It gave him comfort and satisfaction to know his sister would have such a companion as she entered the gauntlet of society. Repeating his joy on their safe arrival, he left the girls to unpack, recommending them to the housekeeper, Mrs. Jones, who was to help them to their rooms.

When Georgiana entered her room, she discovered a letter left for her on her dressing table. Taking it in her hand, she saw it was from her cousin Anne. How unexpected, she thought. At her brother's urging, Georgiana had written to Anne several times since they were together at Christmas, but, until now, there had been no reply. Why Anne should write now was a mystery. Georgiana sat on her bed with the letter and eagerly opened it.

"DEAR GEORGIANA,"

"Mama has ordered the library be closed for cleaning and possibly refurbishment—she has not yet decided which it will be. It is yet too cold for me to be permitted to spend any time out of doors, and so, I am afraid to say, Kent is very dull this spring. I received your letter a few weeks ago, and Mama has not let a moment pass without reminding me how delinquent I am in not yet replying, so I suppose I must apologize for that. I have been very occupied in rescuing from possible destruction a number of volumes from the library that, though dear to me, seem to be of little worth to anybody else—least of all Mama. If she has her way, she will convert our library into a music room to display her immense appreciation of an art in which neither she nor I have ever taken an interest. Thank heavens she is so concerned with the demands of rank, for in her role as a great lady, she knows she must preserve the generations' work and her husband's life interest in the form of the library, but to her, one volume is as good as any other. She by no means wishes to destroy all—for that would be intolerably unseemly—but she so wishes to cultivate the bare handful of mediocre musicians that have started appearing in her friends' drawing rooms that she thinks it a kind of grand compromise to knock down the shelves in only half the room to make room for a dais. What this would do to my father's intact collection of rare Natural Science books—which now stands on the side of the room slated for destruction—I have not the words for. My bedroom is, for now, being secretly converted into a botany library.

"I suppose I must be grateful that our new curate will receive his ordination at Easter, for it has caused her to turn her attention from the library to the parsonage. She has spent countless hours preparing for his arrival, which should be sometime shortly after his ordination. It is a blind pride which compels her in this case, for the curate himself is hardly a person of consequence. And yet, upon reflection, I must conclude that Mama only expends effort on impressing and ingratiating herself to those beneath her own station, perhaps because she has failed to succeed in the circles which she ought to occupy. Her condescension to those beneath her is more welcome than her conversation is among her equals.

"As for myself, I have entirely given up speaking in her presence. It is merely an invitation to grief and frustration. I do not think she has noticed—in fact, I think she prefers it. She never tires of her own conversation; she does not have the opportunity of missing mine. Well, whatever she may or may not have of it now, she shall soon be without it forever. As soon as I receive my inheritance, I shall leave England for good. No doubt, that should shock all my relations, due in no small part to their concerns about my health, but I am not half so ill as they are all convinced I am; a warmer climate is all I want to be the absolute picture of health. It is true there may be a dearth of qualified physicians elsewhere, but I have been treated by every doctor in the kingdom for twenty-two years without, as far as they are concerned, noticeable improvement, so perhaps they are not so qualified as they all claim and their absence will do me no harm. Perhaps it shall even be to my benefit, for who knows what their mystic arts have brought unwittingly upon me. Perhaps it is they who are the cause of my ill health. And I may have my freedom earlier than expected if our friend Miss Bingley has her way. If I marry, I shall receive my inheritance as a dowry, and I shall never be free; but if I reach the age of five-and-twenty unwed I shall receive it for my own disposal. I even hope I may receive it earlier if your brother should marry someone other than myself. I do not know if your brother speaks to you of such things, but my mother certainly does not scruple to speak of it constantly that I am intended for your brother. I was older than you when your mother was still alive and I can assure you there was never any such formal arrangement. It was not in your mother's nature to dictate anything to anyone. There may have been a vague hope and a romantic speculation, but they were very wrong if they thought I meant to sacrifice myself to their notions of the Fitzwilliam Empire. And I doubt very much that your brother should do so either. If he should marry someone else, I am certain Mama would entirely despair of my marrying at all and allow me my inheritance straight away. My father knew well enough to give up hope for me once I reached twenty-five years of age, and though Mama may be deluded respecting your brother, I cannot believe her so blind as to think there may be some other man for me who might appear in the next three years. So you see, much as I ought to love your brother as my kin, I do resent him his enduring bachelorhood inasmuch as it stands between me and my independence. I was encouraged, however, by the blatant determination of Miss Bingley this Christmas. I had half expected to hear a happy announcement by now, for she seemed possessed of all those things which gentlemen prize. She was handsome, fashionable, accomplished at playing, singing and dancing, and not without intelligence. I expect he would tell you first if any such announcement were forthcoming.

"I will leave off here or this letter will never be sent. I hope you like London. Mama insists I add that she hopes you purchased your life's needs in terms of boots and shoes when you were in Northampton. She is convinced there is a famine in footwear and that one can never be oversupplied in that department lest we should all be forced to go barefoot. It is a secret plot of Napoleon, apparently, to target all the English shoemakers in battle and leave us weak and defenceless in our rags. Well, he shall not affect me for I shall buy my shoes in Africa, or the Indies, or the Americas, or somewhere else very, very far from Kent.

"Yours etc.

"ANNE"

Georgiana reeled from this letter. She could not recall ever being spoken to so directly and so boldly in her life. Anne raised and disposed of the most delicate and scandalous subjects as she might do so many tares in her wool. Mr. Darcy had never spoken to his sister of his potential marriage to Anne, or to Caroline, or to anyone else for that matter. Georgiana wondered what other subjects he had failed to raise with her, and whether any of them might affect her even more directly. She was also stunned at the idea that Anne might disappear to Africa—Anne, who had always seemed so timid and shy. It would indeed shock all her relations, and not the least because of her health. Georgiana was stunned to see how great was the disparity between the Anne that everybody thought they knew and the Anne which this letter thrust upon her. She wondered whether this could be true of herself, or of anyone else she knew. She herself was shy and susceptible to sentiment. She considered for some time how this could be perceived in any other way, but she could not. She never spoke in public and was wary of strangers. How could this be perceived as anything but shyness?

Unable to resolve all the questions of her life in a quarter of an hour's reflection, Georgiana dressed for dinner and went downstairs to spend as much time as she could with her beloved brother before he was obliged to leave them.

Following dinner, Clare retired early, being uncommonly fatigued from the day's journey. Mr. Darcy took the opportunity to share with his sister a decision which he and Colonel Fitzwilliam had come to, namely, that they thought it time she came out into society.

"There is no cause for apprehension," he assured her. "I know you are still quite young, and that you find exertions of a social nature rather trying. It is precisely for that reason that your cousin and I thought, though you are yet young, you should come out now so that you may have the liberty of moving slowly into society, taking it a little at a time so that you are not overwhelmed. You can grow accustomed to the idea slowly."

Georgiana nodded but said nothing. She did feel apprehension, but she trusted her brother to know what was in her best interest. He had been in the world and could judge much better than she. He was ever kind to her, and would not require of her anything beyond her capacity.

"Most young ladies have a ball in their honour when they come out," he continued. She looked up in sudden fear. "But," he added, "I believe this is the preference of most young ladies. I expect you would not like such a grand affair for yourself. Am I correct?"

"No, not at all—that is, I mean, yes, you are correct. I would not choose to have any sort of large event. I should not enjoy myself at all."

"That is as I thought. Would it be bearable to have a small dinner at Grosvenor Square to mark the occasion with a few friends? Aside from us, Miss Langford and, of course, Lord Ashwell, I thought Lady Sofia and Mr. Bingley would like to join us. What say you to that? Could you tolerate such an evening?"

He smiled at her. Georgiana sighed in relief and smiled back, feeling very grateful that her brother was always so considerate of her often unreasonable reserve. "Yes," she answered. "I can think of nothing so exceedingly tolerable as that."

They both laughed. "Excellent," said Mr. Darcy. "I am very glad to hear it, for I have already made the arrangements. You may tell Clare that we dine at Lord Ashwell's on Friday."

CHAPTER 21

In her youth, Mrs. Langford had been little concerned with the impact her humble marriage would have on either her fortunes or those of her children. Her younger brother, Geoffrey, had inherited Farrow Hall and the baronetcy and always intended to take care of his sister and her children. He was not yet married and had no heirs, but there was yet another brother, Richard, who was to inherit if anything should happen to Geoffrey. He, like his brother, was good-natured and caring, and there had been no question that he, too, would provide for his relations. Both brothers were in excellent health and it was anticipated they would beget many heirs between them. Three years ago, however, tragedy struck the house of Crawley. Out riding one morning, Richard fell from his mount and split his crown upon an exposed rock. Before the family had doffed their mourning weeds, Geoffrey took to bed with a fever, which carried him off to an early and sudden grave.

Both deaths having occurred so unexpectedly and in such quick succession, neither brother had made any provision for the Langfords. Therefore, Mrs. Langford mourned not only the loss of two beloved brothers, but also the security for her children which they represented. As the uncles passed from the world, the estate and title passed to a cousin of Mrs. Langford's, Mr. Leicester Crawley, now Sir Leicester Crawley, baronet.

Mrs. Langford knew of this cousin, and had even made his acquaintance once or twice in years past, but he had never been a favourite with her and never received more than common cordiality from her or her family. He had little to recommend himself, being coarse in his address, unfixed in his opinions and rotund in his person. Never having expected to inherit the baronetcy, he had been forced to pursue a profession. Though he had begun at several, he had neither the requisite intelligence nor application to succeed at any and was becoming quite desperate when rescued from his poverty and indolence by the deaths of Richard and Geoffrey.

He found the life of a gentleman quite suited his disposition. He particularly enjoyed being elevated above those who had formerly looked down upon him, and was always demonstrative in his condescension towards them. When, some years previous, Clare was first introduced to him, he was struck by the blossoming beauty and grace of his young cousin—a beauty and grace such that he would not have dared to approach before his elevation so inflated his self-regard. He thought one day to make a great example of his charity by making her an offer of marriage. The Langfords, he thought, were quite at his mercy, and he delighted in the contemplation of their gratitude for his future kindness towards them.

Mrs. Langford hoped Sir Leicester would be kind to her family and paid him every appropriate attention, but she did not encourage in her children more association with him than the family connection merited. Whatever he might do for them in the world, she did not believe it was worth the risk of indebtedness to such a character as his, which she had always regarded with suspicion. As she had told Clare many times, to look back on one's life without regret was a privilege that could not be purchased with a thousand inheritances.

As Sir Leicester spent most of his time in London, it was necessary that Clare see him and, as far as prudence would allow, endear him to the Langford family. Mrs. Langford had therefore written to her cousin to inform him of Clare's being in town, also providing her address should he wish to call upon her.

The morning following the ladies' arrival in London, an invitation was delivered to the house from Sir Leicester, asking Clare to come for supper three days hence. Clare did not like to admit her relief on being obliged to refuse. She despatched as quickly as possible a note saying that, with sincere regret, she was unable to attend since she was already engaged to dine that evening with Lord Ashwell at Grosvenor Square.

The following afternoon, Sir Leicester called upon Clare while Mr. Darcy and Georgiana were out. He began by straight away welcoming her to the gay city of London, expressing a wish that, now that they were so much more closely situated, they might become better acquainted.

He stayed only a quarter of an hour, which was long enough for him to assure Clare three times of his mother's excellent health, to invite her to the theatre the following week, and to share with her his worldly wisdom respecting a certain gentleman.

"So, you will be dining with Lord Ashwell this week," he began.

"Indeed, Cousin. It is very kind of him to extend the invitation to me, and I am sure you see that I cannot refuse."

"Well," he said, leaning towards her, "I suppose he *must* make up his table, though I hope you shall not form a habit of submitting to all his invitations without question."

He shifted yet closer to Clare, who remained quite upright in her seat. "You see," he continued, in an accent of confidence, "I have not come here out of simple courtesy. One does not like to speak ill of any fellow, but, as your nearest relation in town—possibly your only sort of protector in this place—I think it my duty to arm you against any possible source of harm."

Clare maintained her composure, but could not entirely conceal her curiosity.

"Lord Ashwell may hide behind his wealth and consequence, and though there are many who will overlook and forget any wrongdoing, however vile, some of us are not so easily swayed. I see no reason to share the facts that give me cause to caution you; only promise me you will be on your guard against him. I assure you that your interests are nothing to him. It would not be out of character for him to take full advantage of a defenseless girl such as yourself. I presume Miss Darcy is as much in the dark as you are, given her young age, and I gather that the Darcys and the Fitzwilliams are quite thick, so I very much doubt anyone would share anything with you even if they were informed of the truth. What concern have they for you that they should reveal their sordid histories and defame their own race for your benefit? Please tell me you will heed my advice, and that you will look to me if you should find yourself in any difficulty."

Clare was uncertain how to respond to this exhortation. She might have thought his warning a kindness had she not been warned by Georgiana against such gossip, by her mother against Sir Leicester himself, and by his own want of breeding against the sincerity of his intent. It was shocking in itself that he should so casually slander the reputation of another gentleman, without any real apology or pressing necessity. She felt she may have more cause to take caution against *his* self-interest than that of Lord Ashwell.

"I hope I shall always be vigilant in my guard against evil," she answered, "in however genteel a form it may present itself, and I hope I shall always be sure of your true and selfless friendship."

Sir Leicester, satisfied with this reply, rose and took his leave, repeating his invitation to the theatre and his hope of their becoming ever-greater friends.

CHAPTER 22

Clare endeavoured to overcome her anxiety in the face of dining at Grosvenor Square. She believed herself equal to the occasion, and she told herself repeatedly that she was merely accompanying Georgiana to dine with her own family. It was not a formal or large occasion, and she would certainly not be the object of anyone's interest. Yet, she could not help but dwell on everything her mother would have said to her on such an occasion, stressing the importance of the connection, and warning her against the evils of any slight misstep. This general state of nervous apprehension was augmented by the mystery surrounding Lord Ashwell. A debauched viscount was just the sort of subject which she feverishly delighted to read about in novels. She knew not whether to fear most her own failings or his. Her heart thrilled with that common mixture of fear and excitement that left her, at some times, anxious beyond measure, and, at others, nearly breathless with anticipation.

In determining what would be best for her to wear for the occasion, Clare was distressed. Her mother had many old gowns from her own youth, which were of very fine quality and barely worn. Twenty years prior, they had been the height of fashion; no expense had been spared on them. Out of a desire not to see her daughter shamed in society, Mrs. Langford had sent some of these gowns to be made over for Clare, so that she might have something respectable to wear in society. However, never having taken more than a cursory interest in fashion, having never possessed more than a common measure of taste, and having lost with years of marriage what little she had of either, Clare's mother was not sensible of the dilemma she created for her daughter. The finery of Mrs. Langford's youth appeared gaudy and absurd on Miss Langford. The fabric as well as the style of the gowns were not only extravagant; they were utterly out of vogue. Clare knew Miss Darcy would wear a simple gown of pale colour and few ornaments, and it would not do to overdress in comparison. Clare was therefore a little panicked, for indeed her parents had not been wrong to think that the gowns she had at school were inadequate for life in town, and her choice was either to be ridiculous in the poverty of her dress, or in the extravagance of it. In the end, she was forced to spend a day's labour undoing the work of the Mantua-maker, removing trims and surplus fabric, leaving her with a simple blue gown. Its silk was heavier than she would have chosen for herself, but it was the best compromise she could contrive in the time she had.

The result of Clare's labours was not without effect.

"Why Clare," declared Georgiana as her friend came into the room, "how beautiful you look! Is this what you have been about these two days?"

"It is." Clare looked down at her gown. "I would never have chosen this fabric or this colour, but this was the simplest to alter of everything my mother sent."

"I think the colour flatters your complexion very well and you have made it so becoming on the whole. I marvel at your skill."

Clare was neither accustomed to, nor comfortable with flattery, and she blushed a little at this compliment from her friend. She had never considered herself a beauty, and little effort had been made to undeceive her. Her pious mother believed it damaging to a girl's natural modesty to encourage any sort of vanity or self-regard. And Clare herself, though always careful to avoid the touch of the sun, was yet unable to prevent a few freckles from making their appearance on her face and shoulders, which tarnish she saw as an insurmountable barrier to her ever being considered truly beautiful. She also believed that her features and her figure were too soft and too round to be considered fashionable or elegant. Thus, she accepted her friend's flattery with sceptical thanks.

Joining Mr. Darcy in the foyer, Georgiana relayed her impressions to her brother. Ushering Clare forward, she said—

"Is not Clare very clever and industrious, Brother? You see, she has made this gown almost from scratch, in just these few days since we arrived. Are not you very impressed?"

Mr. Darcy was unpracticed in such little elegant compliments as are always acceptable to ladies. In fact, he was as uncomfortable in giving flattery as Clare was in receiving it. Clare was not in the least offended by his want of exuberance when he could only contrive to say, "Yes, very good. You both look very respectable."

Mr. Darcy had not remarked upon any particular charm or beauty in Clare in the few days they had known each other, though he was impressed with the evenness of her manner and the wisdom she showed beyond her years. But even he was struck by her appearance when she entered the room. He would not be the last to be so that evening.

When Lord Ashwell had first heard that the school fellow who was to live with his cousin in London was an admiral's daughter, he was concerned. His fears were a little allayed when he learned her grandfather had been a baronet, but his imagination still led him to expect something of a hardy, sea-faring lass, with brusque manners and a weather-beaten face. His expectations hardly prepared him for the gently beautiful creature who was presented to him in his drawing room as Miss Langford of Maplethwaite.

"I am so pleased you were able to join us, Miss Langford," he said, his voice mellifluous and unassuming. She longed to raise her eyes to his and take his likeness, but her nerves overpowered her curiosity. She curtseyed, and without lifting her chin, replied,

"Not at all, I was honoured to have been invited."

When once they were all seated, she felt it safe enough to study his appearance. It was more refined than she had anticipated, his features more delicate, his dress simpler by far than it would have been had he been anything like the heartless dandy Sir Leicester had prepared her for. As she resumed her study of his face, she saw that he, too, was looking at her. Mortified, she looked quickly away, though not without seeing him smile at her an unembarrassed, gentle, forgiving smile that could only be shyly returned.

Not long after the Darcy party had arrived, Mr. Bingley was announced, and Lady Sofia followed shortly thereafter. Clare had not expected to meet with two members of noble families in one evening, and had they not been such easy and obliging representatives of their class, she may have been intimidated at the prospect.

Lord Ashwell welcomed them all to his home with such sincerity and enthusiasm that his guests hardly noticed that he did not leave his seat beside the fire until it was time to go in for supper.

CHAPTER 23

A look from her brother as they sat down to table told Georgiana that she ought to make an effort in conversation. She chose the most familiar of the guests to speak to first.

"Sofia," she said unsteadily, "I am so pleased you were able to join us. I thought I understood from my brother that you would be in Brighton for several months. I hope your sojourn was not cut short for any unpleasant reason."

"Oh, not at all, my dear," Lady Sofia effused. "Quite the opposite. You see, I was there with my brother who, like so many before him, became acquainted with a young lady there. So taken was he with her that he was absolutely and instantly determined that she should be his own. It was all very heroic in its suddenness. I have always believed that a love which ignites instantly is a sign of destiny, and must endure in its strength.

"The lady herself was remarkably amiable. I felt an immediate sisterly bond with her when I heard how she fainted on receiving my brother's addresses, and now we are to be sisters in law, I cannot express my delight. It is so charming for Branston, for you know, he is not usually of such a romantic persuasion, though I will say this of him: he does not tarry long once he sets his mind to something. However," she continued, "our father insists that Branston complete his education with a Grand Tour before he weds. Therefore, we have returned to London to make the necessary travel arrangements. He is determined to leave within a month."

"Astonishing!" said Mr. Bingley. "One must admire his conviction."

"It sounds a great deal like something you would do, Bingley," offered Mr. Darcy. "Cannot you see yourself setting off on a Grand Tour at a moment's notice?"

"Indeed," Mr. Bingley replied. "I should join him in a moment, if the idea seized me."

"I am sure you would; and I am sure you would return again just as suddenly if that idea seized you, whether you had completed your Tour or no."

Mr. Bingley spoke primarily to Lady Sofia when he responded, "There is no one I know can rival Mr. Darcy for steadfastness. I know it to be a quality he holds in very high regard. We are always at odds about whether 'tis better to stick to one's purpose at all costs, or whether one must adapt oneself to the changing demands of circumstance."

"I am very much of your point of view, Mr. Bingley," offered Lady Sofia. "I believe one must be directed solely by one's heart. Our feelings are the defining elements of our humanity, and so must they be our compass and our guide. I deeply admire your commitment to allowing yourself to be influenced by your love of beauty and wonder."

Mr. Bingley was unsure how to meet such a passionate outburst. He had not meant half of what Lady Sofia suggested. Lord Ashwell was smiling broadly in appreciation of the lady's sentiments, which he always found amusing. Mr. Darcy was rolling his eyes.

"There is so much of the world I have never seen," Mr. Bingley said after a short silence. "I hope I shall not reach the end my life without once venturing beyond the shores of England."

"But you have been to the continent before," interjected Mr. Darcy. "You were in Paris only two summers ago."

"Yes, of course. I have been across the Channel, but that is hardly a Grand Tour. Everybody has been to Paris."

Mr. Darcy, remembering that Lord Ashwell was the exception to this rule, darted a look towards their host, who did not seem at all to have taken the remark amiss, but merely said, in an easy tone,

"I have never been to Paris. I have never been abroad at all, in fact, much less completed a Grand Tour. Travel does not agree with me, I am afraid. Though I have read so many accounts of the travels and adventures of others that I feel as though I have seen all the sights myself."

"Mr. Darcy has been pressing me for some time to read Gibbon," said Mr. Bingley, "who I believe conceived his great work while on a Tour of sorts. It is a testament to my friend's power of persuasion that I have actually acquired a copy of it. But I doubt I shall ever get past the first few lines. Though I am certain I should set off for Rome itself in an instant, I regret to say I cannot bring myself to sit long enough to read Gibbon's history of the place."

"Well, I do not at all regret to say that I have not read it either, and nor should I choose to" added Lady Sofia. "Such a work of dates and facts can contain nothing of the sublime, of poetry or universality, which is where the true value of all great works lies, and therefore I should not wish to undertake it."

"Lady Sofia," began Lord Ashwell, "it continues to surprise me that I should be surprised at your view of things. I never met a person so determined to be led by their ideals."

Mr. Darcy, thus far a silent participant in the conversation, interjected with some warmth.

"Gibbon's History is worth an entire library of your sentimental drivel. The depth and breadth of his scholarship paints a picture of the Empire that may never be surpassed. How can you compare such an achievement to your works of vapid sentiment?"

Lady Sofia was unmoved by his attack.

"To those whose interest lies in the strict lines of accuracy, yes, there must be value in such a history," she conceded, "but, for those of us whose pursuit is the fullness and beauty of life, our hearts and feelings will not be bound by such limitations. By the study of the plain facts of history, we grow removed from the pure and tender susceptibilities which are our true and natural condition."

"Haha! It seems we have a debate on our hands," announced Lord Ashwell. Then, turning the conversation to the unwitting object of his concealed attention, he continued, "What say you, Miss Langford?"

"I beg your pardon, sir," replied Clare, looking nervously at Lord Ashwell. "What say *I*?"

"Yes, what say you about Mr. Gibbon and his History?"

Everyone at the table turned their eyes to Clare to hear her answer.

She paused for a moment. Unnerved at being asked her opinion in a controversy, and not wishing to offend anyone at the table, she followed her mother's counsel, always to speak the truth, respectfully and humbly. Looking back at her plate she said, "I believe his work is considered quite provocative by many, given its treatment of the Church."

Clare did not lift her gaze as Lord Ashwell replied.

"Ah yes, but is not everything which stands the test of time provocative in some sense? Our very faith itself, in its earliest beginnings, aroused great opposition from many quarters."

Lady Sofia turned the conversation once more to her favourite topic.

"My dear Lord Ashwell," she said, "I knew you must be with me on this point, that the novels of our time, though regarded by so many as scandalous for their shocking content, are vital for the very qualities that garner them such condemnation. Future generations will revere our novelists for being the first to touch upon the complex depths of our nature."

Mr. Darcy's calmly delivered response ill concealed his exasperation. "Surely, the power to shock the sensibilities of young ladies is not to mark a work out as forwarding the cause of human understanding. They are merely sensationalist, their only goal to scandalize the reader. Even those which purport to offer some moral lesson do not offer any new insight or perspective on the human character. I am certain *The Monk* will not even be heard of by future generations, let alone looked into for profound reflection."

Lord Ashwell was clearly enjoying the debate, while Clare was more than a little surprised at the liveliness of the discussion at such a table, as well as a little wary of the topic of novels, given that she had always considered them her most shameful vice.

Lord Ashwell again invited Clare into the conversation: "And having heard such persuasive arguments, does your opinion shift at all, Miss Langford? Must a work of art be provocative in order to endure?"

"I believe there are many works which endure solely on account of their beauty."

Again, keeping her head lowered, Clare could not see the look in Lord Ashwell's eyes as he quietly replied, "Ah, but is beauty not a provocation unto itself?"

Lady Sofia, noting that Georgiana had not had any part of the conversation, gently sought to include her.

"Have you read The Castle Otranto, Miss Darcy?" she asked.

"I have."

"And did you not find it thrilling? Do not you wish you could visit the place?"

"I confess I have always longed to see Italy."

"Well then, you cannot refuse my proposal that we visit Strawberry Hill. I go there every year, as a sort of pilgrimage, and I should love nothing more than to show it to you. The next fine day, I shall call with the carriage, and we shall go. What say you? The gardens may even have some early blooms by now."

Georgiana looked to Darcy, beseeching approval.

"I have no objection, provided you are suitably chaperoned," he offered. "I do not approve of ladies traveling without a gentleman present. I have no interest in going myself, but if Mr. Bingley does not object, perhaps he may accompany you, as well as either Mrs. Belfry or Mrs. Younge, of course."

"But we should be in Hertfordshire within the week," replied Mr. Bingley. "We may well not have a fine day within that time."

In his haste to throw together his sister and his friend in a romantic setting, Mr. Darcy had all but forgotten about the Hertfordshire scheme. Before he could form a response, Lord Ashwell offered himself as a solution.

"Well then, let me go. All these years I have lived in London, I have never yet seen the place. It should be a delightful outing, and with such company as is before me, I do not doubt I shall enjoy it immensely."

Mr. Darcy regarded his cousin with concern. He did not wish to overstep his place by voicing his fear for his cousin's health, but equally did not wish to see his cousin put at risk for the sake of a simple pleasure outing. Lord Ashwell understood his cousin's look, and responded to his unvoiced alarm.

"If it is indeed a fine day, then I should be perfectly able to face the journey. It is no more than ten or twelve miles each way—hardly arduous."

"You call twelve miles hardly arduous?" Mr. Darcy was incredulous. "Half the day shall be taken in getting there, and that is not to mention the return journey."

"It shall be very pleasant, particularly if we break our journey for supper on the way back. There are plenty of fine inns along the way. We may take the barouche. Robert has so little occasion to take it out; he would be glad of the chance to dust it off. We shall be very comfortable, I am sure. And the roads on that route are very good, are not they, Lady Sofia?"

"I do not pretend to judge of such trifles. You must apply to Branston for that information."

Clare was shocked at Lady Sofia's retort, but, being better acquainted with her Ladyship, Lord Ashwell simply appeared diverted, chuckling to himself and saying, "Of course."

After that, Clare was quite easy, for the conversation continued mostly on the benign and comfortable subjects of roads and weather, which she was quite well prepared to continue for as long as the evening lasted.

CHAPTER 24

More than two weeks passed before a day arrived fine enough to allow for the much-anticipated outing to Strawberry Hill. In that time, there had been several visits between the households—ample opportunity for Lord Ashwell's regard for Clare to further increase, the enjoyment of which Clare worked continually to suppress. Clare was a very good sort of person who felt her very human weaknesses rendered her very evil. She found herself developing one such weakness for the tender and generous manners of her friend's gentle cousin, which lead to flights of imagination far beyond what she had ever before allowed herself.

One may well imagine that a future lord of the English realm would be far above the consideration of a humble admiral's daughter, but everything in Ashwell's behaviour towards Clare suggested otherwise. He always inquired after her family, and showed genuine concern on hearing of her mother's ill health. He listened with lively interest to stories about her brother and, without any air of superiority, he expressed admiration for the honours her father had earned at war. Short of ceremony or fuss, he was always solicitous of her comfort and careful to put her at ease. Each time that Clare felt touched by Lord Ashwell's kind words, she recalled Sir Leicester's warning. Either her cousin, she thought, must be mistaken, or Lord Ashwell must be all the more dangerous for his ability so skillfully to conceal his wicked nature.

The Strawberry Hill party was to be larger than originally planned. As expected, Mrs. Younge had readily consented when asked to chaperone the young ladies. In addition, Mrs. Belfry had also insisted on attending Lady Sofia. Had that not augmented the party sufficiently to test the capacity of a single carriage, another unexpected addition certainly did.

The morning of the excursion, Mrs. Younge announced to Georgiana over breakfast that she had prepared a surprise for her.

"You must not be angry with me," she said, "but I have invited another guest to join us today. I know I ought to have asked your permission, but I thought it would be such a charming surprise that I did not wish to spoil it. The extra passenger may overburden our carriage, in which case, I am quite happy to stay behind. Mrs. Belfry is surely chaperone enough for three young ladies and two gentlemen."

"It is a gentleman, then?" Georgiana replied with evident apprehension.

"Do not fear, my dear," Mrs. Younge replied, noting Georgiana's panicked expression. "It is, indeed, a gentleman, but he attends only upon your pleasure. It is for you to say whether he joins us or no, and, if you do not wish it, I shall make your excuses without your ever having to set eyes on him. I do not expect it shall come to that, though; not if he has been faithful in his representations to myself as regards his acquaintance with you, for he has told me you are the nearest to a sister that he has ever had. Now, shall you prove him true by knowing him by that description?"

Before Georgiana could make an answer, the bell rang.

"We shall see by your face, then, whether I was wrong to have invited him."

The butler entered the breakfast room.

"Mr. Wickham to see Miss Darcy."

Georgiana nearly overturned the table, so sharply did she rise from her seat, a joyful smile animating her face as Mr. Wickham's graceful figure strode through the doorway. He, too, was smiling broadly. He did not have to pretend his joy on seeing her, and he beamed all over the breakfast room. Georgiana made her way hurriedly around the table to greet him, and, for a moment, it seemed she might actually throw her arms around him. Remembering herself suddenly, she stopped and offered him her hand. He took it eagerly. Looking into his eyes, she smiled and said,

"Mr. Wickham, what a delight!"

"Georgi . . . I am sorry. I must say Miss Darcy. It is I who am so delighted to see you. When I learned Mrs. Younge was to have charge of your days, I absolutely insisted that she bring me into your company. I hope it is not too impertinent of me to impose myself."

"Goodness, no!" Georgiana exclaimed. "Mrs. Younge has done a splendid thing to invite you. I thought perhaps she had brought my brother back from Hertfordshire for the day, though I could not see how that might be possible, and I will say that your appearance is the only thing that could rival such a feat."

"Am I to understand that your brother is not in town? I had rather hoped to see him also, for it has been too long since we last met."

"He is gone to Hertfordshire, where I believe he intends to stay some time assisting his friend Mr. Bingley to find a suitable estate on which to settle."

"Well, that would be a disappointment were I not absolutely assured that we shall enjoy ourselves very much with the present company."

Georgiana introduced Mr. Wickham to Clare, and all continued pleasant until the arrival of the Fitzwilliam carriage, bearing Lord Ashwell in jovial spirits, Lady Sofia in exuberant spirits, and Mrs. Belfry in a spirit of iron-plated pragmatism.

Lord Ashwell and Mr. Wickham were introduced and, though the former was quite sure that he had heard the latter's voice somewhere before, he was not able to place him.

The ladies gathered their things and were just assembling to depart when Clare begged a word with Georgiana.

"The carriage may be too full to accommodate us all," she said, "and I do believe your brother would prefer that Mrs. Younge attend you on such an outing. Therefore, I beg you let me be the one to stay behind if there be not room enough for all. I shall not be disappointed to miss the outing, though I do not doubt it shall be a pleasant one. It seems that Mrs. Younge is quite keen to go, and I shall have just as agreeable a time here. You are, as it is, overstocked with chaperones and, as for company, you shall not want for that either since you and Mr. Wickham shall have much to say to each other."

Clare's offer was not as selfless as it may have seemed; in fact, she had not been entirely forthcoming as to her reasons for wishing to stay behind. She was desirous of going, but that desire was tempered by her fear of allowing herself too much pleasure. Though she would never confess it, she had read the Castle Otranto many times. Her mother had taught her to regard the reading of novels as incompatible with womanly virtue. Spending the day in a place of romantic allusion in the company of Lord Ashwell—which she was quite sure would only further indulge her growing infatuation with that man— was hardly something she could allow herself.

Georgiana, however, would not hear of leaving her friend behind and was convinced there would be a means of fitting everyone in the carriage. She could not have guessed all the forces of contrivance and masquerade that caused inordinate commotion in achieving this end.

Mr. Wickham, wishing to appear gallant, offered to ride up front with the driver, but Mrs. Younge objected, saying that he must be allowed to ride with Georgiana, whom he had not seen in many years, thereby furthering by design his more immediate object of winning the young lady's heart. Quick to take the opportunity of sacrificing herself for the cause of reuniting long-separated friends, Lady Sofia insisted that she ride outside the carriage, that her heart had no other wish than to forfeit her own comfort for the sake of her friends and that she would brook no opposition. She was thwarted in her heroism, however, by a single "no" from Mrs. Belfry.

Lord Ashwell spoke up. "Although I admire your bravery, Lady Sofia, I cannot allow any ladies to ride alongside the driver of my carriage. It will not do. I shall ride outside. I shall enjoy having the view that it shall afford."

Lord Ashwell really had no intention of spending the whole journey separated from the lady who was the very reason for his being there. He made the suggestion knowing full well that courtesy demanded it of him, but also that those present who knew of his condition would not dare expose him to the brisk air outside the carriage.

Georgiana was not bold enough to prohibit her cousin from doing anything, but Lady Sofia could be relied upon to play her part.

"You know it is impossible," she said, "that I should countenance such a thing. The risk to me is nothing, whereas it could cost you dearly. It may be a fine day, but a fine day in April. The air is still damp."

Georgiana quietly offered to have another carriage brought round so that none should be required to ride outside. With a gentleman and a chaperone to ride in each, it would be very convenient. This required that Mr. Wickham again offer to ride up front in order to spare such trouble, and Mrs. Younge's objections to this arrangement weakened in the face of the objections to every other option.

Mrs. Younge attempted to put an end to the argument, which, if it continued much longer, threatened to consume the better part of the day.

"I understand very well," she said, "your concerns in allowing a lady to ride out front, and I should agree wholeheartedly in the case of Lady Sofia or Miss Darcy or Miss Langford, but I am not such a lady. I am of a hearty constitution and am quite used to the rigours of fresh air. I have a warm cloak and the day is fine. I shall be very comfortable up front."

She fastened her cloak and tightened her bonnet and made to ascend to the seat behind the horses while everyone stood by in perplexed silence, except Lady Sofia who offered her encouragement.

"Mrs. Younge, how I adore your spirit! Such rare and demonstrable conviction, I commend you."

"This will never do," declared Lord Ashwell. "I cannot have a lady ride on the outside of my carriage, whatever assertions she may make as to her constitution."

Seeing that every other solution had been examined and rejected, Clare calmly and firmly declared that there seemed to be an impasse and that she must stay behind. Nobody should be required to ride outside and the idea of taking two carriages to accommodate one person was absurd, particularly when she had—she said—no particular interest in the location and, even without her, Georgiana had a surplus of chaperones.

She considered claiming a headache, but she could not bring herself to dishonesty no matter how small the lie or how necessary it was to her object.

Lord Ashwell was quick to seize his own opportunity. He ushered the others into the carriage and closed the door behind them.

"Now that Mr. Wickham has arrived," he said, "you are no longer in need of a gentleman. I can hardly allow Miss Langford to remain behind without any company. Ride out, Robert," he shouted to the driver, who set the carriage in motion before any of those inside could voice their opposition. The only person who felt any remorse at the outcome was Georgiana, for she believed, however incorrectly, that the pleasure of her friend and her cousin had been spoiled.

Mrs. Younge, hoping to contrive a way to get Mr. Wickham and Georgiana alone together, was happy to see their company shrink by two. Mr. Wickham, who seemed to feel Lord Ashwell scrutinizing him at every moment, was glad to be free of him and Clare as well. Mr. Wickham could trust to Mrs. Younge to keep the silly and sentimental Lady Sofia occupied, and, since Mrs. Belfry was focused on her charge and nothing else, this would mean that he and Georgiana would be left alone without impediment so that he might reacquaint her with his charms.

Lady Sofia saw no contrivance anywhere—only a great sacrifice made by two people for the love of their friends. Since there could be no greater joy than suffering for one's loved ones, she merely sighed at the tragic beauty of their loss.

CHAPTER 25

The carriage soon disappeared from sight, and Clare found herself, for the first time, completely alone with Lord Ashwell—Sir Leicester's words of warning ringing in her ears. She thought it suspicious that, as soon as she had made clear her intention to remain behind, Lord Ashwell had, in an instant, determined to do the same. The fact that the party was riding in his carriage only made a stronger possibility of ulterior motives on his part. She pushed from her mind the idea that she had escaped a very small evil only to find herself faced with a greater one.

Lord Ashwell broke the silence: "Well, Miss Langford, it seems we have been thrown together."

"I hope it is not for my sake that you forewent this outing," she said. "I did not look to ruin anyone else's enjoyment in staying behind."

"Quite the contrary, I assure you. I really had no wish to see the place myself. I only went in order that the outing might be brought about. In truth, it probably was too long a journey for me. I only hope I do not intrude on your day." He turned to Clare and continued: "I should have consulted you on that point, but I sought to put a swift end to the confusion. I hope you do not mind."

"Not at all," she said.

Clare was unsure whether or not to invite Lord Ashwell into the house. It seemed he had contrived this situation quite on purpose, and she could not help but feel uneasy at the prospect of being quite alone with a man whose intentions she could by no means be certain about. She trusted Georgiana's opinion of Ashwell more than her cousin's, but certainly the Darcy family was more likely to be biased on the subject, particularly as their family connection gave them an interest in preserving Lord Ashwell's reputation. She wished—desperately wished—to think no more of it; he had always treated her so amiably and with such consideration that she felt her suspicions were an affront to his kind nature, but she could by no means dismiss from her thoughts her cousin's warnings.

As far as the present was concerned, there was no polite way out of the situation. They now had no carriage to take them anywhere, and she did not feel that her position in the household was such that she could order that one be prepared. She could suggest they walk somewhere, even if only through the park, but it was clear to her, though no one had actually informed her of any particulars, that Lord Ashwell was not able to exert himself without risking his health. She did not wish to be cruel in keeping him out of doors when the coolness of the air might do him ill. She looked towards the house.

"Shall we go in?" he asked, relieving Clare of the decision, for which she was both grateful and suspicious. Still, she could only concur, and the two entered the house. Clare ordered tea and a fire in the drawing room, for though the sun was beginning to warm the air outside, it had not yet penetrated indoors. Clare took out her workbasket, and Ashwell searched on the shelf for a book.

"I do apologise," she said as Ashwell reached the end of the shelf and turned himself in a circle looking for another but finding none. "We do not have much of a library here, or at least not of the sort that might interest a gentleman. You must know that Mr. Darcy is a great reader, but he does not seem to keep many books here. Georgiana has told me many times of the vast library he keeps at Pemberley, but, while he is town, I think he supplies himself primarily from the circulating library. There are a few books of an instructional nature, and here are just a few novels and other things that I never look into, but I am afraid that is all," she said waving her hand at a few books left on the mantle.

"I thought all young ladies read novels," stated Lord Ashwell, returning to the beginning of the shelf and scanning the titles a little more closely than he had before. "Do you really never look into them?"

Clare was not about to confess what she had always harboured as her darkest secret—that she could not stop herself reading novels, and of the worst possible kind. Still, she could not be entirely dishonest and the situation demanded that they have something to speak of.

"I have read a few of the most popular novels," she answered, seating herself in a chair by the window and taking her needlework out of the basket at her feet, "but only so that I might converse with other young ladies on a topic so frequently raised. I have always thought that novels do not elevate the mind, even when they purport to do so by presenting plots that reward virtue and punish vice. I believe time is better spent actually performing acts of charity than reading about the good that comes to artificial characters by reason of their invented virtue."

"You are, of course, perfectly correct," he stated. "But I believe that their very popularity renders them a point of interest in revealing the true character of our nation. For how better to understand a people than by understanding what they choose to read?" And with that, Lord Ashwell selected a copy of Tom Jones from the shelf and sat himself down beside the fire to read it.

"I believe this one is rather widely read," he remarked, "though hardly a good example of virtue rewarded. Is it one you have reviewed?"

Clare had read it, many times.

"I hope you do not presume that all young ladies are prey to identical susceptibilities. Miss Darcy may read the occasional novel, but she is more interested in Poetry, which I believe shows a greater refinement of mind."

"For myself, I have never considered taste to be a moral issue."

At first Clare read much into this remark. Could it be an indication of a much deeper want of moral judgment on his part? Did he consider morality in any of his choices?

As the morning went on, however, Clare's fears about Lord Ashwell's motives began to dissipate. Every time he looked over his book and ventured some remark or query, it always led to very pleasant and refreshing conversation that she did not wish to leave off. She found herself increasingly at ease with him. She could hardly imagine that anyone could spread slander about such a man, and even less so that anyone should believe any. She wondered what might be the source of her cousin's information, and she gathered the courage to approach the subject.

"I wonder whether you are at all acquainted with my cousin, Sir Leicester Crawley?" she asked, looking up from her work. "He was only recently made a baronet when my uncle died three years ago without issue."

"I do not believe we have been introduced. I am not often at court, and so my acquaintance is not overly large I am afraid. But I could be mistaken. Why do you ask?"

"No reason, really. Only he called on me the day before we dined with you at Grosvenor Square, and I happened to mention that I was to dine with you. He seemed to recognize your name; that is all."

Lord Ashwell responded only, "Ah, I see," and he returned to his reading with a scarcely concealed disquiet. Clare did not inquire further, and he was glad of it. She could not have known how his heart had sunk at her words. It was clear, he thought, that her cousin had said something to raise suspicion in her mind about him, though he knew not to what extent.

As subtle as her questions had been, she still had cause to regret her curiosity when, a few moments later, he shut his book saying, "Diverting as it may be, there is only so much nonsense I can read in one sitting. I fear I have taken up enough of your day already. Thank you for your indulgence in sharing your company with me this morning. I should be going."

Clare wished she had not said anything regarding her cousin. Nothing could have been gained from it. Lord Ashwell was obviously not about to disclose anything to her, and her question, no matter how delicately asked, had had an effect quite the opposite of what she intended. She had clearly caused him to raise his guard.

She attempted to make light of his expressed intention to leave; without setting down her work, she said, "There is no carriage, Lord Ashwell. Surely," she peered up at him from her seat, "you do not intend to walk."

Ashwell was more determined to leave than she had expected him to be.

"I am," he said, "quite confident I can find a Hackney Coach at this time of day. In truth, I ought not to have imposed on you at all. However, it really has been so charming a morning as I cannot recall passing in such a long while that I cannot regret it. Good afternoon, Miss Langford."

Disappointed that her curiosity was to drive him out of doors, Clare rose and curtseyed; Lord Ashwell bowed and departed. In spite of the relief she felt to be clear of the awkwardness that Lord Ashwell's presence occasioned, Clare wished that he had not gone so soon, and regretted giving him so little cause to reciprocate the wish.

CHAPTER 26

The Strawberry Hill party did not dine at an inn on their return journey as originally proposed; rather, they were required to manifest Lady Sofia's pastoral fantasy of life as a traveller, and picnic in a field. The would-be vagabonds supped their humble repast of corned ham, boiled beef, pigeon pie, roast duck, lemon drizzle and plum cake off silver plates, while they took their stewed gooseberries, their cordial and their brandy in crystal glasses, and their tea in china cups.

Sated with victuals and drink, Mr. Wickham lay upon the grass—a bed made warm and soft by the late afternoon sun. Lady Sofia dabbed her face with a lace napkin, which she then handed to a servant who was clearing away the picnic things and loading them into the carriage. In one sweeping glance, she took in the field that stretched from the hem of her dress to the distant boundary marked by a rude fence.

She shook her head and sighed: "What beauty and simplicity there is in a rustic life such as this," she said. "I have no wish for the fineries of society when surrounded by such simple pleasures."

"Your idea of a rustic and simple life is quite to my taste," responded Mr. Wickham, raising himself up on his arm and turning towards the ladies, "particularly the duck." Georgiana and Mrs. Younge hid their laughter from Lady Sofia, whose eyes were closed in smiling reverie. Mr. Wickham returned Georgiana's smile with a look of unspoken understanding. "I declare, this has been the most diverting day," he said, rising to his feet and searching his surroundings for a point of interest. "I think we ought to applaud Lady Sofia for arranging it all."

Georgiana and Mrs. Younge heartily concurred, and congratulated Lady Sofia on a very charming outing. Mrs. Belfry sat silent and motionless at the edge of the blanket, scanning the road and the horizon, on guard for highwaymen.

"I assure you," Lady Sofia spoke in breathless humility, "I have no joy but in bringing joy to my friends. I return your thanks," she said, her palms turned upwards in the mode of a sacred supplicant, "for what enjoyment can be had without the company of kindred souls with whom to pass the time in amiable sympathy?"

"Very well said, Madam," Mr. Wickham agreed with enthusiasm. "Now, Miss Darcy," he said, extending his hand, "before we return to the rigours of the carriage, will not you take a stroll with me and tell me all you have not already said about yourself and your life since last we met. You cannot imagine what a pleasing subject it is to me, and I do not think I could tire of it were you to repeat it all a hundred times."

Georgiana joyfully complied, rising from her place and making her way around the picnic to Mr. Wickham's side. She watched as he stood and, with little ceremony, brushed himself off. She wondered what she could say to him. It was not that she had anything to conceal—quite the contrary. In fact, she thought her secluded life to contain nothing that could hold the attention of a gentleman such as Wickham. Even if she did have anything to tell, she never felt she could make her own conversation as interesting as she always found that of others. And so, not knowing how or if to begin, she remained silent, looking over the fields for a moment before following Mr. Wickham as he began to walk away from the group.

"I hope your friend will not be angry that I have taken her place," said Wickham as they walked along the hedgerow.

She thought it a sign of his thoughtfulness to remember Clare in the midst of his leisure.

"She seems very sweet," he said, considering whether Georgiana's friend might prove an obstacle in the path of his ambition.

"Yes, very," she answered. "We have each of us but one brother and no sisters. I suppose that is why we were so quick to become such fast friends."

"Do you wish you could have had a sister?"

"I wish many things, none more so than that my mother could have lived. But as that was not to be, a sister would have been a great comfort. A sister would have been with me at school, would have been a home to me while I was away all those years."

"Was not your brother a comfort to you?"

"Oh, very much so. I could not have asked for a better guardian. And my cousin, Colonel Fitzwilliam, he is my guardian also. They are both of them so caring, and so wise. I am very fortunate to be under their care."

"But still, they are gentlemen. They cannot be to you what a sister, or a mother would be." Mr. Wickham voiced the feelings which Georgiana's gratitude for all that her guardians had done for her would not allow her to admit. She made no reply.

"It is no discredit either to you or to them that you should need some feminine counsel," he continued. "No doubt that is why they sent you to school."

Georgiana nodded.

"And you are very fortunate now to be under the care of Mrs. Younge. She is a very compassionate soul, and very wise also. I do not doubt you will grow to depend upon her and to love her as you do your friend Clare."

"I hope you are right," Georgiana said, looking behind her at Mrs. Younge; "but I do not sense from her that tenderness that I have always known in Clare."

"She is only nervous," he assured her. "She cannot be expected to be instantly easy in her new position. It is a great responsibility she has assumed in taking on the care of you and your friend. You must have patience with her. But I assure you, she is as sympathetic a kindred spirit as even Lady Sofia could hope for."

Mr. Wickham thought he must tell Mrs. Younge of Georgiana's longing for a mother's love that she might win the girl's trust and confidence by supplying some semblance of it.

The fine weather held well into the evening, and, aside from a universal concession of being thoroughly fagged and ready for tea, the party returned to London in excellent spirits. Having seen them all safely into the drawing room, Mr. Wickham excused himself from the party, claiming an early appointment the following morning.

"Goodnight all," he said with a flourish to the room in general, and turned to go, as Mrs. Younge engaged Clare and Lady Sofia in conversation. Mr. Wickham stopped and turned to Georgiana, who stood near him by the door.

"Goodnight, Miss Darcy," he whispered, his face a good deal closer to hers than it ought to have been. He bowed and held her gaze a moment before swiftly departing. Georgiana saw him out the door, then sat distractedly on the sofa beside the impervious expanse of Mrs. Belfry.

"Is not Mr. Wickham the most charming of gentlemen?" remarked Mrs. Younge. "I was so pleased to see him enjoying himself today. He was so light-hearted once, but his recent change of fortunes has weighed heavily upon him. It is some time since I saw him so cheerful."

With a solemn nod of her head, Lady Sofia mused—

"The most worthy people have the most tragic tales."

She had already been quite won over by Mrs. Younge's tales of the long-suffering Mr. Wickham, and saw in him the pattern of the man of sentiment.

"To be thwarted in love and in fortune at the same time," she continued, "must have been very hard, though he bears it stoically enough."

"Thwarted in love and in fortune?" inquired Georgiana. "He spoke nothing of this to me."

"Nor would he," responded Mrs. Younge, "for he is not one to complain or to burden others with his troubles."

Lady Sofia could not restrain her sentimentality. She threw her head back in despair, saying—

"The world is a cruel, hard place for the earnest seeker of the simple and humble joys of life." She sat forward in her chair, pressing her hand to her heart.

"Mrs. Younge has told me all about it," she continued passionately, "for she knows the interest I take in the downtrodden and innocent victims of life's iniquities. No doubt she has spared you his tale to protect you from too much knowledge of the world, lest it should upset your delicate heart, but I have convinced her of the strength of your constitution, and of the benefits to one's health of overpowering emotions, and she has agreed to share with you what she knows of his troubles. Is not that correct, Mrs. Younge?"

"Quite so, madam," answered Mrs. Younge. She then explained to Georgiana, "I did not think it my place to weigh you down with cares which the gentleman was, out of kindness, reluctant to share even with myself. But I see now that you are such a friend to him as would rather know the truth of his history than be shielded from it."

Such an introduction could not but pique Georgiana's interest. She urged them to tell all they knew, and Mrs. Younge eagerly obliged.

"Only a few weeks ago," she began, "Mr. Wickham was in a way to have everything a man requires of life to count himself blessed—the lady he loved and a living to support them. His father, as you might remember, was not a wealthy man, and anything which may have been his from that source had been spent by his mother in her extravagance, so it fell on Mr. Wickham himself to raise his expectations, and the promise of this living gave him something more than hope that he might soon do so. He has lived on almost nothing besides hope and expectation since his father passed, so you can imagine his dismay when, upon the promised position falling vacant, and his applying for it, he was denied it without cause. And, if that were not hard enough, his lady would no longer have him without it. She, who had as good as promised herself to him, refused him on account of his not being worthy of her without a fortune, though she had plenty money of her own and could have kept them both very well. As it turned out, she had been truly false to him. In rejecting him, she stung him with the news that he was not the only gentleman at whom she had set her cap. She fancied her chances better with another, one more able to offer her the finer things she longed for. Well, I hope that all her finery comforts her the way poor Mr. Wickham could have."

"I am sure," said Lady Sofia, "no lady of feeling could prefer material comforts to the joys of true love."

Mrs. Younge nodded her head in agreement. "I know I could not," she said. "When I think of my late husband and our delights, I could not imagine trading even our unhappiest moments for all the finery in the world.

She sighed and fixed her gaze on her tea.

"I suppose Mr. Wickham too shall have to go into the army now," she said. "I only hope he does not meet with the same awful fate."

The brief silence was broken by Lady Sofia.

"Mrs. Younge," she said, interrupting the lady's contemplations, "you have not told the worst of it." Turning to Georgiana, Lady Sofia concluded the pathetic story: "Could you imagine his horror when he discovered that the gentleman who had been preferred above himself, whose money had lured his love away from his own sincere and devoted self, was the very same gentleman who had denied him the living on which had rested all his future happiness? Such a cruel twist of fate!"

The ladies took it in turns to bemoan the plight of poor Mr. Wickham and to denounce in the strongest terms the heartlessness of he who stood between a good man and his happiness, none of them, excepting Mrs. Younge, having any idea that it was Mr. Darcy they were thus condemning.

Mrs. Belfry alone was silent, being herself wholly engaged in preventing Lady Sofia from eating more cake than was good for her, which she achieved by consuming the entirety of it herself.

That night, as Georgiana was retiring to bed, Mrs. Younge approached her outside her chamber door.

"Miss Darcy, I hope you will forgive my speaking to you like this. For delicacy's sake, I did not wish to say anything in front of the others, but there is something regarding Mr. Wickham that I must share with you. May I?"

"But of course, Mrs. Younge."

"Well, Miss Darcy, I have always considered myself a keen observer of human behaviour, and I believe that your modesty may be preventing you from seeing what I find so plain. As I said, please forgive my presumption."

"Not at all. Go on." Georgiana was all eager attention.

"This afternoon, I could not help but notice the improvement in Mr. Wickham's spirits when he was at your side. Your presence seemed to draw him out of himself." Georgiana shifted her gaze to the floor and began to toy with the cross around her neck. She felt her cheeks turn warm and red.

Mrs. Younge continued. "I have not seen his eyes shine nor his countenance smile so brightly since his recent disappointment at the hands of that lady—if she can be called a lady. She is so unlike you, who would never deal so lightly with a man's heart, much less so true and tender a heart as that of our dear Mr. Wickham."

"Surely you are mistaken, Mrs. Younge," said Georgiana.

"Your humility does you credit Miss Darcy. I believe Mr. Wickham is uncommonly fond of you; it is proved in every gesture, ever word, every look in your presence. What you have done for him today is much more than you can know. His friends and I have done everything to lift his spirits, but nothing could bring him out of the melancholy that gripped him so—nothing until today." Mrs. Younge paused to allow her words to take effect before continuing. "I hope you will allow him as much of your valuable company as your other engagements permit. Pray, do not be offended by this. I would not dare to say as much were I not convinced of your sincere concern for Mr. Wickham and your desire for his happiness."

"Thank you for your frankness, Mrs. Younge," Georgiana said. "Mr. Wickham is, as you know, a dear and long-standing friend, and it pains me to know how he has suffered of late. He shall always be welcome here, and I shall do what I can for him, though I am not as convinced as you of my powers of influence."

"The most deserving often underestimate their gifts. His affection for you is clear enough to me, and if I am mistaken as regards his feelings, I shall be very sorry for it. I never knew two people better suited in temperament and taste than you and Mr. Wickham. But I have said enough. I shall leave you to your slumber now. Goodnight."

Slumber Georgiana could not, fatigued though she was. Nothing in particular had stood out about Mr. Wickham's behaviour towards her that afternoon, but she did not consider herself an expert in human observation. She wondered whether she had been denying the possibility of what she secretly desired—the love of the first gentleman ever to warm her young heart.

Even though they had not been in contact all these years, Mr. Wickham had occupied in her heart a place of near adulation— the adored older brother who was not a brother at all, but a young man of considerable appeal, not so unfamiliar as to be a cause of anxiety, but not so familiar as to want intrigue. She had always been a very steady and sensible girl, but all her steadiness and sense could not withstand the combined forces of a handsome gentleman's attentions and a childhood fascination on the heart of a feeling and inexperienced young lady, sheltered from the world and susceptible to love. In addition to this, she now learned that she could be the gentleman's saviour, which only further encouraged a swift and firm attachment with little, if anything, to stand in its way.

CHAPTER 27

The following morning, a plainly wrapped parcel arrived, addressed to Georgiana. The attached note, penned in Lord Ashwell's graceful hand, read as follows:

"DEAREST COUSIN,"

"I trust you had a pleasant outing yesterday. The horses returned with all their limbs and the carriage with all its parts, so I assume that the journey at least did not prove fatal. Please do not concern yourself with my not having joined you. I had a delightful time with your very charming friend, whom I hope I did not alarm by the imposition of my company. Please convey to her my kindest regards as well as the enclosed drawing implements, which she will know well how to put to use. You may assure her that she may accept them without qualms as they were left behind by a house guest some years ago, ostensibly by accident though I suspect it was quite intentional, in the hope that I might find them and choose to better myself by some artistic occupation. I am afraid that hope never materialized, and I am convinced that her talents will find a more ample use for them than I ever could.

"I hope you will both accept an invitation to dine with me Thursday next as cook has advised she will be preparing a goose large enough to satisfy Arthur and his knights. Fond as I am of eating, I doubt my ability to consume the entire bird myself, and I do not like to give so much of the spoils to my already over-indulged servants. Indeed, I am certain cook planned the goose counting on the fact that I keep so little company and hoping herself to enjoy the better part of it. I hope I may count on your assistance in thwarting her wanton scheme.

"Yours etc.

"ASHWELL"

Georgiana handed the parcel to Clare, who opened it with due hesitation. It contained two embossed sketching books, several pencils and some drawing charcoal, all of very fine quality.

"I cannot accept these." Clare handed the items back to her friend, but Georgiana would not take them.

"Surely there can be no harm in it," she said. "Only this morning, I heard you mention how you longed for some new drawing things, and it is not as though they are improperly offered. Merely passing on some abandoned items to someone who could use them cannot signify. No, I insist you take them. To return them might cause offence, and, in itself, imply some impropriety in the gift. A simple thank-you on your next meeting will show that all is well."

Neither of the young ladies suspected the truth—that Lord Ashwell had spent a great deal of time thinking about both the gift and how it was to be given. The tools were not accidentally left behind by anyone, but had been purchased by his Lordship expressly for Clare. While talking the previous afternoon, Ashwell had remarked upon a charcoal and pencil drawing of a churchyard that hung quite close to where he was sitting. She had commented on the talents of the artist in terms that showed more than a passing familiarity with the subject. When he pressed her, she admitted—with characteristic self-effacement—that she had long maintained an interest in sketching. When he had asked whether she might share any of her drawings with him, she replied that she had given her sketchbook to her brother when they were last together in Leamington. She had hoped her brother might be comforted by having her drawings, including several which she had done of him, and that, perhaps with some small encouragement, he might take up the art and fill up the remaining pages with sketches of his own.

This conversation had stayed with Ashwell some time after he had taken his leave of Clare. That same afternoon, he found himself wandering about the shops, debating the propriety of sending her a small gift of some kind. He knew what he wished to give her, but not how he could convince her to accept it. Settling on the story of the left-behind drawing materials, he selected a set that would be masculine enough to fit their invented history, but delicate enough to suit a lady.

Lord Ashwell's heart was naturally affectionate and quick to love, but for most of his life it had been occupied with a hopeless affection for one long gone from him. None had entered his life with the power to supplant this firm but futile devotion, until now. In recent years, he had met only with affected and grasping ladies who flaunted their faces and their accomplishments in hope of ensnaring a future earl. His title only, and not his person, was the cause of all their interest. A scandal some years back had so damaged his reputation that no worthy ladies of rational judgment and sincere affection would consider him.

Clare Langford was the first lady in some time neither to scorn nor to pursue him. She bore an air of contented disinterest, free from ostentation, and this affected him more than he would have imagined. He did not know how oppressive his existence had been, how starved he was for unpretentious companionship, until she brought her serene and unassuming self through his door. He did not think he would ever tire of such a presence, any more than he would tire of a summer breeze, and he wished never to lose it.

In the end, Clare accepted the gift, albeit with some misgivings. She was determined to discover the nature of the scandal that hung about the giver. Georgiana had already shared all she knew on the subject. The only other person who seemed to have any knowledge of the matter and to whom she could reasonably apply for it was her cousin, Sir Leicester. She therefore invited him to call at a time when she knew Georgiana would be out with Mrs. Younge and Mr. Wickham.

Sir Leicester arrived a full twenty minutes before the agreed hour, and was therefore required to wait for Clare in the drawing room while she hastily made herself presentable. She found him relaxing in a chair by the window, sipping from a rather large, rather full tumbler of Mr. Darcy's sherry. He choked a little as he struggled to rise from his chair, endeavouring not to spill the sherry on his crisp and brightly patterned waistcoat. His coat—far too small—was of purple velvet, his cravat—far too big—silk, topped with a ruby pin. Clare could not escape the impression of a swollen, colour-blind Beau Brummell, dressed for an evening party in the middle of the day.

"I am so glad you could come, Sir Leicester," Clare began.

"At your service, Cousin," he returned with an elaborate bow made awkward by his tight fitting coat. "It is very fashionable of you to have me wait for you. My mother always says that the most elegant ladies always require a gentleman to sit a while before making their entrance."

"I assure you it was not my intention," she said, concealing her irritation as she crossed the room to the tea table. "Please, sit." She began preparing herself a cup of tea. "I would offer you tea," she said, "but I see you are already enjoying something a little stronger. Will you have some cake?"

"Yes, please, thank-you," he replied, sitting back down, his eyes sparkling at the tower of sweet meats. He selected the largest one, looking longingly at those he was required to leave on the plate. Clare inquired politely after Sir Leicester and his family and set the plate of dainties on the table beside his chair. He smiled and answered her inquiries at length, eating and drinking all the while. Clare, meanwhile, was mustering the courage to raise the subject which was the reason she had prompted his visit.

"You know I am very grateful for your friendship, Sir Leicester," she began cautiously. "I hope you do not take it amiss if I am a little curious about a subject you raised when last you were here."

"Of course not, my dear," he replied, leaning back into his chair. "You may be easy with me. We can speak of anything you like. I am always happy to share with you whatever I may know."

"Thank-you, sir. You are very kind. It is something of a delicate topic. It is regarding a certain gentleman." Clare found gossip almost as distasteful as she found her cousin.

"Aha!" he said. "You mean Lord Ashwell. Has he been making himself disagreeable, or worse, agreeable?" he asked, laughing through his nose at his own joke.

"No, nothing like that," Clare timidly replied.

"One does not like to defame another man's character," he continued, ignoring her response. "But since you have asked so particularly, I feel that, if you are to protect yourself, you must be privy to the awful truth. When it comes to the safety of young ladies, I am always excessively concerned. I feel it my bounden duty to prevent your falling prey to any man's black-hearted intentions."

Clare was surprised at the strength of his language. "Is it really as bad as that?"

"It is worse. Once you know the facts, you may judge for yourself whether Lord Ashwell does not deserve all my censure. The story is well known. I read about it in the papers at the time, as did everyone, and have never had it contradicted.

"Three years ago, Lord Ashwell became engaged to a young lady of long-standing acquaintance, a Miss Annabel Gray—a famed local beauty and a very sweet and accomplished young lady. By all accounts, he showed all the signs of utter devotion at the time of their engagement. There was certainly never any question of the sincerity of her affection. She was a woman of fortune, so his wealth held no appeal for her.

"Their engagement was a short one. It was generally accepted that this was due to the impatience of young love. As the wedding day neared, however, many began to notice that the young lady was no longer her once affable self. She withdrew from society and, when she was seen, she was noticeably low in spirits.

"Practically on the eve of the wedding, your Lord Ashwell cast her off. Rumours soon began to circulate that she was with child, the evidence for which soon became undeniable. It is bad enough for a gentleman to break off an engagement without cause—and there was none so much as alleged in this case—but it is another degree of evil for a man to convince a woman to give herself to him on the promise of marriage only to cast her out with her burden and into a world which must reject them both."

Clare was horrified. She could not reconcile this behaviour with the gentle manners and the seeming kindliness of the gentleman she had come to know. It was far worse than she had imagined.

Sir Leicester continued his tale.

"Given her condition, Miss Gray was forced to accept any gentleman who would have her. In the end, it was a sailor, no doubt a fortune-hunter, who, for a hefty sum, agreed to take her on and raise Ashwell's child as though it were his own. She had no choice but to submit to her fate.

"So you see, dear Cousin, for all his titles and his charms, Lord Ashwell is more viper than man. If he could dare do such a thing to someone he knew all his life, who had influence and connections in society, what might he attempt against you, who have no history with him, and so little import in the world?"

Sir Leicester took a large bite of cake while Clare reeled from this news. How could it possibly be true?

"This is very shocking," she said. "I can scarcely believe it. Is it possible there is some misinformation?"

"It is more or less common knowledge. It is old news, and not much talked of any more, especially since he is such a recluse; he does not go out enough to remind people of his indiscretion. But I assure you, it is true. He has never attempted to deny it, though he has had opportunity enough.

And how could he deny it? The child was irrefutable proof! If what I have told you does not satisfy you, you need look no further than his own household. He lives alone and rarely keeps company; and, yet, it is well known he has over a dozen young maids among his staff. He can have no proper employment for so many girls. Do you know he keeps a lady's maid? A lady's maid! For a bachelor! What do you think he means by that? I can hazard a guess but I shan't speak it aloud. No, I am sorry to be the one to say it, but he is a fiend that Lord Ashwell."

He did not look at all sorry to be the one to say anything. Instead, he looked rather pleased to be the messenger. He puffed up his chest and adjusted his waistcoat as he added, in obvious self-reference,

"A gentleman could never do what he has done—not a *true* gentleman."

He then reached for Clare's hand, which he held in clammy gravity.

"I am very glad that you came to me," he said. "It is precisely what I know your mother would have counselled. I hope you know you may always come to me."

Clare withdrew her hand with a word of appreciation.

Leicester consumed the remaining pieces of cake, looking to Clare each time for any signs of disapproval; but, Clare being entirely engrossed in her thoughts, none came, so he dispensed with formalities and ate the last two pieces directly off the tray. He lingered long after the cake was finished, hinting not very subtly at his own eligibility as a husband and at her good fortune in having him for a cousin.

Clare was grateful for the information, but sorry for its source. She did not like to associate with her cousin more than was absolutely necessary, and she was quite happy when she was finally able to usher him out of the house, using Miss Darcy's imminent return as a reason to have him quit the place.

So full was her head of Lord Ashwell and Miss Annabel Gray when the party returned that she failed to witness Mr. Wickham's portrayal of a man in love, failed to witness him gaze on Georgiana with admiration—tenderly press her hand—drop an involuntary tear—and leave the room abruptly.

CHAPTER 28

Georgiana was surprised when Mr. Wickham refused the invitation she had procured for him to dine with them at Grosvenor Square. He claimed as excuse a sense of inferiority to her noble family and a wish not to be made the object of pity and condescension.

"You have been invited for my sake, not out of pity," she said. "I thought for my sake you might come. Wherever you go, you are admired. It does not signify that my cousin stands to inherit a title. He does not act the part, and even if he did, that would not alter my wish to have you there with me. Please reconsider."

She found his excuses weak, but she did not suspect that he had a very good, though undisclosed, reason to be absent—he did not know the extent to which his dispute with Mr. Darcy had been revealed to Lord Ashwell. He thought it better to disappoint Georgiana than to risk exposure.

"I wish you had spoken to me before you spoke to your cousin about it," he said warmly. "I have business out of town the following morning, business regarding my conscription. Even if I wished to, I cannot go."

"Perhaps you could travel early in the morning, or after supper," she pleaded.

His countenance softened. "I am afraid it is not possible. Please forgive me." He held Georgiana's gaze as he took her hand and kissed it gently.

"Oh, Mr. Wickham," she sighed. "I believe I could forgive you anything."

Clare was rounding the corner when she caught the end of this exchange, and she paused, just out of sight, not wishing to interrupt. She saw their eyes locked and their hands held, and she realized suddenly that her own concerns had blinded her to the romance that had been brewing between Georgiana and Mr. Wickham. She trod loudly as she strode into view. Mr. Wickham dropped Georgiana's hand.

"Oh Clare," Georgiana began, taking a step towards her friend. "Is not it a pity? Mr. Wickham cannot join us on Thursday."

"I am sure he has his reasons," Clare answered, unmoved, a challenge in her tone and in her stare.

Mr. Wickham did not like the sharpness in her voice. He sensed her suspicion and he was wary of her. She seemed impervious to his charms and was maternal in her concern for Georgiana. He had been fortunate thus far to find her a little distracted and easily avoided, but he was discovering the bounds of his luck.

"Quite so, Miss Langford," he answered cordially. "Regrettable as it is, I must attend to my future. I cannot spend forever idly enjoying myself, not with my circumstances as they currently are. Nothing shall be improved by my present distractions. Please give my regards and my apologies to his Lordship."

Mr. Wickham said brief good-byes and departed with an awkward bow. Clare's scrutiny followed him out of the house, her own virtue knowing its adversary by instinct.

"Has Mr. Wickham been here every day since the outing to Strawberry Hill?" Clare asked, turning to Georgiana, whose gaze had also followed the gentleman through the door, though with quite a different sentiment. "It seems to me that he has."

"I believe you are right," answered Georgiana. "Is not it fortunate he should be able to visit so often? His company is such a comfort to me."

"I wonder he did not come when your brother was here," said Clare. "Surely such an old friend would have been welcome."

"I wish that were so. Mr. Wickham tells me that he and my brother argued when last they spoke, though he hopes to mend the rift between them. He says that perhaps I might be a force for reconciliation in that regard. I love them both so dearly that I cannot bear to see them at odds."

"I know you do not like to see anyone quarrel, but ought Mr. Wickham to involve you in his conflict with your brother, particularly as it might result in your having to choose sides between the two of them? Does your brother even know that Mr. Wickham has been a guest in this house?"

Clare disliked confrontation of any kind, but she disliked more what she had just seen and heard. She was not so quick to trust a gentleman who claimed intimacy with girl as young and impressionable as Georgiana, particularly if it was not with the knowledge of her guardian. She could not stand idly by, ignorant though she was of what precisely his intentions were. She regretted having been so distracted by her own concerns over the last few days that she was thus delayed in intervening.

"I confess," she said, "I have not told my brother that I have seen Mr. Wickham. Mr. Wickham thinks it best not to speak of him to my brother until they are able to meet in person and discuss their differences. I had suspected for some time that they were not on good terms and had hoped it might be resolved with patience and goodwill."

"Surely, it is your brother's patience and goodwill that must prevail here, not your own. Mr. Wickham has informed you that your brother and he are at odds, but he will not reveal the details of this dispute to you. Do not you see how essential it is to seek your brother's counsel on this matter? If the dispute is not a minor one, your brother may object to Mr. Wickham's calling so often—and if he does object, you must sever relations with Wickham, no matter how dear he has grown to you. For have not you always said that your brother ever has your best interests at heart, and is never wrong?

For the first time in their friendship Georgiana felt aggravated by Clare's interference. Unconsciously biased as she was towards Mr. Wickham, she was unable to see the validity in her friend's concern. Mr. Wickham had commandeered so much of her affection as to leave little space in her heart for anyone else, particularly anyone who might speak against him.

"Do you really think I act improperly?" she asked, turning to her friend. "I am surprised, Clare. I had hoped to seek your counsel in reuniting my brother and Mr. Wickham. My father was always so fond of him, and he and my brother were once like brothers to each other. Mr. Wickham, in any case, is eager to be so again. I am certain there must be some simple misunderstanding at the heart of their disagreement, and, if I write to my brother now, it may jeopardize their reconciliation."

"If you sought my advice," Clare replied as gently as she could, "I would suggest you seek the counsel of your brother before you spend any more time with Mr. Wickham. He knows more than you or I do about the nature of the conflict and is always fair-minded and reasonable. Surely he would regard your openness, and your favourable opinion of Mr. Wickham, as cause enough to abandon any prejudices. If, however, he learns that Mr. Wickham has asked you—no matter what the reason—to conceal from your brother the addresses he has been paying to you, this cannot but make matters much worse between them."

Georgiana felt hurt that her cherished Mr. Wickham could be the object of suspicion and took offence on his behalf.

"Do you believe that there is some mischief on Mr. Wickham's part then? I do not see what cause you have for your misgivings. I believe I know him better than you and can only recall kindness from him. Moreover, nothing has been in secret. Mrs. Younge has been always present, and acts on behalf of my brother. I do not intend to discuss the subject with my brother until he is here in person and I ask you please to allow me this. It is only a matter of weeks."

This was the closest the two ladies had ever come to a quarrel and the closest Clare had ever seen Georgiana come to speaking harshly. Clare could see that further argument would be ineffectual, serving as it would only to further divide them and to drive Georgiana to the side of Mr. Wickham. Her hatred of conflict made her glad to have this justification to leave the subject alone, but she was not satisfied in the main.

She ought to have been able bring her concerns to Mrs. Younge, charged as that lady was with the care of Georgiana, but it was clear on reflection that Mrs. Younge was a better friend to Mr. Wickham than to Georgiana. It was Mrs. Younge who had first brought Mr. Wickham to Berkeley Square, and who was forever speaking his praises and lamenting his troubles. Consequently, Clare did not think it wise to speak her suspicions to that lady. She considered seeking out Mr. Darcy, but she was doubly prevented, firstly, by ignorance of how to reach him and, secondly, by a concern that such a direct violation of her friend's wishes might forever destroy their friendship, and she did not consider the situation so dire as to warrant such a risk. And only the most extreme circumstances could induce her to write directly to a gentleman.

She therefore settled on Lady Sofia as the best consultant on the subject. She was not certain what assistance Lady Sofia might be able to render but she knew she would need some sort of ally, and at least Lady Sofia had considerable resources at her disposal.

Lady Sofia may not be of a clear-minded and sensible persuasion, but surely, the story of an innocent heroine threatened by the designs of a fortune-hunting villain must capture her imagination. Clare was not sure Mr. Wickham was such a villain, but she did believe he was not acting in good faith and that was all she needed to cast him in the role of antagonist in the high dramatics of Lady Sofia's mind.

CHAPTER 29

Clare was relieved that, for the remainder of the week, she did not see Mr. Wickham at the house. As much as the absence of Mr. Wickham made her thoughts easier, she was not without her worries. She had attempted without success to call on Lady Sofia—each time she called, she was informed that she was out or otherwise engaged. No matter how subtly she raised the topic, Georgiana adamantly refused so much as to discuss the subject of Wickham and her brother, and she could see that, every time she spoke of it, the gulf between her and her friend only further widened. What is more, there was the impending dinner at Grosvenor Square. How could she address Lord Ashwell with serenity considering what her cousin had revealed to her? She wished to return Lord Ashwell's gift, but she could not see how she could do so without offending—or at least embarrassing—the evening's host.

Several days had passed since the gift was given; surely, she believed, it would seem odd to return it now. If she did not intend to accept it, she ought to have sent it back immediately. Furthermore, returning it on the eve of her attendance at his home might cast an unpleasant shadow over the evening. And she did not think she could send it to him directly in any event, whether before or after seeing him on Thursday. It had been sent to herself through Georgiana, and only through Georgiana could she properly return it. She knew Georgiana would not allow her to return it without good reason, and though she had one, she could not provide it. She did not wish to give her friend further reason to quarrel with her, and so she was at a loss. What acceptable explanation could she offer, both for refusing it and for delaying in doing so? She considered inventing a false reason, such as that her brother intended to return her own items to her or that her parents were sending her replacements once they learned that she had given hers up. But even contemplating such a deceit made her writhe with distaste. She looked at the items, wrapped in paper, and picked them up into her hand. She knew she must bring them with her to dinner.

On Thursday, she wore her most capacious muff. She was thus able to stow her parcel in it without attracting Georgiana's notice. She fingered the paper as they departed from the house, a feeling of anger and regret towards Lord Ashwell brewing in her heart. On behalf of Miss Gray, and, indeed, on behalf of all her sex, she was offended by his conduct, past and present. She had truly come to care for him, and his kindness had all been false. Any man capable of such villainy as he had inflicted could only mean to treat her ill. She resented deeply the pain it caused her to relinquish her affection for the man he had pretended to be.

"It is not so cold as all that, is it?" said Georgiana, indicating the muff as they climbed into the carriage.

"Oh," replied Clare, fumbling for an explanation. "I got a little chilled earlier, and it is a cool evening."

Georgiana made no further inquiry. She had found so much of her friend's recent behaviour odd that she no longer felt it worth remarking on.

On their arrival at Grosvenor Square, Lord Ashwell welcomed the party with characteristic grace and warmth, and a very slight nervousness which was not so typical. He was still unsure about having sent that gift to Miss Langford, and wondered whether he had played his hand too early.

"My dear friends, how well you all look this evening. Dear Cousin, I believe you are lovelier every time I see you."

Georgiana was still a little shy of her cousin and blushed at this innocent flattery. "Miss Langford," he said, turning towards Clare, "I am so pleased you could join us."

Clare kept her eyes towards the floor as she made her way silently into the room, unsuccessfully willing herself invisible. He thought she looked more woodland queen than admiral's daughter that evening. She had certainly done her utmost to dress as modestly as the occasion would allow, but this had an effect quite opposite from the one she intended, for Ashwell found a woman to be the most becoming when most modestly arrayed. Though she did not—would not—raise her eyes, Clare felt his gaze hot on her cheeks. Her heart pounded loudly in her ears.

"Mrs. Younge," said Lord Ashwell, remembering his other guests, "your name is ever apt, so youthful and radiant you always are. I hope it is not very cold outside. I know the distance is short, but I always feel the cold and I do not like to cause anyone to go out in inclement weather."

"It seems you and I are very different, sir. I never feel the cold, so you may rest easy on my account. And, as you say, the distance is very short." With Georgiana's reticence and Clare's uneasiness, Mrs. Younge and Lord Ashwell were obliged to carry most of the conversation.

"Well, cook assures me that the goose shall make up for any sacrifices you have borne in coming," he said.

"I am sure its sacrifices are greater than ours in any event," replied Mrs. Younge, drawing a round of polite laughter from the company.

"I am afraid the cancellation of your friend has left our table a gentleman short this evening, Cousin," Ashwell well said, turning to Georgiana.

"Oh, I do apologise, sir. He sends his sincerest regrets, and I offer mine."

"I must confess it does not disturb me to have more than my share of your attention." Lord Ashwell chanced a look towards Clare, but found her still looking at the floor.

A silence of some moments followed, broken at last by Mrs. Younge.

"I do hope the weather does not remain cool for long," she said. "We are planning a trip to Ramsgate in a few weeks. We may even try a little sea bathing if it is warm enough. It may be beneficial to the health to bathe in the winter, but it must be a great deal more enjoyable when the air is warm, and since neither of us is ill, I think we shall only try it if it is pleasant. Do not you agree Miss Darcy?"

"We shall only try it if I am able to overcome my fear of the ocean. I am assured it is very safe, but I am sorry to say I am not very adventurous. Mrs. Younge is so brave. She may embolden me yet."

"And what about you, Miss Langford? Do you fear the sea like young Georgiana here, or are you eager to try this new craze?"

"I hope I have been raised to respect the sea." Clare could not avoid answering Lord Ashwell, and she struggled to keep the spite out of her voice. "It has claimed many lives, and I would not treat it as a plaything. Still, I am told that exposure to the sea is very beneficial. Certainly my father has always had excellent health."

Georgiana was surprised at her friend's tone. She had always been pleased to note the conviviality between her cousin and her friend. She hoped, in the deepest corners of her heart, that they might even have begun to form an attachment. She knew that Clare, though a very worthy gentlewoman in her own right, may yet want for offers, much more so if her mother were to succumb to her recent illness, and thus deprive her of her family estate. Georgiana, wise enough to recognise in Ashwell's kindnesses to Clare a blossoming affection, knew not why her friend would endanger such an excellent match as she would most likely never be offered again.

"Have you ever tried the sea, Cousin?" she asked.

"I have not. I did try Bath once, but I found the travel undid any benefit that the place might have done me. I fear it would be the same with the seaside."

Just then the door was heard and a new guest announced.

"Sir Francis Peabody, sir."

"Ah, Peabers, do come in," said Lord Ashwell, ushering his friend into the room. "Allow me to introduce you to this charming company. Miss Darcy, Miss Langford, Mrs. Younge, this is Sir Francis Peabody. Sir Francis and I were at Oxford together. I cannot tell you what a prodigious help he was to me then, and how very obliging he is now, always to accept my invitations when I have need of a gentleman."

Sir Francis was not a very inspiring character. He had often been in the company of Lord Ashwell in their youth, and, since they were both of a rather sickly nature, unlike their peers, neither was much inclined to running and jumping and hitting things. They grew quite fond of each other, sharing intellectual interests, and now, since they both lived alone, they continued to be each other's near exclusive companions.

Sir Francis stood awkwardly in the middle of the room, unsure where to look.

"Sir Francis," said Mrs. Younge warmly, "do come and join us. We were discussing the benefits of sea bathing. Have you ever tried it?"

Sir Francis accepted the invitation to sit on the sofa beside Mrs. Younge, but looked horrified at the suggestion of submerging himself in frigid, open water.

"Sea bathing?" he repeated distastefully. "I should hope not."

As the others began to debate the matter, Clare thought it the perfect opportunity to slip out and conclude the business of the parcel.

"Please excuse me," she said quietly to Lord Ashwell as she rose from her chair. "I seem to have forgotten my handkerchief in my muff. The cold air has left me in need of it."

"But here, you may have mine" Lord Ashwell made for his pocket.

"You are very kind, sir, but you should not wish for it back, and I cannot take it when I have my own just down the hall. If I could just be shown to my cloak," she indicated the servant.

"Sully," Lord Ashwell addressed the same servant, "fetch Miss Langford's muff, would you?" Then to Clare, "They must be given something to do. I have employed so many of them that there is never enough work to share between them."

Clare followed the servant out of the room saying, "I shall just go along and save the trouble of returning it."

As she was lead through the house, Clare took in her surroundings in the hope of judging from them, somehow, the character of their master. She could hear down a corridor the chatter of female voices suddenly erupt into girlish laughter. As they passed by an open door, she peered into the room, which seemed to be a small reception room. She saw on the sofa a girl of about twenty, dressed as a servant, reading a novel in rather a slovenly posture. Clare thought it odd that the girl took no notice of her and Sully as they passed. Could there really be a dozen such girls secreted away in the back rooms of the house, as Sir Leicester had said? As absurd as it had sounded when told to her by Sir Leicester, it began to seem possible.

Clare retrieved her parcel from her muff and asked the servant to place it in Lord Ashwell's study and not to mention it until she had left for the evening. Sully assured her that he would do as asked. Clare thanked him and returned to the drawing room with the handkerchief that had been her excuse for leaving it, passing again the small drawing room and the dishevelled girl, who had since pulled her feet up under her on the sofa and was biting her nails in distraction.

Clare returned to her party to find, to her horror, that the dreaded subject of the gift had been raised by her unwitting friend.

"You did like the sketching things very much, did not you Clare? It was very kind of my cousin to send them on knowing that you were without yours."

"Yes, very kind," was all Clare could contrive in reply.

Georgiana had thought to ease the unaccountable tension she sensed between Clare and Lord Ashwell, but her efforts had the opposite effect. Lord Ashwell seemed to grow shy at the mention of it also, and Georgiana thought Clare rather ungracious in her want of effusion. Sir Francis was certainly at a loss as to his friend's interest in this strange creature, so plainly attired and so awkward in her address.

"I am sure it was nothing," Lord Ashwell muttered, saddened at Clare's indifference. He had been so pleased with his choice of gift, and had delighted in the joy he imagined it had brought her. It had seemed so fitting at the time. Had he judged poorly? Had something caused her to take his gesture amiss? He had done nothing himself. She must have been poisoned against him, perhaps by her cousin, the baronet, who she said had recognized his name.

"But tell me more about your plans for your garden," said Mrs. Younge to Sir Francis. "I know so little about botany."

And on the evening continued in the same vein, with everything meet and civilised in the way of delicacy and strained conversation. It ended with many compliments, many expressions of hope for repetition and many feelings of confusion and regret.

Only Sir Francis, however, could truly be said to have had an enjoyable evening. He had been most keen to accept his friend's invitation when he learned that young Miss Darcy was to be in attendance. Though he considered himself an eligible match, he found it very difficult to advance, or even to make, any acquaintance with young ladies—something his friend, Lord Ashwell, seemed able to do with grace and ease.

Sir Francis had long hoped that it would be through his friend that he should meet the future Lady Peabody, but, since Lord Ashwell himself did not go out as much into society as he once did, the introductions he had procured from his friend in recent years had waned. When he heard that his friend had a cousin who was moving to town and whom he might have the opportunity of encountering at Grosvenor Square, he quickly convinced himself that this would be the introduction he had been anticipating. He had held similar hopes on a previous occasion, before being introduced to his friend's other cousin, Miss de Bourgh, but she had not struck him as a suitable candidate for a wife. Miss Darcy was quite another matter.

Though their introduction and conversation were both brief, he found her to be just the lady he had hoped for. Her manner was demure and gentle, her conversation sensible, her mien warm and kind. When they were married, she would not overwhelm him and would not tease or mock him. And she was yet young, which meant her character would be supple enough that he could easily expunge any fault he might find with her.

He seized his earliest opportunity of pursuing the matter, taking his leave of his host that he might escort the ladies home.

Lord Ashwell stood in his foyer a few moments after his guests had gone, the image of Clare's expressionless face before his mind's eye. He then retreated to his study where he found the parcel that Clare had left for him, and the simple note she had attached.

"DEAR SIR,"

"Thank you kindly for forwarding the enclosed. I pray you take no offence at my finding that, regretfully, I cannot accept them.

"Yours Sincerely,

"C. LANGFORD"

Lord Ashwell felt he ought to have anticipated this disappointment. A more hopeful person might have been crushed by such a cursory rejection from the object of his affection; but, fortunately, Lord Ashwell was accustomed to feeling dejected and, thus was able to reconcile himself all the more readily to be ing let down once more. He sat, staring at the note, his thoughts slowly turning from his own disappointment to Clare's happiness. He might yet be a friend to her. He still had many connections which he might contrive to work to her advantage, or to that of her brother, which must be equally, if not more, welcome to her. He cheered himself therefore in contemplating what he might secretly do for the lady he had resigned himself to being without.

CHAPTER 30

Weeks passed, and Clare was pleased to find that Mr. Wickham did not visit Berkeley Square. Perhaps he really had needed to attend to business regarding his conscription and had given up on Georgiana. Georgiana did not seem like a heartbroken wretch, did not appear to pine for his presence, and so perhaps Clare had misapprehended the nature of her involvement with Mr. Wickham. Clare hoped that either there never was any scheme, or that whatever scheme had been in place had been abandoned. Perhaps Georgiana had heeded Clare's concerns and had decided to wait until her brother returned and allow Mr. Wickham to resolve his differences with that gentleman himself. Whatever the case, there did not seem to be any more Mr. Wickham to concern her, and she was very glad of it. She did not raise the subject again with Georgiana, as the disagreement seemed now moot. In any event, they would all soon be gone to Ramsgate, far from the reaches of Mr. Wickham.

In preparation for their summer at the seaside, Clare and Georgiana had ordered bathing costumes to be made. They arrived one morning and the girls rushed upstairs to their rooms to try them on. It was the first time in weeks that either had felt like the cherished companions they had been at school.

Ever since their confrontation over Mr. Wickham, Georgiana had been a little distant with Clare. She had felt hurt by Clare's suspicion of Mr. Wickham and her cool reception of Ashwell's addresses. Both of these men were excessively dear to her, and neither had shown anything but the utmost kindness, friendliness and goodwill towards herself and towards Clare. In Mrs. Younge, Georgiana had found an unexpected and sympathetic friend, and she had lately given more of her company and her confidence to that lady, leaving Clare with little to concern her and nothing to do about it.

As they raced up the stairs side by side, Clare rejoiced in the occasion to have her friend to herself and to be merry together. The girls had just put on their new garments and were inspecting each other's appearance with self-conscious but irrepressible laughter when the post, containing a letter from Mrs. Langford, was brought up to them. The thought of her mother always left Clare feeling sobered and humble. Receiving the letter, she felt suddenly very foolish in her enthusiasm for the seaside and in her ridiculous state of dress.

"Please excuse me, Georgiana," she said with a sigh. "I really must read this."

"Of course you must," Georgiana replied with a sympathetic smile. "But do return when you have finished. You must help me to decide which gowns to pack. You know I am always so lost without your guidance."

Clare nodded and returned to her own room to read the letter.

"DEAR CLARE,"

"I hope you are well and that you are becoming ever more accomplished every day. You are being provided with the best masters, and we trust you are learning all you can from them, and retaining all you learn through constant study. Your father and I are both well, particularly so because of some joyful news that we have lately received.

"A letter arrived yesterday from Sir Leicester, and was of a very peculiar and unexpected nature. He wishes to give to you and your brother, effective upon my death, a life estate in the house and adjoining lawns and gardens at Maplethwaite. He inquired whether this would be welcome. Welcome does not begin to capture my relief on receiving this news. He cannot imagine how incredible this is, not only for you and Crawley, but for your father and me, to know that you should always have a home of your own, come what may.

"I expected Sir Leicester might ask something in return, but to my surprise, his letter contained only sentiments of a most honourable nature. He says that he is concerned for your position in the world, for your vulnerability, and that he believes a secure home for life would free you from the attendant pressures of want. He expresses the same in respect of your brother.

"As he has never met Crawley, I must assume that this act is due to you. His admiration and regard for you must be strong and sincere for him to make such a thoughtful and generous gift. Maplethwaite is a great possession for him to give up to you so freely. It is truly selfless of him.

"I confess I had not thought him capable of such benevolence, but it seems I have misjudged him. It is true that his manners and his appearance are not the most pleasing, nor is he particularly clever, but, with this act, he has shown himself generous and caring. Such a character is worth a thousand handsome faces and eloquent tongues.

"My darling daughter, it is clear to me that Sir Leicester cares a great deal for you. I write to beg that you not dismiss too hastily any offer you may receive from him. He is not a paragon of romance, I grant you, but it is a man's character, and not his charm, that is the making of a husband.

"I have not detected from your letters any hint of a preference for him, but let me counsel you to search your heart and determine whether you might, in time, find him agreeable, knowing as you do now the depth of his feelings and the sacrifice he makes for you. If I could see you happy and loved by a man of good character, I know I could go in peace and tranquility to my grave.

"Your father sends his love and kind wishes.

"Yours, etc."

Clare held the letter in her lap as she allowed her tears to fall upon it, blurring the script as they landed. She gave in to her sadness, letting the paper fall to the floor and weeping with abandon. It all seemed sealed. She must marry this man whom she had never cared for, out of gratitude and hopelessness of ever making such a match again.

She thought of Lord Ashwell, or rather of the pretty picture of him that she had painted for herself before she had learned the truth. The loss of him, who had never existed, was still fresh, and she could not help but mourn him. She had been angry with Lord Ashwell for taking from her this imaginary beloved, and now her anger turned on Sir Leicester for imposing himself on her mind as a vile and pitiful substitute. She wished their characters could be reversed, that Ashwell could be the one to whom she felt so much obligation, and Leicester the one she must abandon.

In every small matter, Lord Ashwell had acted with more thoughtfulness, more humility, more kindness than she could ever imagine of Sir Leicester. And yet he was capable of such treachery, and Sir Leicester of such generosity. Why could not one man unite the best of each? If such a man existed, surely she could never hope of ever interesting him. Why could not she have been born high so that she might have her choice of suitors? She had always been sensible, always good, always obedient, and all this was to lead her into the arms of the repulsive Sir Leicester Crawley. She was wretched.

She looked towards her bed, where she had hidden a copy of *The Italian*. She pulled it out from beneath the pillow and stared wearily at it, not having even the heart to open it. She held it instead in her lap, in silent and hopeless resignation.

Some time later—she could not say how long—Georgiana knocked on her door and was admitted.

"My dear Clare!" she exclaimed when she saw her friend, red-eyed and despondent. She rushed over and sat herself beside Clare, offering her a handkerchief. "Whatever has happened? Have you had bad news from home?"

Clare accepted the handkerchief and forced a smile as she answered her friend. "No, indeed, no bad news—it is good news in fact. I do not even know why I was crying." Clare dried her eyes and returned the handkerchief, her tears over for the present. "My cousin, Sir Leicester, has given me and my brother a life estate in Maplethwaite."

Georgiana looked surprised. "But that *is* good news. I do not see how that could make you cry, unless you have been shedding tears of joy. But that does not seem the case. There must be more."

Clare turned to face her friend. "I believe, or at least my mother is convinced, that it has been given as a gesture of love, and that I ought not to reject any offer that comes with it."

"Any offer?"

"Yes. Mama believes he intends to propose, and that, as he has shown himself so generous and selfless, he is worthy of my consideration, if not my acceptance."

Georgiana was agape. "But how can you *think* of accepting him? Have not you always found him intolerable?"

"I must marry someone, and it is not likely I shall receive any better offer." Clare's gaze returned to her lap, where her hands lay, a limp and discouraged reflection of her heart.

"But with Maplethwaite in your name, you will be amply provided for. You have no need to rush into a match of any kind."

"The estate shall remain my mother's while she lives, which I hope shall be a very long time. After that, it is to be given to me and my brother jointly, which is as I would wish it, but he shall wish to settle there with his own family one day, and the gift is only of the house, not all the lands, so there will be no income from it, generous as it is. No, I must still marry. It would be foolish to refuse Sir Leicester. He is a good match for me, better than I ought to expect. He is more than able to provide for me and my family, and clearly eager to do so." She let out a long sigh of resignation. "I shall not be the first woman to accept a man she cares little for. If he is as kind as his gift suggests, perhaps I might reconcile myself to his other faults. Perhaps, in time, I may even grow to be fond of him. For do not all marriages have their rubs and disappointments?"

Clare could not restrain her tears and sobbed haltingly into her handkerchief. After a few moments, she calmed herself and dried her eyes. "Even those which, at the start, are full of mutual adoration often decline into estrangement."

Georgiana looked at her friend with pity and sorrow in her heart. She took Clare's hand, which she pressed to her cheek. "Oh Clare, how curious you are—how curious and how dear. You are clearly distraught, yet you tell me you have happy news. Then you tell me how the happy news is really distressing news, and then you explain why you ought not to be unhappy about it, that it is not as horrid a prospect as it seems."

Clare merely stared at her lap, nodding in agreement with her friend, who continued, "It *is* a horrid prospect, to spend your life with a man you do not even *like*, and I should commiserate with you if you were forced into that fate, but that is not the case. He has not yet even proposed. Perhaps he does not mean to. If he does not, then you need not choose between poverty and wretchedness."

"And if he does?" Clare looked at Georgiana.

"You are not obliged to accept him, whatever your mother says. Would you truly be happier as Lady Crawley than as Miss Langford the spinster, living at home with her brother, with little means but no obligation?"

Clare looked down at Georgiana's hopeful face, so full of sweetness and sincerity. Georgiana had everything Clare had not—money, security, and a guardian who would never ask more of her than to be good and gay. What is more, wherever she went, Georgiana seemed to attract nearly universal love, all the while completely unaware of how beguiling she was. Clare found Georgiana's condolence to be a true comfort and solace.

"Whatever becomes of me, I shall always be grateful for your friendship," she said, with a gravity that caused Georgiana to giggle.

"What is it?" asked Clare.

"Oh, I am sorry," Georgiana replied, clapping her hands on her cheeks. "But you are still wearing your bathing costume."

Clare looked down at her dress. A bewildered smile began to form as she considered what a comical sight she must be. Her jagged, laughing coughs so nearly resembled her sobs that she almost began crying afresh. But though her heart remained heavy, her laughter had, for the present, banished her tears.

"As we are dressed for the seaside," began Georgiana, returning to her feet, "Perhaps we should leave for Ramsgate forthwith and thwart your cousin's proposal, at least for the summer months. We can have one last frolic before you go to your doom."

Clare joined her friend in rising from her seat. "Come," she said, laughing off her grief. "I believe I promised to help you choose some gowns."

"Oh, Mrs. Younge already helped me pick them, as you were indisposed," said Georgiana. "But we can review her choices, and you can give me your opinion on accessories to go with each."

The girls walked arm in arm towards the door, where Clare stopped and said, with more solemnity,

"You know, nothing is really different, except that I now have a place to live out my spinster days, should it come to that, and that I must regard my cousin in a new light. I may have misjudged him, you know. Stranger things have happened than a woman's misjudging a man because she did not like his manners. What a joy it would be if he turned out to be my knight in shining armour after all."

"Your stout, dull, absurdly dressed Valancourt." They both laughed as they made their way to Georgiana's room where the conversation turned to talk of balls and gowns and the bizarre but much anticipated thrill of bathing in the sea.

CHAPTER 31

In the weeks preceding their departure from town, the ladies of Berkeley Square began to see much more of Lady Sofia. The early vigour of her brother's wedding preparations had subsided, so that there was more time to spend with friends.

She expressed her relief to those friends during an afternoon visit.

"It is such a sweet sort of exhaustion I have had from giving myself entirely over to my dear Laura, but I confess it is also a sweet respite to be here with you just now. It feels like an age since I was last able simply to enjoy your company."

"It has been six, maybe seven weeks, since the day of the Strawberry Hill outing," Clare remarked.

"Is it so short a period?" mused Georgiana. "It seems much longer."

"It is a very long time for friends such as us who live so near each other," said Lady Sofia.

"Well, I hope there will yet be plenty of opportunity for us all to see each other before we leave for Ramsgate," Clare offered.

"Nothing could please me more," replied Lady Sofia.

Silence followed, during which Clare noticed a meaningful look pass between the other three ladies, as though they all shared a secret and wished her absence that they might speak of it.

Mrs. Younge turned to Clare: "Miss Langford," she said, "a letter came for you earlier this morning. I had it sent up to your room. Did you receive it?"

"I did not."

Clare fought her anger at not having been told about the letter sooner. She had no cause to be upset. No doubt it was merely an oversight. It was not a pretense for sending her from the room. These were her friends. They would not conspire to rid themselves of her.

"Did you happen to note where it was from?" Clare asked.

"I believe the postmark said Warwickshire, though I cannot be certain."

"Is not your brother in Warwickshire?" asked Georgiana.

"Indeed, he is," replied Clare.

"You must be anxious to read your letter, dear Clare," Georgiana offered with genuine consideration. "Please, we would none of us take offence at your going to read it."

"No, indeed," added Lady Sofia. "You need not stand on ceremony on my account. How loath I should be to stand in the way of sisterly affection. Besides, I really must be going presently."

Clare looked to Mrs. Younge, who nodded her agreement, granting Clare the freedom to excuse herself, which she did with alacrity. Finding her letter on her dressing table, she picked it up and sat at her window, opening it with great interest.

"DEAR CLARE,"

"I hope you are not terribly angry that I have not written to you before now. I did get all your letters and I can even say that I managed to read all of them. Mama says it is frightfully wrong of me never to reply, but I just find it so tedious to sit for hours and write about all the fun I could be having if I were not sitting down and writing about it. I tell Mama that you never get angry, that you will not be offended by my failing to write, but she does not understand. She is so devoted to convention.

"Today I have occasion to write, for otherwise you would not know to expect me. Aunt and Uncle Watson are going to town on Thursday fortnight and have agreed to take me. Mama says I may go and that you are to assist me with my lessons while I am there. I daresay I need all the help I can find, though I do not intend to spend all my time poring over books or taking tea with my sister, or worse yet playing the slave to my aunt and uncle. I hope you may introduce me to some good company since you have been mingling with lords and ladies and everything and there must be *some* good dancing to be had, even if the season is almost over. We will be staying three weeks. You can apply to Aunt Watson for the address, or you can simply wait until you hear from us after we arrive.

"Yours Sincerely,

"CRAWLEY"

Only a sister as loving as Clare could smile at such a crude and unpolished letter. She rejoiced at the news and was calculating whether a reply would reach him before he left when Georgiana knocked on her door.

"Mrs. Younge and I are stepping out to the milliner's. Since you are busy with your letter, I thought we might leave you in peace. Shall you be all right here on your own?"

"Of course I shall, thank you. Are you having something new made?"

"Mrs. Younge goes to see about a repair. I merely go for the diversion, not that it should be very diverting."

Rather than admit her hurt at so trivial a thing as not being invited to join in an outing to the milliner's, Clare invented many explanations for the fact and many reasons not to feel wounded at the exclusion. She was occupied with her letter; she had not ordered anything from the hat-maker's; indeed, she had no reason at all to join the ladies on their errand, yet, little as she wished to admit it, she was hurt that her friend was continually choosing the company of Mrs. Younge over herself.

"I hope you have a very enjoyable time. The sunshine ought to be inducement enough to draw you out of doors."

"Well, I shall leave you to your letter. We shan't be long, I expect."

Georgiana quitted the room, and Clare took up her pen. After completing her letter, she went down to the drawing room to await the return of Georgiana and Mrs. Younge. She took out her work basket and sat herself beside the window, where the afternoon light was yet bright and from where she could watch for the carriage. After darning her second stocking, she glanced up at the clock. She had not marked the time when they left, but it could not have been later than half past two and it was now going on five o'clock.

This was rather longer than Clare thought it ought to have taken to visit the milliner's, even on a busy day. A carriage pulled into the square and stopped shortly before the entrance to the house. Through the window, Clare could identify the carriage, and she began to put away her work in anticipation of her friends' return, but, as she did, a gentleman alighted from the carriage. His back was turned to the house, so she could not see his face, but there was something in his gait that was unmistakably familiar. The man who was now rounding the corner and passing from view was, and could be no other than, Mr. Wickham.

Clare was at a loss as to how to react. The outing to the milliner's was obviously a ruse. A concealed rendezvous—and with a chaperone complicit in the deception—could not but augur evil.

Georgiana and Mrs. Younge entered in jubilant spirits. Clare waited to see whether an innocent explanation might be forthcoming, but neither of them volunteered anything when Clare inquired about their outing.

"How did everything go at the milliner's?" she asked. "Were they able to repair your bonnet?"

"Oh, yes, indeed," replied Mrs. Younge, striding across the room and dropping herself into an armchair. "You know, they are so miraculous in what they accomplish there, it is little wonder they are always so crowded."

"It must have been very crowded to have kept you so long."

Mrs. Younge looked around the room distractedly. "Is there no tea?" she asked Clare.

"I shall just ring for some," said Clare. Not allowing the subject to drop, she continued to press her friend, who had not said anything since entering the room. "Did you order anything in the end, Georgiana?" she asked her.

Georgiana, who was staring dreamily across the room, turned her head on hearing her name, but it was clear she had not heard the question.

"No," answered Mrs. Younge on Georgiana's behalf, "she decided not to order anything in the end. More hats would just mean more to pack and transport to Ramsgate."

Clare was not at all satisfied, and she still held on to the hope that her friend would not dare be brazenly untruthful with her.

"Did you happen to meet anyone while you were out?" she asked, giving Georgiana every chance possible to acquit herself. "You were gone such a long time."

This last inquiry caused Georgiana to look sheepishly at Mrs. Younge, who knew, as well as Clare did, that Georgiana could not be openly dishonest.

"We did not meet anyone," Mrs. Younge answered. "The shop was busy with a group of ladies placing an order for a wedding. Georgiana and I stopped in at a tea house next door until the crowd dispersed. We did not mark the time, but perhaps we stayed longer than we thought."

Clare watched Georgiana as Mrs. Younge made excuses for them both. She would not turn her face towards Clare, looking instead towards the door.

Without addressing anyone in particular, she rose from her seat and announced: "I shall just go and see what is delaying the tea." One look further passed between her and Mrs. Younge as she left the room.

This patent deceit deeply disturbed Clare, who knew it to be so far from Georgiana's nature that it must be the influence of Mrs. Younge and Mr. Wickham. If Clare did not succeed in thwarting them, there was no telling what damage they might do.

CHAPTER 32

The next morning, Clare set off for Lady Sofia's house first thing after breakfast, professing a need for a little air and exercise that was not entirely fabricated.

It was a short walk to Park Lane, but Clare still arrived flushed, though more with anxiety than exertion. Lady Sofia had said the previous day that wedding preparations had slowed, so Clare hoped to find her at home that morning and at liberty to receive her.

Such indeed was the case. Clare sighed in relief as she was admitted to the drawing room where she found Lady Sofia alone.

"Why, Clare, what a delightful surprise this is!" Taking in Clare's appearance, Lady Sofia rose to greet her, took her hands with impassioned solemnity and led her to the sofa.

"You have come alone, with reddened cheeks and rapid breath. Please tell me without delay or ceremony; what urgent and vital matter has brought you here in all this state?

Clare was unaccustomed to such directness, but relieved all the same to be spared the demands of politeness.

"It is something of a delicate matter," she began, hesitantly. "It concerns Miss Darcy, you see."

Clare paused, considering where and how to begin. Lady Sofia was all sympathetic impatience.

"You must remember the gentleman who attended the Strawberry Hill outing," Clare continued, " Mr.—"

"—Wickham?" Lady Sofia interjected. "But of course, he..." she trailed off for a moment, then with a flash of realization, "You have discovered the truth then!"

"The truth?" Clare felt very confused.

"Why yes, the truth about Georgiana and Wickham of course." Lady Sofia beamed with delight. "Oh, I am so relieved." She sighed and collapsed upon the sofa.

"Relieved?" Clare was incredulous.

"But of course." Lady Sofia sat upright. "You are Georgiana's dearest friend and, as such, you ought to have been involved from the beginning. I have objected from the start to the keeping of secrets, as I am always in favour of absolute openness and honesty in all matters of the heart. I knew that your heart was too sympathetic to stand in the way of true love. It is such a relief to have been right, and to be relieved of the burden of secrecy. Oh Clare," she said, taking Clare's hands in hers. "You said it was a delicate matter, but surely you must see that love—true love—is many things, bold and courageous and challenging, but never delicate."

Clare felt her face turn pale and her head grow weak as she discovered that her only possible ally was already in the service of the enemy.

"You have known all along," she said in a whisper of disbelief.

"My dear Clare, do not be angry. All will be well now. Only you must not let on that you know. Oh, is not it romantic beyond words? She has always loved him, you know, and he was always so fond of her when she was young, and now, to be reunited in this way and to discover such a passion for each other, a love so pure that it will not be suppressed by the tyrant of reason. My heart could burst with the utter sentimentality of it. And what an honour it is for me to have been given such a place of significance in the affair—to carry messages to and fro between them, to arrange meetings for them that would otherwise have been impossible. London society is so strict on such points that, without my assistance, they never should have been able to meet. It shall be the great satisfaction of my life to have played a part in bringing together such devoted lovers."

Clare was stunned. She had always known Lady Sofia to be a little silly, but she had never considered her nonsense to be such a ready tool for mischief.

"So you would never consider informing Mr. Darcy of the affair?" she asked in disbelief.

"Oh, my dear, heavens no! I hope I should never be so faithless a friend as to betray her trust so cruelly. Besides, it would spoil everything. Mr. Darcy is a very virtuous man, and I would not say a word against him, but he is not of a romantic persuasion. He would destroy the perfect and delicate blossom of this rare and exquisite sentiment. No, we must ensure Mr. Darcy does not find out until all is said and done, for then, even he must be satisfied, having as he shall every evidence of the honour of Mr. Wickham's intentions. "

"The honour of his intentions?" Clare saw nothing of honour in deceiving Georgiana's friends and relations, in wooing her in secret without the knowledge of her lawful guardian, and in clandestine meetings and covert messages.

"Oh Clare, did you have fears on that account also? Rest assured, he does not toy with her. All of this is in aid of a marriage and no less. I would not have involved myself if his intentions were not honourable, for even the most overwhelming emotion must be pursued with honour or it is worth nothing."

"Marriage? But he is without means."

"He is quite penniless, I understand, but what he is offering is of infinitely greater value, and her fortune will more than suffice to supply the humble needs of love. How many marriages are built on so much less than they shall have? In such a mercenary world, it is so refreshing to witness sincere and disinterested love."

"Quite," said Clare. She saw that argument with Lady Sofia would be ineffectual. She was utterly dismayed and appalled, and in urgent need of escaping before she allowed her feelings to be revealed.

"I really must be going," she said. "Forgive the suddenness of my departure. You have given me much to think on."

"Of course my dear!" cried Lady Sofia, throwing her arms about Clare in a tight embrace. "I hope you know you are always welcome here."

As she turned to go, Clare added, "I hope one day you shall understand the full weight of what you have done in respect of Georgiana and Mr. Wickham."

Sofia held her hand to her heart and bowed her head gravely. "Anything for my friends," she said, then peered up at Clare with a sly grin. "Now promise you will not say a word to Georgiana about your knowing."

It was a promise Clare had no difficulty in giving. "Tell me," she said, "when do they plan to elope?"

"Oh, it cannot be until the autumn, sadly," replied Sofia. "She goes to Ramsgate soon and he is required to remain in town, business with the Army which he must conclude before the marriage can take place. It shall be a long and trying summer for them both. I know not how they shall bear the separation."

"How much sweeter will be the autumn then," offered Clare, "and the end of all their woes."

Lady Sofia repeated her delight in Clare's coming and sent her guest on her way. Clare did not think herself in any state to face Georgiana, and so walked some time in agitated contemplation through the streets and greens of Mayfair. How could the situation have become so dire without her notice? Did it require her immediate intervention? Mr. Darcy would be returning soon, and she could unburden herself to him then, and allow him to take action. He would certainly be more effectual than she could be. In Ramsgate they would be out of danger, yet Clare felt there was serious risk in delaying the revelation of the facts by any period. Mr. Wickham must be prevented, whatever the cost.

CHAPTER 33

Before his name had even been mentioned in Park Lane, Mr. Wickham was already in conference with Mrs. Younge below stairs in Berkeley Square. He stood, arms crossed, leaning against the wall of the small room, which was really more of a cupboard.

"I do not like this, Mrs. Younge," he said. "I am grown tired of this plan. I am grown tired of Georgiana already, and it has only been a few weeks. How shall I tolerate a lifetime of her company? She is so tedious, so dull. She is sweet and good, to be sure, but I find that does not suit me so well as you insist it ought to. And, what is worse, marriage to her shall make me brother to Mr. Darcy, who is ten times the bore she is. I shall be forced to hear his name every day of my life. I wish to be rid of him, not to bind myself to him."

Though she did not say it, Mrs. Younge was growing tired also—tired of Mr. Wickham's complaining and his apathy. She stifled her aggravation with a smile and said soothingly,

"Oh, Mr. Wickham, I know it must be hard. You deserve much more than little Miss Darcy. You ought to be able to choose a wife you like. But life *is* very hard. I should not have to pay my Tom's debts, but I do. You, however, have a door to freedom before you. All you need do is walk through it. Once you are married, Georgiana shall have no power over you. She may nag at you and cry every night when you do not come home, but she shall have no recourse. You may live your life just as you choose. It is true she shall be the only woman to be legally bound to you, but that legal bond will not keep you from being whatever kind of man you wish to be—indeed, the benefits of the union will all accrue to you."

"You are always so rational, Mrs. Younge," he said, resting his head against the wall. "But I am led by my heart, and I have no heart for this union, however much I may ignore it in future."

Mrs. Younge took a step towards him. "You must think of this as a very small investment for a very great gain. You shall see. A few months from now, you shall laugh at your hesitation."

Mr. Wickham looked down at her face, so full of reassurance and determination, and shook his head. "I do not think I shall laugh," he said. "Not with a wife so wanting in wit."

"Do not you hate Mr. Darcy?" Mrs. Younge continued, changing tack. "Was not it Mr. Darcy who turned Miss Bingley against you? Is not it Mr. Darcy who courts her now, and whom she intends to accept? Is not it Mr. Darcy who refused even to consider your application for the living that was left you by your godfather as your legacy?"

"Yes, though I *was* paid compensation in place of that living," responded Mr. Wickham.

"Yes, in your youth you were paid some money to leave Mr. Darcy alone and not to remind him of the obligation his father wished him to uphold in regard to your welfare. You were but young then. How could Mr. Darcy really believe that you could be satisfied for life with three thousand pounds? And now, when you have matured and wish to make your way in the world, he will not so much as hear you. He rejects you outright. His father would have helped you to that living, would have succoured you in your hour of need. He intended that you should be provided for. His dying wish to his son was that he watch over you, whom he loved so well. But this hateful son, so cold as to dissociate himself from one who was as a brother to him in his youth, so miserly as to refuse aid to one in need, so proud as to defy his father's dying wish, dishonours even the memory of his own father."

Mr. Wickham grew increasingly angry as she spoke. He began to pace the room, contemplating the wrong that had been done to him and growing in frustration with each turn as he could take no more than two steps without arriving at a wall.

"You should have been the Darcy heir, Mr. Wickham. You should have done much more with his wealth. You should never have forgotten those beneath you, never have slandered them and made them miserable."

"That is very true," remarked Mr. Wickham.

"How should you like to have Mr. Darcy utterly at your mercy? Should not you like to see *him* grovel as he has made you do? And what irony, what justice would there be in his suffering at the hands of you, the very object of his contempt?"

"You know I should like it above all things," he answered. "He has ruined everything for me. He should be my greatest friend and ally, yet he makes himself my enemy. He ought to promote my happiness, yet he thwarts it wherever I go. But what am I to do? I cannot force him to be reasonable. How is such a man to be worked on?"

"There is but one subject which Mr. Darcy loves above himself, one quarter from which Mr. Darcy can be pained more than any other. You have within your power the very means of tormenting and even ruining Mr. Darcy. And this weapon you yield is the very thing you are so anxious to throw off!"

Mr. Wickham stopped and turned towards Mrs. Younge, a smile slowly spreading across his face as he began to comprehend her meaning. "My dear madam," he said sweetly, taking her hands in his. "How patient you are with me in my simplicity. I could kiss you. Please forgive me. I have been such a fool."

"You shall marry her then?"

"How can I refuse?" He turned ceremoniously to the door and addressed it. "Mr. Darcy," he began with a flourish. "I shall need another five hundred guineas. No? No matter. I am sure Georgiana shall not mind taking in some washing to cover the bills. Oh, you think maybe you *can* spare it? Yes, bank draft shall suit very well. Much obliged, sir." He bowed to the imaginary Mr. Darcy then turned to Mrs. Younge, clapping his hands. "Oh, this shall be a bit of fun after all, Mrs. Younge. How he shall regret crossing Mr. Wickham."

The conspirators were interrupted by a knock on the door. Mr. Wickham opened it impatiently, revealing a maid with a letter in her hand.

"Post for Mrs. Younge." She handed the letter to Mrs. Younge, who took it and waved the maid away. Mrs. Younge opened the letter and scanned it quickly.

"Excellent," she remarked as she scanned the letter. "Come, I shall show you out."

As she led him to the servants' door, she handed him the letter, which he took and quickly reviewed.

"Excellent indeed," Mr. Wickham concurred, laughing as he refolded the letter.

"There is much to do," she said, taking back the letter and pushing him out of the door. "We will be seeing you presently?"

"You most certainly shall," he replied with a grand bow, tripping away gleefully as she closed the door behind him.

CHAPTER 34

When Clare returned home, she found the house buzzing with activity and Georgiana in her chamber packing.

"Whatever is happening? Are we being evicted?" Clare's levity was markedly artificial. Georgiana, focused on her task, did not notice.

"Oh, there is no cause for alarm," she said without looking up. "We have decided to leave for Ramsgate tomorrow. It is excessively sudden, I know, but we were only delaying in order to wait for my brother's return. Word arrived today that he will be absent for another month at least, and he insists we go on ahead without him. I am very sad to be leaving you and…" Georgiana paused and Clare suspected she had been about to say "Mr. Wickham." Instead, Georgiana finished her thought with, "…well, everything familiar. You know how I dislike novelty. I should be so happy if you were with me, but I would not dare to keep you from your brother, who will be arriving so soon."

"Am I to stay here alone until then?" asked Clare, feeling panicked.

Why did Mr. Darcy have to delay his plans at such a crucial moment? Of course he did not know there was any mischief afoot, and he believed he had left his ward in the best care. He did not know he had left his lamb under the watchful eye of the wolf.

"Lady Sofia," Georgiana answered, "has told me on several occasions that you may stay with her at any time if I am ever obliged to be out of town without you. I know she would be very glad of the company. I have sent word to her already. She shall send her carriage tomorrow for you and your things. I know you always want time to practice your drawing. It might be an excellent opportunity to put to use the sketching materials my cousin gave you." Clare flushed at the mention of the gift, which Georgiana still did not know had been returned.

"Where does your brother write from?" she asked, hoping to discover an address where she might reach him. Even if Mr. Wickham was remaining in London, Mrs. Younge would be with Georgiana, and that lady had shown herself as adept as the serpent.

"Oh, I believe the postmark was from Hampshire, or was it Hertfordshire? I do not recall. Mrs. Younge posts all my letters and always knows where to reach him, so I am afraid I never pay much mind to where he is. His friend Mr. Bingley thinks he may have found a property at which to settle—Netherfarm, or Northernfield I think—and the arrangements will tie them up for a few more weeks, perhaps longer. "

"I shall leave you to your preparations then. If I am to remove to Park Lane tomorrow, I must begin my own packing."

Clare went directly to Mrs. Younge, who was giving instructions to the housekeeper, and inquired how she might send a letter to Mr. Darcy.

"You wish to write directly to Mr. Darcy?" Mrs. Younge looked as shocked as she did suspicious.

"I do, and Miss Darcy tells me you have his current address." Clare was embarrassed to be openly proposing writing a letter directly to a gentleman, but she saw no way around it and her reputation in the eyes of Mrs. Younge was not of supreme importance to her in light of all she knew.

"I am responsible for the household," said Mrs. Younge. "I am sure I may do as much for you as Mr. Darcy might."

"I am afraid I really must speak to Mr. Darcy directly about this matter."

"Well, if you must write to him, then I suppose you must. I do not have the address at hand, and, as you can see, I am a little occupied at the moment, but I have some other things to send, so if you give me the letter I shall be happy to post it for you."

Here was an end to Clare's hopes. She could not entrust such a letter to Mrs. Younge, and she could think of no excuse for needing to post it herself. Mrs. Younge would surely not send any letter to Mr. Darcy now without reading its contents first, and, having once read it, would certainly not send at all. While Clare could still feign ignorance, she might have been able to make an unwitting ally of Mrs. Younge, but that time had passed. If Clare was to alert Mr. Darcy to the mounting danger his sister was in, she would have to find another way.

Georgiana may have been choosing her own fate, but Clare could not lay the blame entirely at her door. Georgiana was very young, and Mr. Wickham and Mrs. Younge were clearly very cunning. Clare was Georgiana's elder, and whatever differences had of late come between them, Clare still loved her friend, and felt some responsibility for her. If Mr. Wickham were to succeed, Georgiana would be lost forever.

CHAPTER 35

Early the next morning, Georgiana and Mrs. Younge left for Ramsgate, their farewells to Clare earnest and brief, respectively. Lady Sofia's carriage arrived shortly thereafter.

Clare hoped to find an opportunity as soon as possible to speak to Mr. Wickham, at his residence if necessary. It was a brazen thing to do, but she had spent a sleepless night in weighing her options, and finding that she alone could prevail on Mr. Wickham, she felt she must do so, though it be alone. If nothing else, she could at least confirm for herself that he was still in town as Lady Sofia had said, and had not followed Georgiana to Ramsgate. She was prevented from calling on him for more than two weeks by the breathless pace of Lady Sofia's social engagements, in which Clare was obliged to participate.

She convinced Lady Sofia to allow her to stay home one day, claiming a need for solitude and poetry and the gloomth of the indoors. Lady Sofia readily assented to such a sentimental request, and, when she left to pay her calls, Clare finally was presented with the opportunity to pay an important call of her own. She watched Sofia's carriage disappear out of sight, then hurried upstairs to collect her things. She was just on her way out again when the doorbell rang and she heard a most unexpected and unwelcome voice in the hall.

"Sir Leicester Crawley to see Miss Langford," she heard her cousin say.

She had been so occupied with Georgiana and Wickham that she had all but forgotten about Sir Leicester. Her immediate response to hearing him in the hall was a desire to return to her room and pretend to be indisposed, or out, or dead. But she did not. She chastised herself with a recollection of her mother's wishes and of her own distant hope that her distaste for him might alter with time and a more profound acquaintance. She told herself it was foolish to feel such strong aversion for one who had been so kind to her, and that a sense of obligation at least ought to prevail. Besides, he could not be put off forever. She recalled the suggestion of Georgiana, made in jest some weeks ago, to depart immediately for the seaside, and she wished that indeed they had left for Ramsgate that very day. They could have avoided the inevitable for a few months at least.

Clare descended the stairs, smiling as unconcernedly as she could.

"Sir Leicester," she said. "What a pleasant surprise."

"I am sorry not to have given you any notice of my coming," he began, removing his hat. "My mother tells me that ladies are in the habit of receiving calls at about this time, so I did not think of it. But it seems you are on your way out."

Clare looked at her reticule and gloves. "Oh, yes, I was, but that is no matter. It can wait."

"No, no, I do not wish to keep you from anything. Can I take you somewhere?" Sir Leicester looked down at his hat, and fidgeted with the rim.

"That is not necessary," Clare replied.

"It is nothing, really. The carriage is right outside. Just say where you are going and you shall be there."

Clare could not tell him where she was going.

"I was just going for a walk," she answered. This was not really a falsehood since she had intended to walk to Mr. Wickham's.

"Might I accompany you, then?" he asked. "A lady should not walk alone, if it can be helped. And my mother is always saying I ought to have more exercise."

Clare could think of no cause to exclude him—at least, no cause she could reveal.

With no other avenues available to her, she was obliged reluctantly to submit to Sir Leicester's request.

Sir Leicester returned the hat to his head and offered her his arm, without meeting her eyes. Clare was not accustomed to this side of her cousin. She had always thought he could benefit from a little reserve. His averted gaze gave her an opportunity to study him briefly. He was not handsome. His features were coarse, and his hands were bulky like the rest of him. He had good teeth, and his hair was not without hope. He certainly attempted to dress the part of a gentleman, and perhaps with the guiding hand of a tasteful wife, he might be made at least tolerably presentable, if not actually attractive.

They strolled through the gates into the park, taking a leisurely route through the trees towards the Serpentine. The heat of summer had arrived and the shade of the park was a welcome relief from the bright pavement. Sir Leicester walked at a remarkably slow pace, stopping occasionally to look up at the sun through the leaves, or around the park, remarking on the small number of people it contained. Clare painfully restrained her pace to his, all the while wishing she could run, wishing she could bring this charade to a swift conclusion and pursue her purpose with respect to Mr. Wickham. If her cousin could but show a little less indolence, she might yet have time upon their return. Concealing her impatience with a smile, she calmly remarked,

"I suppose most people have gone back to the country by now."

When at last they arrived at the water, in twice as much time as they ought to have taken, Clare was about to suggest they take the shorter route back when Sir Leicester asked her if she would sit for a moment. She did. He took a seat beside her and removed his hat, then placed it back on his head, then, quite sure of himself this time, took it off again and placed it in his lap. He tugged at the wrist of his gloves, momentarily tightening them before he decided to remove them, placing them first on the seat beside him, then on top of his hat. Clare simply sat through all his awkwardness, watching the water with her hands clasped in her lap. She found herself smiling with unexpected amusement at his fretting. Finally, he inhaled audibly and began to speak.

"I hope you will find it acceptable," he said in a low voice. "I have arranged for you and Crawley to be able to stay at Maplethwaite for as long as you may have need. I am sure it was a great shock when both your uncles went to their maker in so short a time, and I reckon they would have taken care of you, if they had lived. I have heard that your mother is not well, so I hope it will be something off your mind to have a home to go to, whatever might come to pass."

Clare cocked her head a little to the side and looked hard at him. She had expected him to be brash and bold in raising the subject of the gift of Maplethwaite. She thought he would manipulate her with it, but instead, he seemed embarrassed and apologetic. Could it be that he was truly a humble, caring soul and that the manners she had previously observed were merely a misguided attempt to appear important?

"It is far more than acceptable, sir," she said gently. "Ever since mother told me of your intention, I have been most anxious to express my gratitude. I only hesitated because I did not know whether it was a secret. It is a great thing you have done, and it will indeed be a great weight, not only off my mind, but also off that of my brother and my parents. Were they here, I know they would join me in thanking you most sincerely."

"Well," he said, finally exhaling fully. "I am so very pleased to hear you say that." He leaned back in his seat and visibly relaxed. His whole person seemed to lengthen as his anxiety departed. "You know, I have never been to Maplethwaite. Perhaps I will visit next time I am in the north. You can always come to Farrow Hall, you know. I mean, all of you, Crawley and your parents and everything. I should send you an invitation next time I am up there."

"That is very kind," said Clare. "Are you there often?"

"No, not very—to own the truth, I find the country rather boring. Mother spends most of her time there. No doubt, she would like to have a London season, but she is getting too old for that." Here, he leaned towards Clare and spoke in a whisper: "Please, don't tell her I said as much. Besides," he continued, straightening up again and resuming his jaunty tone, "she likes it at Farrow Hall—being a lady of a manor and all that. You could probably visit *her* there, even if I am not at home. I am sure she would enjoy receiving you all. I cannot say as I will be at Farrow Hall any time soon, though. I prefer Bath to the country. I am thinking of going there in the autumn. Plenty of amusement in Bath, and all the best people."

"I have never been myself," said Clare. "I did spend some time at Leamington Priors this winter with my aunt and uncle, though. It is not quite Bath, I grant you, but they do have some of the same society. I had hoped to go to Ramsgate with Miss Darcy for the summer, but I will likely travel back home after my aunt and uncle have come and gone from London. Crawley will be with them, which is why I have stayed behind in town."

"You should go to Bath in the autumn," Sir Leicester added enthusiastically. "You tell Miss Darcy you wish to go to Bath. I reckon Mr. Darcy could get you there, set you girls up somewhere nice. There are balls and parties every night, and a decent bit of theatre. And you shan't want for friends. I could introduce you to plenty of people. I would not forget my little cousin in such a place."

Clare suspected the sort of connections to be found in Bath were not such as she should wish to make, but thought the offer was kindly meant.

"Thank you, sir," she said. "I do not know what Mr. Darcy plans for the autumn, but I have never heard him mention Bath with any fondness. He will probably bring Georgiana home to the country after the summer, and I should return to Maplethwaite. I will be very glad to see my parents again. By then it will have been a year since last I saw them."

By this time, Clare had given up hope of getting to Wickham's and back before Sofia returned. It would take her at least an hour to walk there, and another hour to get back, plus whatever time she spent there. And upon her return, she would need some time to change and appear as though she had not ventured anywhere. There had barely been enough time before Sir Leicester arrived, and he had used up more than she could spare.

"Shall we return to the house?" she offered, rising from her seat. "I know it was not much of a walk, but I would enjoy some tea."

"Enough of a walk for me," replied Sir Leicester, "especially in this heat." He hoisted his lumbering form into a standing position.

Clare had found it rather cool in the shade beside the water, but in all his rich clothing and all the bulk of his person, she supposed he would find any bit of temperature oppressive.

Although it was hardly ten minutes' walk back to the house, Sir Leicester was short of breath enough from the exertion to make conversation impossible until the tea was served in the drawing room.

"I don't suppose you have any ice?" Sir Leicester asked, looking about himself as if he expected to find a block behind the sofa.

"I really do not know what there is, sir."

"I reckon I could get some. All the best houses have ice," he said. Clare feared he was about to send his servant to purchase some, or worse, demand that the staff search the cellar.

"I am sure I saw some advertised in Oxford Street," he said. "You should come and see me when your brother comes, and bring your aunt and uncle. We shall have ice. I will get you some."

"I am sure they would all like that very much," Clare responded with the utmost sincerity, for she knew all three to be always keen on receiving hospitality and novelty, and all the more so from a Mayfair gentleman with a title.

"Very good," he said, adding, "I hope you shall spend much more time at my table in future, you know, as you wish."

Clare wished not even to contemplate, much less discuss, her future at his table and whatever else he might have intended. She continued as though failing to catch his meaning.

"The next time I write to my mother, I shall certainly pass on your invitation to visit Mrs. Crawley at Farrow Hall," she said. "I imagine she would be very happy to accept. It was her childhood home, after all."

"Depending on when she goes, she may find it even better than she left it. Mother is planning some improvements. She is a lady of very superior taste, you see, and wishes to make it as elegant a home as possible. She is planning a considerable improvement to the grounds."

"Improve the grounds?" Clare repeated. "But they were designed by Capability Brown."

"I hope he will not take offence at the alterations," he responded, unmoved. "Mother thinks it a little drab as it is. She plans to add a reflecting pool and an ornamental garden, and possibly a labyrinth."

Clare had not thought anyone interested in such designs since before even her mother's time.

"And where does she plan to put these gardens?" she asked, wondering how they could be made to work with the existing landscape of gentle asymmetry and peaceful slopes. The incongruity of the scheme defied any taste, archaic or otherwise.

"Oh, in the orchard—or rather I should say, where the orchard is at present, for that must all go first."

Clare's puzzlement turned to disbelief. "The orchard is to make way for a labyrinth?" She could not imagine anyone of even the meanest sense doing such a thing. It seemed almost criminal.

"You do not approve," said Sir Leicester curiously.

Clare looked down at her tea, measuring her words. "It is not for me to approve or disapprove what you do with your own home. I find it an unusual choice; that is all."

Sir Leicester grinned. "My mother does have unusually elevated taste. I confess I would be lost without her guidance

217

on matters of fashion and the like." He looked down at his garish waistcoat. "You may not guess it," he said, "but I have no sense of style myself. I would never have known what to order from the tailor, nor how to put it all together, if she had not directed everything."

It was not in Clare's nature to laugh at people, but she was sorely tempted by this last remark. She thought, if she were driven to marry this ridiculous man, her consolation would be the salvation of Farrow Hall and possibly Sir Leicester himself from the dictates of his mother's wayward notions of elegance.

When Sir Leicester's visit was quite concluded, which, due to the gentleman's want of perception, was some time after it ought to have been, Clare watched him struggle to hoist his unwieldy frame into the carriage. As he drove away, waving his stout hand at her with exaggerated humility and feigned grace, Clare wondered whether, in time, she might see beyond what she believed must all be the work of his mother, and discover in him a man worthy of her affection. She felt such affection was still a great distance away. His manners were so unsuited to the man she knew him to be, a man capable of such thoughtfulness and condescension as to give up Maplethwaite for the benefit of her and her brother, who were nothing to him and who could offer so little in return. It taught her not to trust to first impressions when it came to a person's true character.

CHAPTER 36

Several days passed before Clare again found herself alone in Park Lane. She meant not to waste another moment in making her way to Mr. Wickham. The instant Lady Sofia's carriage disappeared around the corner, Clare set off on foot across the city. Passing through the glaring streets, her anxiety increased. What might she say to Mr. Wickham if she were fortunate enough to find him at home? What would her mother say about her presenting herself alone to a gentleman at his rooms, or even about her traversing the city alone? What might become of Georgiana if she failed to prevent her elopement with this rogue? She arrived at her destination fatigued and a little disheveled, but with courage in her heart enough to overpower her discomfort as well as her nerves.

Upon applying within for Mr. Wickham, she was told that he did not usually receive ladies at that hour.

"Does not usually receive ladies?" she repeated. "Is he in the habit of receiving ladies to his room then?" she asked.

The servant curtseyed and shook her head. "I'm sure I don't know, ma'am," she said with a confused and embarrassed smile.

"Of course," Clare said impatiently. "But I really must speak with him. Will you please tell him I am here?" She took a calling card from her reticule and held it out to the servant.

"I am sorry, ma'am," said the servant without taking the card. "He is not usually about at this time, and he gets ever so cross if I rouse him."

Clare put the card away again. It was past noon, but if she must yet wait for Mr. Wickham to stir, then she would do so.

"I will wait then. What time will he be prepared to receive visitors?" she asked.

"Usually about one o'clock," the servant answered, "but he won't be receiving anyone here today."

"Perhaps if you tell him that I have come, he may consent to see me," said Clare.

"I'm afraid that won't be possible, ma'am," said the servant, curtseying again.

"And why, pray tell, is that?" asked Clare, in the closest she ever came to a rash tone.

"Why, he ain't here."

Clare's considerable irritation gave way to panic.

"When do you expect him back?" she inquired, hoping he might only have failed to come home the previous night, or be absent for some other reason unconnected to Georgiana.

"I an't sure, ma'am," replied the servant. "He's been gone some weeks already. Gone to the seaside he is—Margate I think, or was it Ramsgate? It definitely wasn't Brighton because I asked him to say hello to the Prince for me if he happened to see him, but he said the Prince only went to Brighton."

Without taking her leave, Clare ran from the house and back up the pavement in the direction she had come. The servant called after her, asking if there were a message to leave for Mr. Wickham, but she did not reply.

Her mind raced with the weight of her discovery. She had been negligent in her duty to Georgiana and to Mr. Darcy. She ought to have found a way to reach him when she first discovered Mr. Wickham's plan. What if it were now too late? She ought to have known Mr. Wickham would not remain in town while Georgiana was so unprotected in Ramsgate.

What must she do now? She must find a way to reach Mr. Darcy. She could take the post to Ramsgate and plead reason with her friend, but could she undertake that journey alone, and if she did, would she meet with any success? To walk across London in daylight and call, alone, on a single gentleman was hazardous enough, but to travel by public conveyance to the seaside without friend or companion seemed prohibitively daunting.

Clare returned to Park Lane in a distracted state. Upon entering the house, she cast about as if for some clue as to how to proceed. In so doing, she caught sight of a calling card left in the tray, which had been empty upon her departure. The name on the card was Ashwell. She picked it up and turned it in her hand. On the reverse, he had written,

"Should Miss Langford require anything while my cousin is away, I am at your service."

Clare stared at the card. The handwriting was elegant and neat. Could she go to Lord Ashwell? She saw little alternative, and, collecting herself, set out again, this time towards Grosvenor Square. Her head was full of questions on the short walk through Mayfair. Would he know how to reach Mr. Darcy? Would it be worse to place herself at his mercy than to ride the post alone to Ramsgate? Was his assistance any more likely than Lady Sofia's? Whatever the case, she knew she must exhaust every avenue in aid of her friend.

Cautiously, she rang the bell. A minute or so passed. She rang again. A suspicious-looking servant slowly opened the door. Clare could hear coughing from within the house.

"Miss Clare Langford to see Lord Ashwell," she said.

The servant stood without responding, taking in her ragged appearance with a look of wary suspicion at finding a single young lady at the door. Clare handed him her card. The servant took it, studied it silently, then looked back up at her. She raised her eyebrows at him impatiently, and reluctantly he said,

"This way, madam." He showed her into the drawing room where he asked her to wait for her host. His Lordship, moments later, came hastily into the room.

"Miss Langford, this is unexpected."

Clare rose from her seat to greet him, and immediately sank back down. Her fatigue, her anxiety and even her hunger conspired to exhaust her. Had she been able to rally herself against these forces, she would have been prevented by the flood of emotions that attacked her as Lord Ashwell rushed to her side and, kneeling beside her, took up her hand in his.

"Miss Langford!" he cried in alarm. "Whatever can be the matter?"

Clare found herself momentarily unable to respond. Despite all her cares and her exhaustion, she could think of nothing but the cool and gentle touch of Lord Ashwell, which convinced her instantly that she could never be happy with Sir Leicester.

"May I bring you some refreshment? Some wine perhaps?" offered Lord Ashwell. "Or are you hungry? I was just sitting down to some bread and cheese, but I can send for something more fitting." Without allowing Clare to answer, he ordered the servant bring the wine and a plate of something. He did not say that he had left his friend, Sir Francis Peabody, in his study. Neither did he tell her how it affected him to receive the unexpected announcement that Miss Langford was at his door.

"Thank you, sir," Clare finally managed, withdrawing her hand and seating herself more upright in her chair. "I am sure I am quite well. I am sorry for troubling you. I would never have presumed to—it is only, I have just tried everything else, and, well—" she struggled to hold back her tears.

"Miss Langford, please," he interrupted her. "If you are quite well as you say, then this agitation shall certainly cure you of it."

"Do you know how I might reach Mr. Darcy?" she asked, barely able to calm herself. "I mean, do you know where he is staying just now? I know he is in the country with Mr. Bingley, only I have no way of finding him, and I must write to him on a most urgent matter. I did ask Mrs. Younge but, you see, I could not give her a letter because...well...it is no matter. Do you have an address for Mr. Darcy? That is what I need, if you have it, please."

"Of course I shall furnish you with Mr. Darcy's address. Clearly, you are in need of it. You may write your letter here and now if you wish, and I shall dispatch it this very night. But may I be of no further assistance?"

Clare's tears finally burst forth spontaneously at such sympathy and condescension. She knew Lord Ashwell to be a wicked man, but all she could see in his expression was humble self-effacement and sincere goodwill. In such an hour, when she felt so friendless and desperate, she found in Lord Ashwell the genuine concern and wish to be of honourable service that had been so wanting elsewhere. Her emotion overwhelmed her in the face of this unexpected kindness.

"Please, Miss Langford, do tell me what this is about." He handed her a handkerchief. "You must accept it this time." She did.

"It is Georgiana. I fear she may be in very great danger. I have tried every approach to prevent it: I have spoken to Georgiana, but she will not hear me, and all warning has only pushed her further from me, making it impossible to help or even advise her. I have attempted to enlist Lady Sofia's help, but her head is so full of sentimental nonsense that she actually favours this…this catastrophe. Mrs. Younge, who is supposed to be guarding her charge from exactly this sort of thing, is, as far as I can tell, in league with Mr. Wickham.

"Today, I walked all the way to his lodgings to attempt to talk him out of it, though I cannot see how I could have affected him. But I shall never know that for certain, for he is gone to Ramsgate already. It may, in fact, be too late. So you see, I must write to Mr. Darcy immediately. It is the only way."

"You walked to Mr. Wickham's house?"

"Yes."

"Does not he live on the other side of the city?" Clare nodded. "Why did not you order the carriage, or hire a cab?"

"I do not have the authority to order a carriage. I could never be so bold. And I haven't money for a cab, as well as the tolls."

"You would present yourself unchaperoned to a gentleman at his lodgings, yet you have not the boldness to order a carriage. You are remarkable, Miss Langford." He looked at her with admiration. "But what is this about Georgiana being in danger?" he asked. Relieved to unburden herself, Clare gathered her strength and shared all she knew.

"Oh your Lordship, it is too terrible. Mrs. Younge has taken Georgiana to Ramsgate, and Mr. Wickham has followed after. He has been seeing Georgiana in secret for weeks, and I believe he plans to elope with her from Ramsgate. He is so cunning, I am sure he shall succeed. And there is no one to stop him, that is, unless I can bring Mr. Darcy here immediately, for I know Georgiana will obey him where she would not heed my advice."

As she spoke, Lord Ashwell's already fair complexion whitened. He stood and walked quickly to the door, calling out for Sir Francis then walking just as quickly to a writing desk in the corner of the room and scribbling something on a piece of paper. Sir Francis entered the room in confusion. Lord Ashwell handed him the paper saying, "Send a courier immediately to Mr. Darcy at this address in Hertfordshire. Tell him to come instantly to Ramsgate and inquire after me at the post office. I shall leave word there for him of where to find me. There is no time to explain. It is of the utmost urgency."

Sir Francis stood for a moment in awkward silence, before he turned on his heels and strode out of the room.

Lord Ashwell turned to Clare. "Come, I shall return you to Park Lane. You have done very well to tell me about this. Georgiana is more fortunate than she knows to have you for a friend. I shall leave forthwith for Ramsgate, where I shall stall things until Mr. Darcy arrives."

"But how can I rest in ignorance of what is happening?" Clare asked. Lord Ashwell paused.

"But of course you cannot. You must come also. That is obvious."

Lord Ashwell walked to the door, calling out to the servant in the hall. "Sully, fetch the lady's things, and have Robert bring the carriage round. Oh, and fetch Maria, would you." Then, returning to Clare and assisting her from her chair, he added "she might as well have something to do for her wages. Maria shall be a fine companion for you. She is a lady's maid."

"A servant?" asked Clare.

Ashwell took Clare's things from Sully and helped Clare with her pelisse. As he put on his own coat, he answered her.

"Well," he said, "she is in my service, but she is, in fact, a great lady, who fell on hard times in her native France after the Revolution, or, at least, that is what she told me when she applied here, which induced me to hire her, even though there are no ladies here whom she can serve. No doubt she deceives me, but it affords me the distinction of being the only gentleman in London with his own lady's maid."

Maria came downstairs and was ushered out to the carriage. Lord Ashwell left instructions that, among other things, a message was to be sent to Lady Sofia stating that Clare would not be joining her that night, due to her having run away with a band of gypsies.

CHAPTER 37

For most of the journey from London, Clare could pretend sleep. However relieved she felt for his assistance, she thought it imprudent to display too much gratitude to such a man as Lord Ashwell, and she spoke as little to him as possible. For a time, he slept, and she watched him, studying his face, so full of goodness and sincerity. She could understand entirely how Miss Grey had been taken in by him, but she could not imagine how it was possible that he could have treated her so ill. His good nature extended even to the smallest gestures, yet in such a great matter he had played such a villain.

Maria slept most of the way, and Clare was inclined to believe that was how she spent most of her days as well. The silence of the carriage was therefore almost exclusively interrupted by Lord Ashwell's repetitious coughing which Clare thought grew louder and more frequent as the hours passed.

The night was spent in a quiet, draughty inn at Gillingham, from which they departed early in hopes of reaching Georgiana and Wickham by evening. Clare continued her act of fatigue, and kept her eyes closed for the first leg of the journey. She was not entirely deceptive, for she truly was weary, but her state of anxiety kept her quite alert. When the carriage stopped at Sittingbourne, she was forced to abandon her mock sleep and she took in her surroundings. As they took some air while the horses took their refreshment, Clare avoided the gaze of her traveling companions, but when she chanced a look towards Lord Ashwell, she was struck by the dark shadows beneath his eyes and the pallor of his complexion. She had only seen him in dim light the previous night and had not noticed any alteration in him then. Without the sounds of the carriage to drown it out, she could hear now how craggy and laboured his breathing had become since the day before. It had been a late night and a restless one for everyone, no doubt, and even Clare could feel that the air in the inn had been bad.

"Are you quite well, sir?" she inquired.

"I can never truly call myself well, I am afraid, but you need not be concerned. I have survived far worse than this." Lord Ashwell turned suddenly from her, doubling over in a relentless bout of hoarse coughing.

"Let us just step into the inn for some tea. I am sure it would do you well to warm yourself and have a drink." Lord Ashwell may have been a blackguard, but Clare could not but have compassion for any of her fellow creatures in distress, particularly when they had risked their tenuous health in aid of her friend.

"Please," he said, "do not trouble yourself. It is nothing, or at least nothing to which I am not accustomed. We shall stop again at Faversham for a little longer and we may take tea there. For now, let us carry on. We must get to Georgiana as soon as possible, and there is a long way to go yet."

A few minutes later, they were back on the road. Clare looked out of the window, eager to arrive at their destination and occupied with her own failure to prevent this state of affairs. Her own feelings had prevented her from approaching Lord Ashwell for assistance, and she regretted this omission deeply. After a few minutes' reflection, she chanced a look across at Lord Ashwell, who had leaned against the wall of the carriage and closed his eyes in sleep.

The rig pulled up to an inn at Faversham. Clare and Maria, both eager to stretch their limbs, descended from the carriage, but Lord Ashwell did not stir. Clare asked the footman to rouse him.

"Lord Ashwell!" the footman called, climbing into the carriage himself to see to his master.

"Lord Ashwell, Lord Ashwell!" the footman's voice grew louder until his face emerged from the carriage, clearly in a panic. "Miss, he is not waking up miss. He seems very hot."

Clare froze, stunned by the sudden gravity of the moment, then collecting her wits, looked about for someone who ought to take charge. There was no one besides herself. Maria and the footman both looked at her and, with a steadying breath she began to give direction.

"Ask the driver to help you bring Lord Ashwell into the inn," she said to the footman. "Maria, go inside and tell them we need a room on the ground floor, that it is most urgent."

Before Clare had finished speaking, Maria began to sob.

"No, no" she cried. "What will I do? The master cannot die. Where shall I go? Who shall be kind to me now? This cannot be. It cannot be."

Clare left her to fret and went herself into the inn where she saw Lord Ashwell settled into a room, sent for the apothecary and led Maria inside to the tea that she had ordered. She then asked for writing supplies and began a letter to Mr. Darcy explaining their current predicament. Not knowing where he would be at that moment, the best she could do was to send her letter to the post office in Ramsgate and hope he would receive it there when he called for his cousin's address.

The apothecary came, cursorily examined Lord Ashwell, and recommended that the patient not be moved that day, nor probably for several days. He departed with a promise to return in the morning, leaving a tonic to be administered every three hours and an exorbitant bill the exaggerated amount of which Clare attributed to his learning of the nobility of his patient. Clare would see how Lord Ashwell responded to the treatment before determining whether to admit him again or not.

There was nothing for Clare to do but wait. Her anxiety at being forced to sit idly, knowing the treachery which awaited Georgiana in Ramsgate, was unbearable to Clare. She sat staring out the window of her room. She was joined by Maria, who sat on the bed, and their mutual silence was punctuated only by the occasional sound of Lord Ashwell's violent coughing in the next room.

"I wish we were not trapped here," Clare mused aloud. "My friend needs me, and I have failed her so shamefully already. If only I could reach her."

"But you must not leave!" the maid implored. "We cannot abandon the master. He should never abandon us. No, it would not do. I shall not go. You shall go if you must, but I shall stay with his Lordship, though I can be of so little use."

Clare wondered how such a man could inspire such loyalty in his staff while being himself so callous and disloyal. She looked at Maria, so trembling and desperate. She walked over to her, sat beside her and took her hand.

"Of course I shall not leave," she said. "But tell me, how is it you are so devoted to his service, though you are a lady's maid in a household with no lady?"

"But of course!" Maria looked up, eyes wide. "Lord Ashwell has been very kind to me. He took me on with the excuse that I might assist his mother when she was in town, but she has only come once since I have been there. She is a great lady, and I should have served her well, but of course she brought her own maid with her, as one might expect."

"Lord Ashwell tells me you were once a great lady yourself."

"My mother was a great lady in France." Maria did not show any sign of artifice or hesitation but spoke quite plainly and simply. "Her father was a Peer of France. My father was from a noble English family, and they met in Paris at the start of his Grand Tour. My father expected to inherit a Barony, including the family seat in Oxfordshire. His cousin, the Baron, was elderly, single and childless. All believed he would be dead by the end of the year. My father married my mother on the strength of his expectations. Asylum from the revolutionaries was reason enough to quit France. When they arrived in England, they discovered that the Baron had secretly married a young widow who was carrying a child by him. The child was discovered upon his birth to be a son, and so my father was disinherited at the last. My mother's property in France had been seized, and so my parents were left with only a small annuity between them. They moved from London to Surrey, where they could live more cheaply, and where my mother was able to tutor a few young ladies in French. I was their only child, and my mother taught me the manners and ways of courtly life, though I never saw any of it for myself. Two years ago, she left this life to be with God, and I left my father's house to go into service. Lucky I was to have been so well trained, for I had nothing else to recommend me and would have been fortunate to be a scullery maid." Clare thought Maria must either be an excellent liar or a very exceptional case.

"It is an unlikely story, I know," Maria responded with a shrug to Clare's incredulous expression, "but it is true. If I were to invent a history, I should more likely be believed if I made up something less dramatic, but I never could lie with any skill, and so I must be disbelieved by everyone. I applied so many places, but when I told them I was descended on one side from a baron and on the other from a Peer of France, everyone took me for a brazen liar – that is, everyone but his Lordship. He allows the world to believe he is duped by me and by all his staff, but really it is he that he is too humble to admit his own kindness and generosity to us."

Clare could not reconcile this description of Lord Ashwell with his behaviour towards Miss Grey. How could he be so kind to his servants, and yet so cruel to a lady of fortune and breeding? How could he be so generous in private, and yet so demonstrably wicked in the matters so significant to his reputation? Clearly, something was amiss.

Clare began to wonder whether there really was anything more she could do besides bide her time and administer the questionable tonic left by Mr. Sparks. She knew of no other medical professional, or really anyone of any description, within dozens of miles, and the only recommendation that was provided by the inn was of Mr. Sparks, in whom she had little confidence. She considered whether she did have any acquaintance in the vicinity when it came to her quite suddenly that Faversham was not 10 miles from Rosings Park. She wondered at herself that she had not thought of this earlier for surely the de Bourghs employed the best physicians in the country to care for Anne and of all people they would be most keen to furnish the means of preserving the Fitzwilliam heir.

Not quite up to addressing Lady Catherine directly, Clare addressed her letter to Anne, writing it hastily and dispatching it by courier. Clare left it to Anne to arrange the details of the matter, all of which was done with more ease than the highest hopes could wish. Lady Catherine had gone to London for the week to oversee the purchasing of furniture and draperies for the rectory. The new rector had lately arrived and was discovered to be the most grateful recipient of all her Ladyship's officious condescension. Consequently, Anne could send for the physician without any suspicion or interference from her mother.

Dr. Marsh arrived shortly after sunset, going directly to his patient, whose bedside he did not leave all night. Two hours after the physician's arrival, the inn was again in a fuss, for Anne had decided to profit by her mother's absence and follow Dr. Marsh to Faversham, with Mrs. Jenkinson and a whole band of staff in tow.

Despite the boldness of this action, Anne's demeanour was as reticent as always. She did not seem eager to see her cousin and retired promptly to a private room for the evening, ordering that some supper be sent to her there and leaving Clare to wonder why she had come at all.

CHAPTER 38

Dressed in pure white, her mother's amber cross about her neck, Georgiana welcomed Mr. Wickham into the small but well-appointed drawing room where she and Mrs. Younge had been awaiting him.

"You look nice," he began.

His flattery was hollow. He thought she looked rather plain. Simple dress like hers was elegant enough on a dainty, pretty girl, but on Georgiana, whose face was more pleasant than it was beautiful and whose stature was more grand than it was delicate, a touch of decoration would, he thought, go a long way. With her wealth, she could afford to dress so as to dazzle all Ramsgate; he wished she would. He was tired of always being seen with such a dull creature. When they were married, he would ensure she was always more fittingly adorned. A little lace, perhaps, and a few jewels might make her presentable.

Georgiana smiled and blushed a little. "Thank you," she said quietly.

She was still somewhat in awe of Mr. Wickham, and, even after months of courtship and a direct proposal, she could still hardly believe his interest in her. She would never have thought herself worthy of such a man's notice—so handsome, so charming, so universally admired as he was. Everywhere they went together, she felt every other young lady must long to take her place. She had but to take one more step with Wickham, and she could look forward to a lifetime of such envy.

"Come," he said, offering his arm with a flourish. "Your carriage awaits."

They departed the house, followed by Mrs. Younge. Mr. Wickham helped them both into their seats, then walked around the carriage.

It had been a warm day, and the evening breeze off the sea was fresh and invigorating. As the smell of the sea struck him, Mr. Wickham felt a burst of hope for his future. He leapt up into the driver's seat, taking the reins and offering them to Georgiana.

"Would you like to drive?" he said with a playful smile.

"Oh," Georgiana looked at the bridle, then up at Mr. Wickham, exceedingly vexed not to be able to accept. "I do not think I could," she replied, "That is, I do not know how."

Mr. Wickham's smile hardened. His burst of enthusiasm was gone as quickly as it had come. Turning away from her he said flatly,

"No, of course not."

"Perhaps you could teach me, some other time, you know, when we were not driving through crowded streets," she offered, a pleading strain in her voice. When he did not reply, she lowered her head.

"Are you angry?" she asked.

He forced himself again to adopt his cheerful tone. "Impossible. How could I be angry? I only thought it might be a bit of fun. I only wish for you to enjoy yourself."

"I enjoy being with you," she replied.

She watched him as he expertly manoeuvred the carriage through the crowded streets, the evening sun showing his profile to full advantage; she saw in him a man of the world, a man whose spirit and courage she would have to learn to match if she wished to hold on to his love. She knew that he had been little pleased when she had shown herself to be timorous, and she felt that she was sure to lose him if she continued to be so.

Looking squarely at him, she said in a clear voice, "I will do it."

With a grin returning to his face, he pulled the carriage to a halt and offered her the reins. Georgiana did not take them, but looked up at him earnestly. He turned to face her in skeptical understanding. Taking up both her hands, he felt them tremble in his.

"Can you be serious?" he asked. "You will accept me? You will be mine for all the days of our lives?"

She smiled and nodded, growing giddy with the thrill of her boldness. "Yes," she said. "And it must all be as you said—Gretna Green and everything." She clasped her hands to her face and added, "It is too much. I shall faint."

Mr. Wickham lifted her hands from her face and kissed them both.

"Do not fear," he said, his breath quick and shallow. Looking back over his shoulder towards the house he asked, "Should we leave now?"

He had waited over a week for her reply. He had spent every day and almost every evening with her since she had come to Ramsgate, an arrival that had been preceded by weeks of clandestine meetings and secret messages, every acquiescence a battle. At every stage, she had asked to inform her brother of their growing attachment. She wished to tell Darcy about his coming to Strawberry Hill, about his visits to Berkeley Square, about his coming to Ramsgate. When he proposed, her first words were of her brother. He had told her that she must make up her own mind, that if she were to become his wife, she could not always seek her brother's approval on every matter. This had been a constant theme of their courtship—that she was too reliant on her brother's judgment, that she must become independent of him if she were ever to become the woman she wished to be, the sort of woman he could truly love. He had even threatened to leave if she wrote to Darcy. She had agreed to make up her mind about the marriage without consulting her brother, but here she was consenting to an elopement. To say he was impatient to seize upon her sudden acceptance was greatly to understate the matter.

"We need only pack a few things. We can be gone in an hour

or two."

Georgiana looked at Mrs. Younge, then back at Mr. Wickham. "Tonight?" she said. "It is rather sudden." She paused and looked towards the sea, then back towards the house. "The sun is going down," she mused. "We cannot get very far before it becomes too dark to travel, or at least I would not like to travel through the night. Cannot we go to the ball tonight, and celebrate together? We can leave at daybreak tomorrow. We shall have the whole day to travel, and we shall be properly prepared."

It was not difficult to convince Mr. Wickham to stay one more night in Ramsgate. He had been looking forward to the ball that night. There was to be some good sport at the card tables, and some agreeable society.

All happily agreed, therefore, to enjoy one last evening's revelry before embarking upon their fate in the morning.

CHAPTER 39

Ramsgate's pious few were just departing from Vespers when Mr. Darcy raced into the town, driving at unconscionable high speed and attracting the impertinent remarks of more than one by-stander. Mr. Darcy had no interest that could have caused such rash and imprudent conduct on his part, save the well-being of his sister, who he was thoroughly convinced was in very grave danger. Though he knew not from what quarter she was threatened, he left nothing to chance. Despite Lord Ashwell's reputation as a frivolous character, Darcy knew him to be as genuinely concerned for the welfare of young Georgiana as he himself was. Therefore, when the courier had brought him a note from Grosvenor Square—a note of such brevity and poor penmanship that it was clearly despatched in great haste—he did not hesitate to act immediately under Ashwell's vague instructions. Ashwell was, the note said, en route to Ramsgate, and he asked Darcy to meet him there without any delay, which he instantly set off to do, stopping only to change horses, which he insisted be driven at top speed. He slept only in the carriage, and that only in short and restless bouts, the jolting of the carriage and his anxiety for Georgiana keeping him mostly in wakeful discomfort.

So disheveled was he upon presenting himself at the house he had let for the summer that the servant who opened the door., and who had never before seen Mr. Darcy, refused to grant him admittance and required that he produce his card before allowing him to be the master of the house.

"Where is she?" Darcy snapped as he strode into the hall, looking about him as though she might be concealed somewhere on the premises.

"She is not in at the moment, sir," the servant responded, terrified that he was about to find himself ejected from the house.

"Yes, but where may I find her?" Mr. Darcy repeated, turning once more to the luckless servant, who was still not entirely convinced that this hot-headed and bedraggled creature could really be the proud and reserved Mr. Darcy of Pemberley.

The servant considered his reply a moment and determined that the harm that could come to him if a gentleman who already knew Miss Darcy's address located her at a public ball was greatly outweighed by the harm which might be his if he thwarted the actual Mr. Darcy from finding his sister as he seemed urgently desirous of doing. He answered,

"I believe she and Mrs. Younge have gone to a ball. You will find them at the assembly rooms."

Without a word, Darcy returned to his carriage and continued his pursuit. He applied for admission on arrival at the assembly rooms, but he was denied due to his attire being found wanting, particularly the state of his gloves. He thought he might try another door to see whether he might at least steal a look inside and attempt to locate his sister. He found just such a door at the side of the building, through which he could make out a corner of the dance floor. Georgiana happened, at that moment, to be occupying that very quarter of the room. She seemed in good health and good spirits, and in fact more care free than he thought he had ever seen her. Knowing her to be very shy of strangers, particularly gentlemen, he wondered who her partner was that could set her thus at ease in a setting in which she had never before shown anything but awkwardness.

It was only a moment before Mr. Darcy learned the identity of her partner, for as the dancers turned in an allemande, an all-too-familiar countenance came into view. For a moment Mr. Darcy stood, stunned, watching his sister and Wickham dance together. He could see now why his cousin had written to him in such haste. He knew the signs of infatuation well enough to see that he had arrived not a moment too soon.

Behind Wickham and Georgiana, another familiar face soon appeared. Mrs. Younge, who should have been protecting Georgiana, was watching with seeming delight as Mr. Wickham whispered in her charge's ear. Rather than sheltering her from the mischief of that gentleman, Mrs. Younge appeared to be abetting him.

Mr. Darcy addressed the servant at the door.

"Please, you must let me through," he insisted. "It is of the utmost importance."

"Of the utmost importance?" the servant repeated, arching his eyebrows. "What? Shall you perish if you do not dance this evening?"

Mr. Darcy reached into his coat pocket. "I am not accustomed to being spoken to in this way," he complained with rugged impatience. "Here is my purse," he handed to the servant a pouch heavy with coins. "If I do not return in five minutes, you may keep the lot."

The servant took the purse and, before he could make any reply, Mr. Darcy pushed past him, knocking him into the doorframe. The dance had concluded, and Mr. Darcy caught Mr. Wickham's eye through the crowd. He was standing with Mrs. Younge, but Georgiana was not with them. Mr. Wickham froze for an instant, then turned quickly towards the door, jerking Mrs. Younge away from her conversation.

"Brother!" Georgiana's voice rang out through the ballroom. Mr. Darcy turned to see her rushing through the room towards him. All around, heads turned to watch the scene, which included Georgiana's would-be partner who stood in a state of confused abandonment.

"Georgiana," he replied, as she threw herself with alacrity into the warm embrace of her beloved brother.

Overflowing with exuberance and questions and delight, she did not see Wickham and Mrs. Younge depart from the room and drive hastily away in the carriage.

"But where is Mrs. Younge?" Georgiana cast about the ballroom for her companion, "and ..." she did not say Mr. Wickham's name. "Never mind; we shall find them presently. How is it you are here? I did not think you would arrive for another fortnight at least."

"Come," he said sternly, leading her from the room. "We must go."

"But what about Mrs. Younge?" Georgiana asked. "She will not know where I have gone."

"I have seen her already," replied Darcy, without looking back. "Never mind her for now."

Mr. Darcy could not bring himself to force upon her the painful truth. The true reason for his sudden appearance in the ballroom would be revealed soon enough. For now, he offered only a sympathetic smile.

They passed out of the assembly rooms, Darcy collecting his purse from the servant as they went, neither remarking nor caring that it was half the weight it had been when he had given it.

Georgiana was all questions as they left the ballroom, but Mr. Darcy said very little as he led her to the carriage. It was a strange sight as the two departed together, one with such a brooding countenance, the other evidently in the gayest of moods. As he helped her into her seat, he broke his silence.

"Come," he said, "let us return to the house. We can light the fire and you can tell me everything over some bread and cheese, for I have not had any supper yet and I am too weary for anything else."

Unaware of the grave reasons for which her brother had so unexpectedly appeared in the assembly rooms, Georgiana believed his grim demeanour to be the result of his fatigue and she did not wish to try him with excessive chat. And so, though her heart was full, she matched his silence as they rode through the town. Georgiana still expected Mr. Wickham to call on her later and she rejoiced in having her brother to herself on such intimate terms. When she and her brother had both been young, and when their father had been away from home, their mother occasionally allowed them to sup on bread and cheese by the fire—no governess, no servants, just her and her brother at ease. On such enchanted evenings, she told him all the secrets of her heart, all her juvenile dreams and fears; he would simply listen to her, not advise her and not laugh at her childish ideas. It was a rare treat to be excused from the formality that ever presided at Pemberley and those occasions comprised some of her most precious childhood memories.

Georgiana was very glad to be given such an invitation to unburden her heart once more, for it had long been full, and she had wanted the freedom to break the secrecy which Mrs. Younge and Mr. Wickham had enforced. Now that everyone would be gathered in one place—so she thought—all misunderstandings could surely be addressed, and the two men she loved most in the world could be made brothers both in spirit as well as in law.

Although the night was warm, Mr. Darcy ordered a fire, and brother and sister sat together over their simple meal. Mr. Darcy attempted to sate his diminishing appetite as he listened to the whole story of Mr. Wickham's duplicity towards his innocent and unspoilt sister.

As she spoke, Georgiana overheard herself making excuses for the increasingly obvious improprieties of Mr. Wickham and Mrs. Younge. By the end of her tale, she could not help but see her folly in the plain, unflattering light of the facts. She was particularly struck by her refusal to heed the advice of her friend, Clare, in whose judgment and whose love she had always trusted, and who had been such a friend to her. Had she but listened to Clare, and not to her vain imaginings, all of this might have been avoided.

She raised her eyes to her brother's. Seeing his frowning face, she quickly looked down again, knitting her hands together in her lap.

"I am afraid I have played the fool," she said quietly. "You must think very little of me to be so easily convinced to act so disgracefully, but I swear I would not have been party to any scheme I did not think you would approve in the main. I am sorry. I never thought I could be so foolish. I have caused so much distress for you, whom I only ever meant to please. Everyone seemed so certain that it would all end happily, well, everyone except Clare. She knew nothing of it, of course. She would have prevented it, but I was persuaded that she must not find out, and I am afraid I have let it come between us— she who would be my only friend."

"Dear child, do not rebuke yourself," said Mr. Darcy, placing his hand on hers. "I am as much to blame as you, for it was I who left you in the care of Mrs. Younge, who has, I think, done more to bring these things to pass than even Mr. Wickham. He has been long in the world and is very skilled in the art of deception. He is a ruthless man, and we must all be on our guard against wickedness of his kind. I believe, in fact, that it is out of malice towards myself that he chose you as his victim. You see, I would not allow him to take the living at Kympton which Father promised him, in part because he did not meet the conditions to receive it, but mostly because, a few years ago, I compensated him very generously for giving up any claim to it. He must have spent the whole sum already. I ought to give you a lecture of sorts, tell you how careless you have been and what trouble you have caused, but I believe you feel it all too keenly already. Believe me, you are not the first and no doubt will not be the last victim of Mr. Wickham's brand of avarice."

With these words, Georgiana was flooded with misery. The love she had borne Mr. Wickham was premised on the false apprehension of his regard for her. Knowing what she knew now, it was clear that he did not care for her at all. Though she knew him to be unworthy, it did not diminish the wound in her heart, to which was added the shame of having been so easily duped. She was utterly wretched.

Unwilling to be expose her tears even to her own brother, she excused herself and removed to her chamber where she could unleash her anguish to her pillow in private.

CHAPTER 40

Dawn brought to Mr. Darcy the recollection of Lord Ashwell, who had been quite forgotten in the previous day's events. He dressed quickly, had tea and toast in his room, and passed Georgiana on the stairs as he was making his way out.

"Good morning, Brother," she began. "Where are you rushing to?"

"I quite forgot that I must go and find Ashwell."

"Find Ashwell?" Georgiana queried. "Whatever do you mean?"

"I must let him know I am arrived and that I have found you."

"Is he really here?" she asked, following her brother down the stairs. "Oh, do let me come with you. I feel so wretched and have no appetite for breakfast. I was only coming down to table to sit with you. It would do me so much good to see Ashwell. He always improves my spirits.

"Come then," said Mr. Darcy, hoping that seeing Lord Ashwell would indeed do her good.

They made their way to the post office, where Lord Ashwell had said he would leave word of his location, but instead, Mr. Darcy found the message Clare had sent for him from Faversham.

"What is the matter?" Georgiana saw her brother's expression alter as he read the note.

"We must go at once," he replied. Faversham was nearly 30 miles away. There was no time to lose.

Brother and sister departed forthwith. Georgiana wondered that Ashwell had left London. He does not travel, and a seaside resort could hold little appeal for him since he does not dance and does not enjoy going out in general. Could his proximity to Ramsgate be somehow related to her own self? It was only once they were driving out of town that Georgiana was able to apply to her brother for more information, though she sought more to allay her fears as she had already guessed the truth.

Mr. Darcy sighed heavily. "We are going to Faversham," he said. "It is there that we shall find our cousin. He is the cause of my coming here, for he wrote to me saying that I was to come to Ramsgate as quickly as possible. I expected to find him here, but the note I received this morning states that he is laid up in Faversham and is not well. That is all I know. I wish it were better news, but such is not the case. You know enough of his condition to understand that this cannot bode well."

Georgiana's heart was strong, having lived through the death of both her parents at such a young age, but on the heels of the disappointment of the previous day, the prospect of yet another tragedy, of her losing yet another beloved family member, this was too much for her. Her head began to ache with the strain of her tears, which began to roll once again down her cheeks. Mr. Darcy placed his arm about her and handed her his handkerchief. Strong emotion always left him even quieter than usual, and little was said by either passenger for much of the journey.

By the time they reached Canterbury, Georgiana's grief had run its wearying course; her mind drifted from the tragic objects which had been occupying it, and she began to wonder at Lord Ashwell's intervention. How had he learned of Mr. Wickham's plans when such pains had been taken to keep them secret? She did not think Lady Sofia would have told him. Indeed, she did not think Lady Sofia even knew Mr. Wickham was coming to Ramsgate. Georgiana herself had been ignorant of his coming until Mrs. Younge had admitted him to the house one evening. God willing, Lord Ashwell would be well enough to answer such questions by the time they arrived.

Quite a large party met Darcy and Georgiana as they pulled into the Faversham inn. Mr. Darcy had worried that his cousin, away from all the comfort and company of home, should be suffering quite alone. In addition to Clare, whose message he had received at the post office that morning, there was also Lord Ashwell's lady's maid and even less explicably, Anne de Bourgh and her constant companion, Mrs. Jenkinson.

He was pleased, however, by the relief it brought his sister to be reunited with her friend, who rushed to greet her as soon as they saw each other.

The circumstance of their reunion must excuse the fervour of it, even in such a public place. Georgiana mistakenly believed the day could hold no more tears for her, but they were renewed afresh as she embraced her friend.

"My dear Clare, what providence is this that I find you here? I am so wretched and undeserving, and yet here you are, as always, so constant and such a solace."

"Do not cry. It is I who am relieved to see you, for I worried it may have been too late."

"Too late?" It took only a moment for Georgiana to comprehend the truth. While it was her cousin who had sent for her brother, it was her friend, Clare, who was responsible for her salvation. It was she who had revealed the difficult truth to Lord Ashwell, and it was this that had compelled him to hasten to her aid with an abandon that had placed his very life in danger. It was Ashwell's letter to Darcy that had brought him to Ramsgate, but Clare's intervention had urged the writing of it.

"Oh Clare," cried Georgiana, "what have not you done on my behalf? What have I put everyone through? I shall never forgive myself."

Clare led Georgiana up to her room with many assurances that all would soon be well, that the affair with Wickham had been prevented before it had done any great damage, that any trouble she had taken upon herself to prevent the elopement brought happy returns with her safe and sound, and that Lord

Ashwell would be quite well again after a few days of rest. Georgiana hoped rather than believed that there was truth in Clare's soothing words, but she knew that such hopes with respect to Lord Ashwell were feeble.

Clare, too, knew better than to be sanguine. She had seen Lord Ashwell's state in the carriage—his pallor and his limpness when he was carried into the inn. Dr. Marsh, whatever his skills, had been anything but optimistic in his prognosis. He refused to make even the smallest of promises concerning Ashwell's recovery. Clare kept all this from Georgiana, of course, for pessimism, however justified, could not ameliorate the truth. Georgiana was already agitated, and further bad news could not but have ill effects.

Mr. Darcy, ever more pragmatic than his sister, immediately drew Dr. Marsh aside. The news was not promising. The good doctor had spent every minute since his arrival ministering to his patient, and, by the time Mr. Darcy and Georgiana arrived, he had already reached the limits of his art. The air out of doors was good in that place, particularly given its proximity to the sea, and, the evening being a warm one, he recommended that the windows be opened to allow the bad air in the room to escape, but the rest, he advised, was out of his hands.

The fresh air did seem to improve the patient's breathing somewhat, and, by nightfall, he had fallen into a deep sleep. And yet, all braced themselves for the calamity. At Clare's suggestion, the ladies attended the church to offer prayers for Lord Ashwell's recovery as well as for his soul. While at the church, Maria took the liberty of advising the priest that, before the night was through, his services might be required at the inn.

CHAPTER 41

The ladies found the inn very quiet on their return. Mr. Darcy was sitting up with Lord Ashwell, Maria went straight to her room to keep her own vigil and Georgiana found herself too spent to stay awake any longer. Clare and Anne, having spent most of the day in captive anxiety, expected not to be able to sleep immediately and so sat up together a while, a deck of cards untouched between them.

Clare found herself no better a conversationalist that evening than her companion, and the silence continued for some time as each of the ladies remained absorbed in their own reflections. Clare was carried off by thoughts of the gentleman who had shown her such kindness and who had made such a sacrifice for his cousin, who was her dearest friend. She did not wish to be as attached to him as she had discovered herself to be. She had very rational cause to believe he felt nothing for herself. His father was an earl and hers was an admiral. That alone was sufficient cause for him never to think of her, and if the story she had heard from Sir Leicester were true, it was not likely his heart would be easily touched.

Yet he did think of her at least once when he sent her the gift which she had felt obliged to return. She suspected more and more that the story she had learned from Sir Leicester must have been materially incomplete if not inaccurate and that her friend had advised her well not to pay heed to old scandals.

If the tale were not as it had been represented to her, if Lord Ashwell were as kind and generous and humble as he had always appeared, then she must regret all her coldness towards him with more than a common regret for she should not have another chance to redeem herself if he should go that night.

Her grief turned to torment at this thought, and were it not for the consequence to his eternal soul, she would have wished him the evil perpetrator which her cousin had represented him to be.

These thoughts and others turned in her head until the sound of heavy footsteps returned her to her surroundings.

"Is Georgiana gone to bed?" Mr. Darcy inquired, approaching the two ladies.

"Yes, she is. I believe it has been a very trying day, or two days, for her," replied Clare, "as it no doubt has been for you." Georgiana's welfare and Lord Ashwell's health had so occupied Clare that she had not stopped to consider the stresses that Mr. Darcy must have borne.

"May I?" Mr. Darcy indicated a chair close to Clare, who nodded her assent and turned her chair towards him as he sat with a fatigued sigh.

"Wearied as I may be," offered Clare, "I am afraid I can never sleep after a day such as this—not without some time to sit and allow my nerves to settle a little."

"Please accept my apologies for your having been brought into all of this business. I owe my sister's whole future to you. It is a debt I suppose I shall never be able to repay, but I beg you will allow me to make you some amends for your trouble."

"Please sir. Georgiana is my dearest friend. There is no debt. Were I in peril, I know she would come to my aid without hesitation, and her friendship is compensation enough for my trouble. It is to Lord Ashwell that we are all truly indebted." Her voice caught on his name as she spoke it. "Have you come from seeing him? Is he improved at all?"

"He has been coming and going from consciousness since I arrived. He has been ill a long time, many years in fact, and I believe it had been getting worse in recent months, though he has never seen an episode such as this. Dr. Marsh speaks of it as a final battle, a crisis, and time alone will reveal the victor. In a spell of wakefulness, he asked me to thank you for coming to him, for allowing him to be useful in Georgiana's salvation. He spoke very admiringly of your courage and your faithfulness."

"Oh?" Clare's veil of disinterest was thin. She wondered whether Mr. Darcy could hear as loudly as she could, the sound of her heartbeat in her ears. Seeing the interest in Clare's expression, Mr. Darcy chose to convey the whole of what his cousin had confided in him, that Lord Ashwell's last hours might be made a little sweeter for it.

He leaned forward in his chair and she leaned in towards him. She followed his eyes as he glanced towards Anne, who sat staring in silence at the fire. Looking back at Clare, he began in a low and confidential voice, "I believe Lord Ashwell regards you in a light that your modesty conceals from you. In his lucid moments, it has been you, not Georgiana, whom he has most keenly enquired after. Indeed, once I had assured him that his cousin was out of danger, you were the only subject he would discuss. Does it surprise you to learn that he has made arrangements for the comfort of you and your brother?"

Clare's mouth fell open. Her silence being answer enough, Mr. Darcy continued.

"From what I can gather from him, he made these arrangements some weeks ago. If you seek the root of his concern, you must look for it elsewhere than his gratitude."

Clare could scarce draw breath so suspended was she by this information, and so confused by this reference to arrangements for her comfort, of which she had never before heard. She began to ask, "Would he wish me to...that is to say...would it be proper...would the circumstances be such as to excuse the impropriety of...is the hour too late..."

Mr. Darcy spared her the effort of marshalling her thoughts into a sensible utterance.

"I shall confirm with Dr. Marsh that the agitation would not endanger him further and that the moment is favourable. I shall return presently."

As Mr. Darcy exited the room, Clare sunk into her chair, then suddenly remembering that she was not alone, turned to Anne to see if she showed any indication of having heard her conversation with Mr. Darcy.

"I am sorry," Clare began, "to have taken such private counsel in your presence. I hope I have not offended you."

"No" was all the return that Clare received. With no one else to whom she could speak her feelings, and in desperate need of a confidante Clare continued in spite of the listener's apparent indifference. She described to Anne the dilemma she faced: should she judge Ashwell in the light of her own knowledge of his conduct or that which she had learned from others?

"You must mean that business with Miss Gray, as was," Anne offered without looking away from the fire. "I am sure everyone is forbidden to speak on it, but since no one ever considers that I might know of it, much less speak of it, no one has ever bothered to forbid me, so I shall tell you."

Clare was quite shocked at the alacrity with which Anne entered onto such a subject, but then considering who her mother was, she really had only Mrs. Jenkinson and the flowers to instruct her in the ways of delicacy and sympathetic conversation. Fortunate it was for Clare that, though Anne remained silent in the face of the most meet and common subjects, she was ever ready to discuss all matters relating to the far less likely topic of family scandals.

"Ashwell loved Annabelle. Even when they were both children, he loved her, but she never returned his love, and, as many times as Ashwell proposed, she refused him. She was not very affected like so many ladies who undertake to marry him at every dinner table he eats at, and I would hazard a guess that is why he liked her so well. Anyway, what the world does not know was that she fell in love with a sailor she encountered one summer, walking on the Cobb in Lyme. For all her modern ideas, they knew her family would never permit her to marry him, and it was a great secret. Her parents did not even know he existed. And then, as you might predict, she finds herself fallen from grace and she was with child and knew not what to do, because she would be disinherited and banished from all society. So she goes to her old friend Ashwell, who, honourable and constant to a fault, says he will have her, child and all, knowing full well that she loves him not. And for the sake of her child, she accepts him. A hasty wedding was arranged so that her child might not be a bastard, but still Annabelle could not be happy. I believe she endeavoured to be, and that, in those months, she loved Ashwell—though it was a grateful love, not a passionate one—but she was always so sentimental, and Ashwell could see that she was unhappy and would ever remain so, so he gave her up and let everyone believe he was the cause of her condition, which forced her family's hand. They considered her the victim of a perfidious scheme, and they spread this story far and wide, forever tarnishing Ashwell's good name.

"In the end, Annabelle got everything she desired. Her parents offered a substantial dowry to any that would have her. Her sailor emerged, not as her destroyer, but as her saviour. They were married immediately, and they are even now raising their child together in the country. It is still widely assumed that Ashwell is the father of this child. Annabelle's position has always been that the child is her husband's, which of course it is, but the layers of deception are such that everyone takes that one truth to be the lie. If her family were ever to learn the truth, they would cut off all support leaving her and her sailor destitute, for he has not been so lucky in the wars. Rather than ruin one that was once so dear to him, Ashwell continues to bear all of the shame and scorn that society can heap on him."

Anne took up her tea and said no more. Clare sat in stunned silence for some time before managing, "Can this really be true, that he should allow his reputation to be so sullied for a woman who never loved him?"

"I do not say that I understand it, but I suppose he is entitled to do what he likes with his reputation, for he has weathered the scandal far better than she would have weathered the shame of her affair. I know you must think it very shocking of me to tell you such long-held secrets, but I confess, I only reveal them to you because of how fond Ashwell obviously is of you. I know what he has done for you and your brother and it is no common act of gratitude. Even if it were, it was done before he knew he had any cause for gratitude, so I have deduced his motive must be love. You might gather from what he has done for Annabelle that he is all for great acts of selfless sacrifice."

With every utterance, Anne grew in fascination to Clare, such an unsuspected trove of hidden knowledge she was revealing herself to be.

"You are sure to learn of it soon enough" Anne continued, not requiring encouragement. "He has purchased from your cousin, Sir Leicester, a life interest in Maplethwaite for you and your brother. From what I hear, Sir Leicester was grateful for the ready cash as well as for the opportunity of appearing magnanimous, for the business was to be a secret and you were not to know the true source of the gift. However, since Ashwell does not seem long for this world, I see no harm in telling you the truth."

Anne had spoken in the plainest tone news of the weightiest significance to the listener, and Clare could not but begin to sob. Her affection for Ashwell was not only justified but returned. Her home would remain her home, unencumbered by any debt of gratitude to her distasteful cousin. Lord Ashwell must not die before she could beg his forgiveness for the offense she had given him, thank him for what he had done for her, and return in full measure his love.

Clare was barely able to compose herself before Mr. Darcy returned to the room and advised that it would now be opportune for her to visit Lord Ashwell's bedside.

CHAPTER 42

Clare followed Mr. Darcy down the dark and noiseless hallway towards Ashwell's room. She held her breath as he slowly opened the door, and ushered her in, past Dr. Marsh, who rose silently to acknowledge them. Mr. Darcy held the only candle in the room, but after the darkness of the hall, it seemed brightly illuminated for the large casements were flung wide, allowing the full light of the moon to enter with the fresh night air, warm and fragrant with the scent of summer.

Clare could see Lord Ashwell's face, outlined in silver light, and hear his craggy breath. His eyes were closed and he lay very still. She took a step towards him and froze when the floorboards let out a loud creak. Her eyes darted towards the physician and back to Lord Ashwell whose face cracked into a faint smile.

"I am awake," he whispered without opening his eyes.

Clare opened her mouth to speak, but did not know what to say.

"I have brought Miss Langford, as you asked," said Mr. Darcy, lighting a bedside candle with his own. Lord Ashwell's smile broadened. Clare curtseyed out of habit. Turning to Dr. Marsh, Darcy added, "Come doctor, let us leave them a few minutes."

Dr. Marsh followed Mr. Darcy from the room, stopping in the doorway and turning back to Clare to say, "Do not let him speak too much. It causes him to cough, and then he cannot stop." Clare nodded and the door closed. She stood, frozen in her place at the foot of the bed. She could not find words to speak, and she was too overwhelmed by emotion to move.

After a moment, Lord Ashwell stretched his hand out towards her. Instantly she stepped forward and took it in both of hers, kneeling beside the bed. "Oh sir," she said. "I know not how to begin." Lord Ashwell remained motionless, eyes closed, but his breath deepened, as though he were breathing her in. "You have been so good," she said, "and I had got it all wrong, and now who knows what may happen." Her voice caught on her words and she began to cry. Ashwell opened his eyes and slowly turned his head towards her. She could see, even in the dim light, that his eyes were red from the effort of coughing. His mouth formed the word "no" and he faintly shook his head.

"Please, you mustn't speak," she said, her voice breaking. "You must not exhaust yourself. Let me speak instead. There is so much I wish to say." She took a deep breath. Though the room was warm, she felt herself begin to tremble. "Allow me firstly to thank you for your incomparable gift. I know that you have given me Maplethwaite for life. There is nothing I can imagine that could be more thoughtful, more generous. I shall be forever grateful. And this, after I was so cold to you. I shall never forgive myself for having believed gossip over what I knew in my own heart. I have just learned the truth about Annabelle, and I am ashamed to have doubted your goodness when there was so much evidence of it. Will you please forgive me? I could never live with myself if I had not your forgiveness."

Ashwell searched her anguished face.

"I am sorry," she struggled to say. "I shall not ask you any more questions, for you must not answer them."

A warm breeze wafted in through the window and he breathed it in deeply. Clare felt him squeeze her hand as he shook his head. "There is nothing to forgive," he whispered.

"Hush," said Clare, raising her hand to stop his speech, holding it, quivering above his mouth.

With his free hand, Ashwell reached up and took Clare's

hand, bringing it to his face and kissing it. "Clare" he whispered, pressing her hand to his heart and holding her gaze. He spoke all in a rush and barely audible. "You must know that I love you. Let me die happy; say that you will marry me, or that you would have if I had lived. It is my final wish."

"Yes!" Clare exclaimed without hesitation. "Yes, I should marry you this instant if I could." She leaned in to him. "But you shall not die. I forbid it."

He reached up to touch her face. "Sweet Clare," he said, "if I live it shall be your doing. And if I do not, it shall not be for want of effort." He smiled as tears escaped from his eyes and rolled onto his pillow.

"Dear sir," she said, wiping them away with her hand. "Your tears are too costly to be spent on me, for if the doctor prohibits speaking, surely weeping is out of the question. You have asked me to make you happy, and I have consented. Now you must be happy." Clare's own tears had already soaked the coverlet.

"I am sorry," said Lord Ashwell. "A prostrate proposal is rather indecorous."

"No more talking," Clare rebuked gently, holding a finger to his lips. "You must be well presently. Think of the years we shall have to fill with conversation."

The door creaked, and Clare sat back from the bed, but Ashwell would not release her hand. She looked up at Mr. Darcy as he entered. Mr. Darcy stopped, looking between them with a stern expression. Lord Ashwell only smiled in sorrowful apology. Dr. Marsh passed by Darcy and walked towards Clare saying –

"That is quite enough agitation. The patient must rest now. Come." Clare stood with unsteady limbs, Ashwell still clinging to her hand. He only relinquished her when Dr. Marsh led her away from his bedside. The couple did not look away from each other even as Darcy led Clare out of the room, and only when the door was closed could she turn away to face the dark.

CHAPTER 43

The sun rose on a restless and tormented Clare Langford. Her fears and her anguish made her wish the past days to be a dream, while her wonder and her anticipation made her long for confirmation that they were not. She had not slept but lay on her bed listening through the wall for the sound of Ashwell's breathing, and drenching her pillow with her muffled sobs. As the early light began to brighten the room, she finally succumbed to sleep.

When she awoke, it was breakfast time. She arose, said a prayer for her beloved and made her way to Georgiana's door. She knocked and was invited in. She entered to find her friend sitting upon her bed, head bowed in somber contemplation. Clare crossed the room and sat beside Georgiana, the elder letting the younger be the first to break the silence.

"I cannot help but conclude that my regret shall haunt me all the days of my life and beyond," Georgiana began without looking at her friend. "How could I have been so foolish? My brother tells me Mrs. Younge and Wickham have gone from Ramsgate now. I doubt I shall see either of them again. And now I must bear the weight of my cousin's demise. Lord Ashwell is the kindest and best man I have ever known save only my brother, and in my folly I am afraid I have endangered him. There can never be forgiveness for me." Georgiana did not look up, unable even to weep at her fate.

"I saw Lord Ashwell last night," said Clare, her voice hoarse. Georgiana looked up at her in a surprise which deepened at the

255

sight of her, in yesterday's dress, her hair tangled and her face swollen and wan.

"Oh Clare!" she exclaimed, placing her hand on her friend's.

"I shall not raise your hopes by saying that he appeared improved." Clare's speech grew faster and her voice began to break as she continued. "He did not seem so, and now I am in such suspense, for I must tell you that my whole happiness depends upon the outcome." Clare withdrew a handkerchief, smiling amidst her tears. "I am afraid the truth is too incredible even for me to believe without scepticism. I hesitate to voice it aloud lest it should prove false in the telling."

"Whatever do you mean, Clare?" Georgiana asked. "Dare I hope that I should have cause to wish you joy at such a time as this?"

Clare nodded, and her smile widened to engulf her tear-soaked face. After a moment's speechlessness, Georgiana embraced her friend and, in the warmest terms, assured her that this was the most incredible, most wonderful news that she could imagine.

"Please say it aloud, Clare. Utter it and make it real, for you seem as unable to believe it as I am."

Drawing a deep breath, Clare stated with hesitation, "He has asked me to marry him, and I have accepted."

Georgiana clapped her hands over her mouth to stop from crying out. "But how can this be? Oh, my dear Clare," she said, tenderly straightening her friend's hair. "I never thought I could have *more* cause to pray that my cousin should live. But now I must redouble my prayers. He must live. Surely God is too merciful to deprive you both of the happiness which He has only just bestowed." Georgiana's eyes grew moist at the contemplation of Lord Ashwell's death. Clare looked earnestly at her friend.

"If he should not survive," she said softly, "you must know that I, at least, shall not begrudge you, for without this episode I should never have learned of his love for me, nor of my own for him. And if his hold on life has been so fragile as to break under such light strain as one night in a draughty inn, then he was never long for this world. At least this way he may spend the last hours of his life in a happiness which would never have been his but for these circumstances. I only wish I had trusted in my own heart, which has always known his goodness. If I had done, perhaps we might have been brought together before now, and under less trying conditions. But one cannot tease apart the regrettable outcomes from the happy ones in matters such as these."

The two sat in contemplative silence for several minutes before Clare suggested they descend for breakfast, if only to distract themselves from the weight of their own hearts.

The table was a silent one. Anne and Mrs. Jenkinson were characteristically mute. Georgiana, Darcy and Clare sat in suspense awaiting news of Lord Ashwell, stirring sugar into the tea they could not swallow, spreading jam on the toast that lay, unbroken on their plates. After several anxious minutes, Dr. Marsh appeared, asking Mr. Darcy to follow him into the next room. Georgiana and Clare sat frozen for well-nigh twenty minutes, their hands clasped tightly beneath the table, until Mr. Darcy returned and requested that Clare follow him. She darted unapologetic from the table and hastened towards Mr. Darcy, who, with a nod, granted Georgiana's unspoken request to join them.

They all three entered the room to find, to their amazement, Lord Ashwell, sitting upright in his bed, a breakfast tray, now empty, just being cleared away. On setting eyes on his smiling face, Clare rushed forward to his bedside. Georgiana took Mr. Darcy's hand and led him from the room, motioning for Dr. Marsh to follow them and leaving the couple to experience in private their first moment of unmitigated happiness.

"Good morning, my dear. Did you sleep well?" said Lord Ashwell, suppressing a grin. "I must say, I did, and it seems to have been just the thing. You know, I feel so much better than I did yesterday."

Clare was unable to match his lighthearted tone, and indeed unable to utter a syllable of sense. Lord Ashwell, seeing her thus affected, abandoned his mock triviality, and, with tender sincerity, he took her hand in his and addressed her.

"Dr. Marsh says I am out of immediate danger, but it will be some time before I shall even be able to leave my couch. I am afraid I shall not make you a very good husband, at least not for many months."

Clare shook her head and wiped her eyes with the very handkerchief which he had given her back at Grosvenor Square only two days past, though it seemed in her memory to have been in another age entirely so much had altered in her heart and in her life since then.

"The doctor says I am daft, but I insist that it is due to you that I have come through this. My prospects were very grim yesterday. Dr. Marsh believes it is all due to the air here being so beneficial, but I believe I should not have woken this morning had not you given me both cause to struggle so against death and the strength to defy it. When you accepted me, I was determined that I should never give in to illness and forfeit your happiness as well as my own. The world may find many a fault with me, but I hope that want of a strong and affectionate heart is not one of them."

Clare smiled. "I believe the world should be very hard pressed to find any fault with you except perhaps that you are too good, and too quick to set your heart on the likes of me."

Lord Ashwell threw his head back in a release of laughter. "Ha! Were I not already devoted to you, I should wish to become so, if only to shock my relations, which gives me such joy. There are some who call my cousin Darcy proud, but they have seen nothing to compare with Lady Catherine's ill-founded ideas of her own superiority. For what has she that you do not? A title and a large income? In marrying me, you shall surpass her in both of these; but she shall never have your goodness, your faithful heart, your brave spirit. Let the world say what it will. They cannot harm me with their opinions."

From that moment, all anxiety and fear left Clare's heart and she felt only a dizzy elation which heightened every perception of beauty and made her wish her own delight on all the world.

CHAPTER 44

Mr. Darcy could only be persuaded to leave the couple unchaperoned for a few minutes before rejoining them. He could not bring himself to approve the match. He disliked the idea that an admiral's daughter could be elevated to the station of a countess through marriage into his own family. However, he could not speak against it. He could say nothing against Clare herself, and, for gratitude's sake, he also could deny the lady nothing. If it had not been for Miss Langford, his sister—and by extension, he as well—would have been united with Wickham, which union would have been dire in its consequences. More important still, Lord Ashwell's decision as to whom he should marry was his own. His love for the young lady appeared in all ways to be genuine, as did hers for him. Perhaps, in receiving his addresses so favourably, she had also been Ashwell's salvation.

And so, in the jubilation over Lord Ashwell's recovery, even Mr. Darcy found himself in a benevolent and joyful mood and, in spite of himself, he allowed his heart to feel only happiness for his cousin, and to sincerely wish him joy.

Dr. Marsh insisted that the patient be allowed to rest, and the happy crowd relinquished his company in favour of his health.

Clare and Georgiana returned to their breakfast, indifferent to its having turned cold. The pair sat alone at the table the until well past noon, talking over the events of the last few days.

"I must say, your cousin Anne may be the most curious

creature I have ever met," said Clare. "She said not a word to me from the time she arrived two days ago until last night, at which time she proceeded, almost unbidden, to reveal family secrets of the most shocking nature."

"Family secrets?" Georgiana repeated.

"In essence, your worthy cousin has been allowing himself to be defamed in order to protect a friend" responded Clare. "You remember the scandal you warned me not to credit? I learned the truth of it last night. Lord Ashwell was once prepared to marry a young lady whom he loved, despite knowing she was carrying another man's child. When that was not enough for her happiness, he let her go, forcing her family's hand and enabling her to marry her lover, while the world believed him to be the child's father and a blackguard of the worst kind. In the years since, he has done nothing to correct the rumours lest doing so might turn her family against her. Can you imagine it?"

Georgiana stared at her friend. "That is astonishing!" she said. "And you learned all of this from Anne? Incredible!"

"I can no more account for it than you can, but she has explained so well the circumstances which gave rise to the scandal, that I must believe her either to be in earnest or to be very skilled in the art of contrivance, for her account seemed so likely that I, at least, have wagered my future on the truth of it." After a moment of reflection, she continued. "I will say, that as his wife I shall not see such wrongs continue to be perpetrated against him, though they be at his own instance. He is such an exceptional creature; he must not allow himself to be so demeaned. I may risk hypocrisy in so saying, considering his condescension in marrying myself."

"My dear Clare," said Georgiana. "My cousin does not demean himself in the slightest by choosing you, whatever the size of your dowry. The wealth and consequence of your character surely exceed the value of twenty high-bred ladies."

Clare knew better than to expect such a welcome reception from the rest of the world, but was willing to indulge herself in the hope of it with her friend, and many magnanimous and unlikely things were said on the subject before Clare remarked upon the state of her appearance, and retired to her room to make herself presentable.

Clare dressed, and sat upon her bed, where she remained for most of the afternoon, her head resting on the wall that separated her from Lord Ashwell, and her heart feeling the length of every minute she was out his company. She considered with mixed apprehension and relief the grace that had spared both Georgiana and Lord Ashwell. One more day would have seen Georgiana lost to Wickham, and without the attendance of Dr. Marsh, the local apothecary may well have seen Ashwell to his grave.

Many letters were dispatched that day, and the recent events were gone over many times by all those assembled. As evening fell, Clare felt the weight of fatigue from the emotion of all that had passed, but she found, as she lay on her pillow, that many questions kept her from sleep, and that all such questions were in relation to Anne, whose timely revelations had played such a significant part in Clare's fortunes. How had Anne become so knowledgeable on subjects so seemingly beyond her sphere? The intimate details of Ashwell and Miss Gray's affair, the arrangements regarding Maplethwaite, Sir Leicester's involvement in the same—how had she come upon all this information?

Perplexed by these questions, Clare slept very little that night. In the morning, she sought Anne out and asked her directly how she happened to know so much about the secrets of Ashwell's household. Little ruffled by the enquiry, Anne responded simply and directly.

"I can take no credit for my information. I learnt it all from Miss Peabody," she said.

"Miss Peabody?" Clare repeated.

"You are acquainted, I believe, with Sir Francis Peabody?" Clare nodded.

"His sister, Emily, is a dreadful gossip," continued Anne, "or I should say she would be had she any audience besides myself. Her parents never let her out into society as she is very pretty and unspoilt, and they fear for her exposure on any terms to men of the world. She comes to town every spring as her parents will not leave her alone in the country and her mother cannot survive without taking in the London season, but she chiefly remains in the house or on tightly supervised constitutionals with her governess. I was introduced to her by chance when there coincided the two rare events of my being in town and her being permitted to join her brother in dining with us at our house there, which she was only permitted to do because there was nobody to stay home with her. Her usual companion had just been transported for theft, and so she came and sat with me and Mrs. Jenkinson upstairs. In general, she relies solely on her brother for news of the world, which he readily supplies, though I wonder if he would do so as freely if he knew it were all being sent on to me in detailed letters. I do read them all, though they are long and frequent and often tedious. Still, they are something of a diversion from the monotony that is my life at home and I have even on occasion had cause to reply to a few of them, so I suppose we could be called correspondents."

"And it is from her that you learned the truth regarding Miss Gray and Lord Ashwell?"

"Yes. Lord Ashwell confides in no one more than Sir Francis. No doubt he was sworn to secrecy, but I suppose he saw little harm in telling his sister—who he assumed had no avenues by which she could spread this information any farther. Indeed, until the night before last, only Sir Francis, Emily and I were privy to it. I am not abroad in society much more than Emily is and had you not spoken of it, I might have carried Lord Ashwell's secrets to my grave, for I have never otherwise heard the subject raised in my presence."

"And what about Maplethwaite? Did Miss Peabody inform you of that also?"

"She wrote to me about that the night you left London. She said her brother came home quite troubled. He had gone to Grosvenor Square to act as a witness for the transfer of interest in the estate from Sir Leicester to you. It seems Sir

Leicester has been spending well above his income since inheriting his title, and he was quite happy to be handsomely paid to give up his claim to a property he did not need, particularly as he was not required to give it up entirely. Lord Ashwell wished also for you to have the adjoining lands, to provide some income, but Sir Leicester would not consent to transferring anything that might earn him some money. The three men were gathered in Lord Ashwell's study with the solicitor when you arrived and interrupted the proceedings with more pressing concerns. When I heard that everyone was gathering here, so close to Rosings, I thought I might come and see for myself how it would all end."

As odd as she found Anne to be, Clare was undeniably grateful to her, for had Anne not shared the truth with her, Clare should have gone on struggling against her heart. She would not have gone to see Lord Ashwell in his room that night, and would not have allowed, much less accepted, his addresses. And who knows what effect her acceptance did indeed have on his health. The patient himself seemed convinced that it was the chief cause of his recovery, and though she would not advance the claim herself, she could not deny the salutary effects of the discovery of their mutual affection. Perhaps it was Anne after all who should be credited with saving Ashwell's life.

Anne left that same afternoon, so that she might return to Rosings well before her mother and avoid being missed at all. The vacancy she left was quickly filled thereafter by Colonel Fitzwilliam, who had been sent for on account of both the indiscretion of his ward, Georgiana, and the health of his brother, Lord Ashwell. He had been equally distraught by the news of each.

He was deeply fond of his brother, and carried with him at all times the burden of concern for his health, a worry that was aggravated by Lord Ashwell's almost cavalier disregard for it. Colonel Fitzwilliam's esteem and affection for his brother meant that the two rarely quarreled, but, when they did, it was the elder's almost complete disregard for his own well-being that was the subject.

Colonel Fitzwilliam received a courier from Clare, written upon their arrival in Faversham, stating that Lord Ashwell was taken seriously ill, and that Georgiana may be on the brink of a dreadful scandal. With respect to the latter, he was told that Mr. Darcy had already been dispatched, and that there was nothing he might do. Clare only thought that, as her guardian, he ought to know. The Colonel pleaded for, and received immediate leave to attend his brother and spent the following three days in restless travel, hoping that he would not arrive too late, either for Ashwell or for Georgiana. The tenderness which he had lately come to feel for the latter left him in torment. He considered the nature of the threatening scandal, which must surely involve some unworthy gentleman, and his feelings on that subject were even stronger than a guardian's duty or a cousin's regard might produce.

He arrived at the inn to find Mr. Darcy smiling and at ease. The two men embraced, and Mr. Darcy assured his cousin that both of the threatened parties were out of danger. He led Colonel Fitzwilliam to Ashwell's room, where they found Ashwell, Georgiana and Clare, chatting and laughing together.

"Brother!" Ashwell cried out upon Colonel Fitzwilliam's entry. Unable to speak, the Colonel responded with a smile that overtook his face, causing his eyes to narrow and his joyful tears to spill. Stepping forward, he knelt down to his brother and embraced him. As the Colonel returned to standing, Ashwell squeezed his hand and said, "It is good to see you brother." Then, turning to Clare, he added, with a sparkle in his eyes, "allow me to present, the cause of my survival, and the soon-to-be mistress of my household, Miss Clare Langford."

"How do you do," said Clare with a flourish and a playful smile.

After a dumbfounded moment, Colonel Fitzwilliam readily embraced Clare, whom he very much accepted as his brother's saviour, and he would not have been more pleased with her were she Duchess of Kent, nor less so had she been a Gloucestershire milkmaid.

All continued in joyful spirits over the news of the engagement, which seemed to have eclipsed all the gloom and distress arising from their recent trials.

As Lord Ashwell could not be moved for some time, Clare wished to remain with him in Faversham and Georgiana wished to remain in the comfort of her friend's company. Mr. Darcy, happy to indulge his sister in this way, remained with them also. Together with Colonel Fitzwilliam, they made a merry time of Lord Ashwell's convalescence and found more joy and more amusement than could ever reasonably be expected at a Kentish coaching inn.

CHAPTER 45

The closest that Clare and Ashwell ever came to a quarrel was regarding Maplethwaite and Ashwell's allowing her to believe that the gift of it had come from her cousin, Sir Leicester. Clare had nearly been persuaded to marry that man on the strength of such a noble gesture. Ashwell assured Clare that there had been no other way. If Clare had refused a few charcoals from him, how could she have accepted an entire house and its contents? And besides, no one would have forced her to marry Leicester. In fact, having Maplethwaite for life made her less obliged to marry anyone. If she must blame someone, let it be Sir Leicester himself, for taking credit for the gift, and leading Clare to believe he was quite a different man from what he really was.

Therefore, having written to her parents regarding Ashwell's proposal, Clare took no small delight in next writing the following letter to Sir Leicester.

"DEAR SIR,"

"I hope this letter finds you in excellent health and good spirits. I am happy to say that I write it in full possession of both. I write with joyous news, and with the greatest delight in sharing with you, who have always been such a friend to me, the fact that I have just become engaged to be married. Do not be shocked to hear that it is to Lord Ashwell that I have promised myself, for I know you warned me against him most sincerely on more than one occasion, but I have learned from a very reputable source that all rumours regarding his past were unfounded and woefully misinformed.

"I am eternally grateful for your sacrifice in allowing myself and my brother to reside at Maplethwaite for as long as we needed. I will soon have another home, but I do not doubt that Crawley will be as thankful as ever I could be for your generosity and condescension.

"I look forward to seeing you in town again in future if our paths should cross. I do not think I shall be able to take up your suggestion of joining you in Bath, for Lord Ashwell does not travel. I remain, humbly and faithfully,

"Yours etc.

"C. LANGFORD"

Clare never received any reply from Sir Leicester, which was just as she wished and expected. From her parents, however, she received the following:

"DEAREST CLARE,"

"After significant deliberation, your father and I have given our consent for you to marry your friend's cousin, Lord Ashwell. His application, which we received two days ago, showed him to be both intelligent and unassuming. He did not betray, at least, any of that sort of abhorrent arrogance that is so often associated with members of his class.

"You must understand, however, that we rely principally on your judgment in accepting him, as we trust that you have been raised with enough care and sense not to allow yourself to be won over by the promises of luxury and ease, but that you will always be wary of the dangers to your soul that a life of privilege bears.

"In light of these considerations, we offer you our blessing and our greatest hopes for your eternal happiness. To see you well settled and happy is all that we could wish.

"Your loving parents."

Upon receiving news of the engagement, Clare's brother,

Crawley, was less restrained in his pleasure in light of all the balls to which he might now be invited, while Mr. and Mrs. Watson vigorously renewed their professions of devotion and service to Clare, their kindness to whom they hoped would not pale and be forgotten in the brilliance of her new situation.

To everyone's surprise, Lady Catherine kept her displeasure to herself. So devoted was she to rank that she would not dare to voice even the slightest disapprobation to her nephew, whose station was, of course, above her own. Instead, she was forced to subvert her disapproval into acts of extreme but ironic condescension towards her new niece.

Lady Sofia merely fainted upon the sofa.

Throughout their circle of friends, relations and acquaintances, none was so unbridled in her happiness as Georgiana; she was forever grateful that the events that had made her so wretched had brought about such complete happiness for such beloved friends.

Clare and Ashwell were married from London before the summer was through. Clare always imagined she would be married from Maplethwaite, but was happy to give up that expectation in favour of being safely joined to her beloved Ashwell in as short a time as possible. Despite carrying a cane to the altar, the groom professed himself to be in the finest health and the best spirits he had ever known. The crisis that he had faced and survived in Faversham that fateful weekend seemed to be of greater significance than anyone could have foreseen. His recovery was not instantaneous, but it appeared that the climax of his immediate illness exorcised him of his long-standing condition for his health and strength steadily improved in the months that followed the wedding, and continued, without a moment of regress, through the many years of his long and happy life.

Colonel Fitzwilliam—his brother's best man at the wedding—smilingly renounced any expectation of inheriting the earldom in anticipation of many nephews to precede him. Some small part of him fancied himself a martyr in his brother's cause, as he was a little prone to self-pity, but he suffered his sacrifice with a stoicism born of brotherly affection. He felt he suffered a double blow, for, until then, he had considered himself destined for Georgiana's hand. It had never been actually promised, but he had felt sure of it so long as he thought he would one day be an earl. As it now seemed he would never inherit his father's title, the Colonel felt he could no longer expect to marry his cousin. He therefore pined also for the loss of a love which was no less his now than it had ever been.

Despite the haste of Ashwell and Clare's engagement, they neither of them came to regret their choice of partner. His character was not without its flaws, but most of his failings stemmed from an overabundance of generosity, forgiveness, and hospitality. He merely gave away more of himself and his wealth than she approved of.

As a result of Lord Ashwell's unwavering affection and acceptance, Clare even began to slacken her own self-remonstrance, particularly regarding her clandestine love of novels. So dramatic was the transformative power of his love that she even allowed one or two of the shameful things to be displayed on a shelf in the library without any attempt at concealment.

As she had promised in Faversham, Clare pursued her commitment to prevent any further injustice to her husband's reputation. He tacitly permitted her to correct the misinformation where possible, and, when asked about the matter, he would at least allow that the facts were not as had been reported, if he could not bring himself to share the whole and complex truth

The potential victims of this rectification, namely Annabelle, her husband, and their child, did not, in the end, suffer too terribly, for by the time the truth became established, Mr. and Mrs. Gray had grown attached to their grandchild and were not so willing to give up support of their daughter insofar as it would mean giving up all connection to the child. Their son in law had also shown himself to be a good husband and a kind father, and his fortunes began to turn a little for the better, which endeared him only further to the family. Therefore, all connected with that family simply allowed that rumours could not be trusted and, while implicitly forgiving the indiscretion which resulted in the couple's forced marriage, they asserted with increased certainty and vehemence that the child was born of both her parents, and that their marriage was no less honourable than any other.

Finally having a mistress to serve, Maria proved herself to be much more worthy of her position than Clare ever would have anticipated on their first acquaintance, and Lady Ashwell found herself to have the best French lady's maid in London ever not to be a French lady's maid.

In time, Lord Ashwell's family came to mind less the humbleness of Clare's beginnings, if not for the constant sweetness and mildness of her disposition, the efficiency of her household or the happiness she brought her husband, then for the son they came to expect in the spring.

In short, Lord and Lady Ashwell might have been called the envy of all society, to be as rich in love and happiness as they were in fortune and consequence; and, deserving as they were of each other, none could even be persuaded to resent them for it.

Made in the USA
Columbia, SC
22 April 2020

92892479R00169